M000121525

Pennsylvania
State Facts

Nickname: Keystone State

Date Entered Union: December 12, 1787
(the 2nd state)

Motto: Virtue, liberty and independence

Pennsylvania Men:
Daniel Boone, *frontiersman*
James Buchanan, *former U.S. president*
Lee Iacocca, *auto executive*
Reggie Jackson, *baseball player*
James Stewart, *actor*

Bird: Ruffed grouse

Flower: Mountain laurel

Fun Fact: Hershey, PA, is considered the chocolate capital of the U.S.

Dear Diary,

I had the dream again last night.

I saw the children huddled, cold, hungry, in a dark and empty room. The little boy was crying, and the girl held him on her lap. She tried to mother him, but she's hardly more than a baby herself. I woke up with an increased sense of urgency, as if time were running out. I know what I have to do, and like a coward I've avoided it as long as I could. The thought of going to the police with what I know sends cold chills over my skin.
I hate the thought of exposing myself like that again... to watch their disbelief, to feel their ridicule. I have no way to convince them that what I say is true.

But I can no longer live with myself if I don't try.

American
HEROES
AGAINST ALL ODDS

KYLIE BRANT

McLain's Law

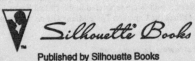

Silhouette® Books
Published by Silhouette Books
America's Publisher of Contemporary Romance

If you purchased this book without a cover you should be aware that this book is stolen property. It was reported as "unsold and destroyed" to the publisher, and neither the author nor the publisher has received any payment for this "stripped book."

This book is lovingly dedicated
in memory of my mother,
Jean Welter,
whose faith in me never faltered

SILHOUETTE BOOKS
300 East 42nd St.,
New York, N. Y. 10017

ISBN 0-373-82236-7

McLAIN'S LAW

Copyright © 1993 by Kimberly Bahnsen

All rights reserved. Except for use in any review, the reproduction or utilization of this work in whole or in part in any form by any electronic, mechanical or other means, now known or hereafter invented, including xerography, photocopying and recording, or in any information storage or retrieval system, is forbidden without the written permission of the editorial office, Silhouette Books, 300 East 42nd Street, New York, NY 10017 U.S.A.

All characters in this book have no existence outside the imagination of the author and have no relation whatsoever to anyone bearing the same name or names. They are not even distantly inspired by any individual known or unknown to the author, and all incidents are pure invention.

This edition published by arrangement with Harlequin Books S.A.

® and TM are trademarks of Harlequin Books S.A., used under license. Trademarks indicated with ® are registered in the United States Patent and Trademark Office, the Canadian Trade Marks Office and in other countries.

Visit Silhouette at www.eHarlequin.com

Printed in U.S.A.

About the Author

Kylie Brant lives with her husband and five children in Iowa. She works full-time as a teacher of learning-disabled students. Much of her free time is spent in her role as professional spectator at her kids' sporting events.

An avid reader, Kylie enjoys stories of love, mystery and suspense—and she insists on happy endings! When her youngest children, a set of twins, turned four, she decided to try her hand at writing. Now most weekends and all summer she can be found at the computer, spinning her own tales of romance and happily-ever-afters.

Kylie invites readers to write to her at P.O. Box 231, Charles City, IA 50616

Books by Kylie Brant

Silhouette Intimate Moments

McLains's Law #528
Rancher's Choice #552
An Irresistible Man #622
Guarding Raine #693
Bringing Benjy Home #735
Friday's Child #862
**Undercover Lover* #882
**Heartbreak Ranch* #910
**Falling Hard and Fast* #959
Undercover Bride #1022

*The Sullivan Brothers

Dear Reader,

McLain's Law will always remain a very special book for me. It was the second one I wrote and the first to be published. I still remember getting the call from Silhouette Books saying they were interested in it. I happened to be home from work that day, sick with laryngitis! My dream of becoming a published writer had come true, and I could barely croak out my excitement!

But it's the hero, Connor McLain, who makes this book truly memorable. He's the ultimate alpha male, dedicated to his job and wary of commitment. So settle back and prepare to enjoy his journey as he meets the woman he has no reason to trust...and soon can't live without!

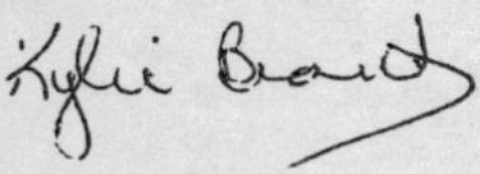

Please address questions and book requests to:
Silhouette Reader Service
U.S.: 3010 Walden Ave., P.O. Box 1325, Buffalo, NY 14269
Canadian: P.O. Box 609, Fort Erie, Ont. L2A 5X3

Chapter 1

The cacophony of sound in the headquarters of Philadelphia's southwest police district made Michele Easton pause momentarily, her gray eyes widening as her senses adjusted to the chaos. Phones rang shrilly, and officers raised their voices to be heard over the melee. One handcuffed man nearby shouted obscenities at the impassive officer escorting him out of sight.

She remained still for a second longer, slowly sweeping the huge expanse with her gaze. Rows of desks filled the room, cordoned off from others with partitions and file cabinets. No one paid her any heed as she stood there, silent and still, looking as out of place as she felt. No one except a man sitting next to a desk, answering an officer's questions resignedly. His eyes swept Michele leeringly, before giving her a lascivious wink.

Michele pulled her eyes away and raised her chin bracingly. It had taken her too long to muster the courage to come here today to allow her hard-won resolve to flee at the seemingly chaotic atmosphere. She headed toward a large corner to her left, behind which sat a man at a desk.

She waited quietly for the officer, whose nameplate identified him as Sergeant Alberts, to transfer his attention from his paperwork to her. As seconds stretched into minutes and this did not seem likely to happen, Michele spoke hesitantly. "Excuse me, Sergeant."

"Yeah?" he said, without raising his eyes.

"I'd like to talk to one of the officers investigating the disappearances of those children."

The man's attention magically shifted from his forms to the woman standing in front of him. His pencil stilled. "Are you one of the parents?"

"No." Michele's tone was startled. She had never considered that she would be mistaken as such. "I believe I have information that may be pertinent to the investigation."

"Pertinent," the man repeated as he squinted at the woman in front of him. She sure didn't dress or talk like many he saw come through here. He took in Michele's immaculate appearance, from her navy suit and pumps to the almost midnight dark hair swept up in a neat chignon. She looked every inch of what she was—a professional woman.

He shrugged. Maybe she was a social worker. "Over there." He pointed toward one of the endless rows of desks. "Second row, third desk. Officer Riley is working on the case. You can talk to him." His attention drifted back to the pile of forms before him.

Michele turned away and walked swiftly in the direction he had indicated. She stopped at the desk that bore the name of Officer Michael Riley. The occupant of the desk was nowhere in sight.

She stood there uncertainly. She hadn't suspected it would be this difficult just to find someone to give her information to. Perhaps she should accept this final chance to leave before subjecting herself to the ordeal of facing a police officer.

Instead Michele squared her shoulders and slipped into a straight-backed chair at the side of the desk. She wasn't going to change her mind now. She wouldn't, *couldn't*, be that much of a coward. She would wait as long as she needed to.

As it turned out, her wait was a short one. It was only a few minutes before a young officer with curly brown hair approached her.

"Hello," he said appreciatively, his open face breaking into a smile. "Sorry if you've been waiting for me. I just went for a fresh cup." He held up his coffee mug. "Can I get you any?" When Michele declined, he slipped into his chair and twirled to face her. "Now, how can I help you?"

"I came, Officer, because I think I may be able to help you." Michele steeled herself to face his curious gaze unflinchingly. "The sergeant said you're assigned to the disappearances of those children?"

Michael Riley made a deprecating face. "Yeah, me and a half-dozen other guys. I'm just a rookie, so it's my job to do all the paperwork, you know? Take statements, file reports, separate the real informants from the crackpots..." A quick look at Michele's frozen expression made him break off. "Oh, hey, I didn't mean you. That you're a crackpot, I mean. Or an informant. I mean, I don't really know..." His face got redder and redder.

Michele forced a reassuring smile. This was obviously going to be every bit as hard as she had feared. "It's all right," she soothed. "If we could just get started?"

Still blushing, the officer nodded vigorously, almost knocking his coffee mug over in his haste to grab a pen and paper. "First I need some preliminary information from you—your name, address, that kind of thing," he told her, trying to regain his former composure.

Michele nodded resignedly and gave him the information he sought. She had been sure that she would have to identify herself in order to be termed reliable. Wasn't that why she hadn't called the information in anonymously?

"Okay, that's about all I need from you. Except for any information you can give me about the case, that is." The officer grinned at her.

Michele took a deep breath. "First of all, there are five children who have been abducted, not four. Three boys and two girls. They're being held together, in a ramshackle building of some kind."

"This is great, really great!" the young officer enthused as he wrote furiously. "This may be the break we've been waiting for. Do you have the address of the building, ma'am?"

"No."

At her abrupt response, the officer raised his earnest gaze to Michele's. "Well, that's okay. Do you think you could take us there? You know, maybe retrace your steps with our help...." At the sight of Michele shaking her head he stopped. "You do know where this building is, don't you, ma'am?"

"Not exactly." Michele chose her words carefully, silently damning herself for coming, for ever believing that once she told someone she would have a modicum of inner peace. Her gaze was level as she looked at the officer and said, "I've never actually seen the outside, you see. Or the inside, exactly. Everything I've seen has been in a dream."

"Lieutenant?"

At Riley's diffident voice, Connor McLain stopped in midsentence. He ignored his friend's smirk as he said with exaggerated patience, "Yeah, Mike?"

The rookie entered the tiny cubicle and stood uncomfortably under the two detectives' scrutiny. "Uh, Lieutenant, I think I have someone here you may want to talk to. She has some information about the missing children." The officer stopped and waited.

The detectives looked at each other, and then Connor's eyebrows rose inquiringly. "You took her statement?"

At the older man's prodding, the rookie shifted uncomfortably. "Yes, sir."

"And?"

"And I think you may want to talk to her yourself, sir. She seems to know an awful lot about the case."

Connor resignedly held out his hand, and Mike put the statement in it. He perused it quickly, before raising his eyes disbelievingly to the rookie's. "A psychic? You want me to talk to a psychic?"

The young man flushed as the other detective snickered. "Not a psychic, exactly." The officer corrected him uncomfortably. "She's not a mind reader or anything like that," he reported as he tried to remember how Michele had described it to him. "She just...dreams things."

At this, the other detective in the room guffawed out loud. Connor sent him a pained look, before looking at the officer in front of him with lowered brows. "Now look, Mike. You know that long talk we had about relevant information?"

The younger man didn't quail. "Yes, sir. But, sir? She knows about the jacket."

Connor stopped. The other detective, Cruz Martinez, leaned forward. "What about the jacket?"

"Everything," Officer Riley went on doggedly. "And I remember what you told me, Lieutenant, really I do. But I wondered, how could she know these things if she wasn't for real? So I just thought you'd like to talk to her."

The two detectives exchanged glances. "Yeah, I would like to talk to her, Mike. Bring her in, will you?"

"Yes, sir!" The rookie eagerly left the cubicle.

"A psychic who sees things in dreams," scoffed Cruz. "C'mon, Connor. I know how you feel about people like that. Why didn't you lay into that kid?"

Connor leaned back in his desk chair. His tone was mild when he answered. "That *kid*," he stressed, "deserves a break, Cruz. Lay off him. Besides, you heard him. She knows about the jacket."

"She can't know about the jacket. We kept it out of all the papers, it hasn't been on the news. So how could she know?"

"How indeed?" mused Connor, a hard light entering his eyes. "That's exactly what I want to find out."

Cruz rose to leave the small room as Mike came back. As the officer ushered Michele past him, Cruz did an exaggerated double take. Connor frowned at his partner's too-typical reaction to an attractive female.

"That will be all, Detective," Connor drawled with deceptive mildness.

Cruz sauntered from the room, turning before he exited. "Anything you need, Connor, just...whistle." With that he strode away chuckling.

Michele paid little attention to the exchange, so nervous was she about this upcoming interview. She had thought that once she'd given her information, the whole ordeal would be over. When the young officer had asked her to talk to his superior, her heart had sunk to the level of her polished navy pumps.

It sank even farther when she heard Mike Riley say, "Michele Easton, sir." He looked at Michele and said, "The lieutenant wants to go over your statement with you, ma'am." Over Michele's protests, he turned and left the room, closing the door after him.

Connor indicated a chair and waited for Michele to slowly sink into it before seating himself in back of his desk. Cruz's reaction to the woman before him had been well deserved, he thought detachedly. Tall and slender, Michele Easton was more than attractive—she was downright great looking. Her fine-boned face had the aloof loveliness of a fashion model. Her dark hair was matched by sooty lashes, which framed large gray eyes.

Something inside Connor twisted with distaste. She reminded him of a porcelain statue of a princess his sister had received as a child. Although beautiful, this woman possessed the same distant demeanor. He supposed she would be a challenge to some men. That untouchable aura would provoke the most primitive instincts, make a man want to be the one to muss her a bit, tumble that prim hairdo and change the ice goddess into a writhing woman driven by her senses.

Other men—not Connor. He'd been down that road before, and the experience had taught him a valuable lesson. Women like this were all surface glitter; there was no warmth, no genuine humanity, beneath. Scratch them, and they bled dollar bills. She was beautiful, all right. She was also probably nuttier than a fruitcake. Or worse.

He faced the woman knowing that none of his suspicions would be reflected on his hard face.

"Look, Lieutenant Connor, I don't see the need to repeat the information you already have in front of you." She gestured to her statement, which Officer Riley had left.

"McLain."

At the terse reply Michele's startled gray gaze flew to the detective's. "Pardon me?"

Connor tapped his nameplate laconically. "Lieutenant Connor McLain."

"Oh," Michele responded inanely. Her eyes flickered from the nameplate to the detective. She felt foolish for not noticing the plate before. It was an unusual name, as was the man to whom it belonged. She didn't know how she would have envisioned a detective lieutenant, but she was sure this man wouldn't have entered her mind. Didn't the department have regulations about the length of his hair? she wondered. Dark blond waves were cut around his ears and left long enough in back to spill over his collar. And his eyes... Michele experienced an involuntary shiver when their gazes locked. They were narrow chips of pale green ice, framed by lashes as thick and gold as his hair. They were a predator's eyes, and they were trained on her with the unblinking gaze of a bird of prey.

Michele trained her features into a calm mask and forced herself to meet his gaze squarely, revealing none of her inner trepidation. "As I was saying, Lieutenant McLain, I've told your officer all I can. I really see no reason to repeat it. Everything I know is in that statement."

"Humor me, then," suggested Connor silkily. "I just have a few more questions for you, before you go." He looked down briefly at the statement Riley had prepared. "You work at Counseling and Psychological Associates?"

Michele hesitated, then nodded.

"What do you do there?"

"I'm a child psychologist."

At Connor's raised eyebrows, Michele elucidated. "We specialize in emotional and learning problems of children and adolescents."

"Have you ever had dealings with any of the missing children or their families in the past?" asked Connor. At Michele's negative answer he continued. "Any knowledge of them through some of your clients, perhaps?"

"I have had no previous contact with, or knowledge of, any of the victims or their families, Lieutenant," she replied with far more equanimity than she was feeling.

"Except in your dreams," corrected Connor.

Michele studied the man in front of her closely, but his features were totally impassive. It was impossible to tell what he was thinking or feeling about her statement. He probably thought she was crazy, she thought wearily, wishing with all her might that she had never come here today. "Except in my dreams," she agreed quietly.

Connor tossed the sheet containing the information she had given

Michael Riley onto his desk, then leaned back in his chair. "Tell me about these psychic phenomena of yours," he invited.

Michele was fairly certain that she heard sarcasm laced in his level tone, and suddenly her earlier trepidation faded. She hadn't been forced to come here, hadn't in fact wanted to. She didn't need this man, who looked like he would be more at home in an action movie than in a Philadelphia police station, to sit there and treat her like some kind of loony-tune. The fact that it was what she had expected and feared before coming here didn't excuse it.

"I don't claim to be a psychic," she informed him, for the first time allowing some of her frustration to creep into her voice.

Connor arranged his face into innocent surprise. "What do you claim to be, then?"

"Just an ordinary person."

"One who has dreams about crime victims."

"One who sometimes dreams about people and events that have no relation to herself." Michele leaned forward earnestly. "If I had to give it a name, I suppose clairvoyance comes closest to describing it. But definitions don't really matter. All that matters is that you listen to me. Lieutenant, I'm sure you're skeptical. I don't blame you for that. All I ask is that you try to listen with an open mind and act on any information that may be of value to you."

Connor eyed Michele for a long moment. "Continue," he invited. They were both aware that he had promised to do neither.

Michele took a deep breath. "About a month ago I started having disturbing dreams about some of the children who have been disappearing."

"That's not surprising." Connor chose his words carefully. "The media have covered all the stories, the chief of detectives and the police commissioner have addressed the topic several times. The mayor and his running opponent have each seized on the issue to grab poll points."

But Michele was shaking her head impatiently. "What I see isn't what has been on TV or in the papers. My dreams are more like—" she searched for the words to describe the scenes that flashed through her sleep "—as if I'm there, at a distance. A spectator." She glanced at the detective to see if he understood.

Connor picked up a pencil from the littered top of his desk and twirled it between his fingers. "If you've been having these dreams for a month, why did you wait? Why didn't you come in four weeks ago?"

Michele hesitated. He had unerringly found her point of weakness. "Because there wasn't really anything to tell," she said finally. "At the time, all I saw were flashes of the children's faces, nothing that would make you believe it was any more than a reaction to a dramatic news story." Nothing but the children's terrified struggles and screams for help that had reverberated through her nights and left her wide-awake, shaking and haunted.

"But now they're different?" questioned Connor.

Michele looked down for a moment and hoped that her face reflected none of her inner turmoil. "Now they're different," she agreed. "I see all five of the children together. I see where they're being held. They're kept bound and gagged, and they sleep on pallets of some sort."

Connor looked at her without speaking for a long moment. "There's just one thing wrong with your information," he said finally. "We believe only four children have disappeared."

"Then you believe wrong," Michele asserted flatly. "There are three boys and two girls. The youngest is a boy who appears to be only three or four."

Connor's gaze sharpened. "As I'm sure you're aware from the publicity, the victims have ranged in ages from six to nine."

"The rest of the children would fall in that age category, I think, but I'm telling you there's another child involved," Michele reiterated firmly. "He's blond, blue-eyed, with a pointed chin and a pug nose. He's wearing denim overalls, a red long-sleeved shirt and red tennis shoes."

Connor felt as if someone had dropped a brick on him. Michele Easton had just described Davey Lockhart, a three-year-old who had been taken out of his stroller while his mother had dashed into a grocery store for a pack of cigarettes. She had described him perfectly, but as he had told Michele before, the boy's disappearance was not considered by the police to be connected to the other four. It didn't fit the profile, for one thing. The child was much younger than the other victims. The store he had been taken from was miles away from the twelve-block area from which the others had disappeared. The mother had expressed her belief that Davey had been snatched by her estranged husband, and the police were proceeding on that belief, as well.

He told her none of this, however. Instead he inquired, "Your statement said you believed they were being held in a building? What kind, exactly?"

"I'm not really sure," Michele admitted. "It doesn't appear to be a house, though. It's very unkempt, dilapidated. I assume that it's abandoned."

Connor nodded, as if considering that. After several moments he asked smoothly, "And the jacket you mentioned to Officer Riley? Can you tell me anything more about that?"

Michele felt a semblance of the sick feeling she experienced every time she dreamed of the jacket. Valiantly she attempted to force the feeling down, to respond normally. "It's pink, hooded," she said woodenly. "It has a broken zipper on the front, and a white lining." She raised anguished eyes to the detective. "The right sleeve is soaked with blood. It belongs to the little girl with the dark hair and eyes."

Despite himself, Connor felt goose bumps rise on his flesh at her words, and he was annoyed at his involuntary physical reaction. The jacket did indeed belong to the little girl she described. But she was hiding more than she was telling. Of that he was sure. He was silent for a moment, mentally weighing his words. He locked both hands in front of him and leaned his chin against them. Finally he remarked, "That's a pretty detailed description. Where, exactly, was this jacket when you 'saw' it?"

"The girl was wearing it when she was taken," Michele responded. "But she isn't wearing it anymore."

"Then where is it?" he challenged silkily.

Michele eyed him steadily. "I have no idea, Lieutenant. But I'm sure that you do." Feeling at the end of her emotional tether, she rose from her chair on shaky legs. "I'm afraid I have nothing else to add to the information in the statement. I really have to go now."

Connor didn't object this time, only rose and followed her to the door.

Her hand on the knob, Michele was struck with a thought. She turned back quickly, unable to believe that she had almost forgotten to ask. "Lieutenant McLain? My name won't be made public, will it? Or the fact that I've talked to you about the case?"

"I can assure you, Miss Easton, we're even less willing than you are to have it become common knowledge that we've consulted with a psychic. Excuse me," he apologized at her frigid look, "with a person who's not exactly clairvoyant. You have my assurance that none of this will be made public."

Michele's gaze locked with his. Whatever else this man might be, he didn't appear to be a liar. She nodded at his assurance and left the room.

Connor sighed heavily as he leaned against his doorjamb and watched her wend her way gracefully through the maze of desks and people and out of sight. Just what he needed on top of a high-profile investigation, frantic parents, a rabid press and the top brass breathing down his neck. A woman who was probably wacko, who could damn well have something to do with those missing kids herself, for all he knew.

"What I want to know," said a wounded voice next to him, "is why you always get to talk to the gorgeous women with legs a mile long, while I get to chat with old ladies wearing rollers in their hair and reporting UFOs in their backyards."

Connor slid his gaze sideways to meet Cruz's. "Those old ladies are the only females we can trust you not to hit on," he gibed. He pushed himself away from the door and stood there. "Come on in," he invited. "I need to talk to you about this one." Cruz preceded him back into his office and slouched into the chair Michele had just vacated. Connor sat on the edge of his desk, facing his friend.

He needed to run this bizarre conversation by someone, and he trusted no one in the world as he did the man before him. He and Cruz had been rookies together, partners when they had first joined the force. They had been in some tight situations and had saved each other's hides too many times to count. Somewhere along the line they had also become friends. When Connor had been asked to supervise this investigation, he had immediately suggested that Cruz be added to the team of detectives working on the case. Despite his usual carefree demeanor, Cruz had the well-honed instincts of a street fighter, and he was a meticulous investigator.

"Well?" Cruz prompted. "Did the mind reader tell you how she knew about the jacket?"

Connor made an exasperated face. "She didn't tell me anything that's not in this statement." He handed the sheet of paper to his partner and waited silently while Cruz perused it.

When he finished, Cruz raised quizzical eyes to Connor. "A psychic and a psychologist?" At Connor's pained look he chuckled. "Must be your lucky day. I know what high esteem you hold mind pickers in."

Connor snorted derisively. His low opinion of the counseling profession as a whole was not a well-kept secret in the district. It stemmed from a deep-rooted privacy about himself and his life that was as much a part of him as his hair and eye color. He had detested the times he had been forced to follow district regulations and talk to the police psychologist after an arrest that involved a shooting. The psychologist hadn't enjoyed the experience much more.

"Maybe it's time to put aside your aversion to using psychics in investigations," suggested Cruz. "I know you've never put any stock in them, but Delmer and Clive swear that the man they used busted their homicide case wide open."

Connor looked impatient. "And did you and I ever have any luck the few times we followed up leads from so-called psychics?" he demanded.

Cruz looked uncomfortable. "Not exactly," he admitted.

His friend snorted. "Damn right we didn't. We spent extra energy and man-hours following leads that sent us on one wild-goose chase after another." He shook his head firmly. "The only information you're likely to get from those circus-tent swamis is so cryptic and open to interpretation that no one could know what to look for." His mouth twisted. "Not to mention the mayor's reaction if the press ever got wind that we were consulting psychics to solve the case. His opponent would have a field day with it, and my butt would be out the door."

Cruz grimaced in agreement. "Well, how do you explain this lady knowing about the jacket? Ever since Torelli found it in that Dumpster, we made sure it wasn't made public. Only a handful of us know about it. You think there's a leak?"

"Possibly," Connor conceded, rubbing the back of his neck reflectively. "Or maybe Miss Easton knows just a little more about this whole thing than she's telling us."

Cruz was silent for a moment. "Was she able to tell you where it was found?"

"She either didn't know or wouldn't say," Connor answered grimly.

His friend's eyebrows shot up. "Something tells me, *amigo,* that you suspect she may be involved in this. How?"

"I don't know," Connor admitted. "That's why I want you to run a check on her. Her job, her background, her friends, where she's from, who she sees. If there's any connection to these kids, we'll find it."

"And if there's not?"

"There's got to be," Connor said flatly. "There's no other way for her to have that information." He and his partner looked at each other for a long moment. "Unless she's involved in some way."

Michele gratefully reached the front doors of the station house and pushed them open. She breathed deeply of the fresh air, trying to regain a semblance of calm. Remaining composed during those interviews had taken almost all of her considerable equanimity. She felt a chill chase down her spine, remembering. Just the verbal recounting of the dreams had been enough to bring all the horror, all the terror, back. Her head was thudding with the aftermath of the event. She wanted nothing more than to get home to bed, where she could burrow under the covers and put this ordeal out of her mind.

She hurried down the front steps of the building, pushing through the throng that had unexpectedly appeared there. She was detained near the bottom, the crowd so thick it was impossible for her to pass through. Impatiently she strained to see what the holdup was.

At first she was unable to see anything, but she heard a vaguely familiar resonant voice boom out, "I can assure the citizens of our city that their lives, those of their children and their safety are my utmost concern. I have been in daily contact with the chief of detectives and the commissioner about this case, and I'm assured that the D.A.'s office is ready and eager to see that any suspect they apprehend is prosecuted to the fullest extent of the law."

A shift in the crowd brought Michele a glimpse of the speaker, even as she identified him by his voice alone. Lawrence McIntire, Philadelphia's incumbent mayor, was obviously making a campaign speech, and Michele had unwittingly stepped into the middle of a media frenzy. Microphones were waving in front of him, and reporters shouted questions at him and his opponent. Michele shrank back self-protectively, even as she acknowledged the improbability of her being seen on camera.

"Reverend Carlson, what do you have to say about the failure of the police to bring the kidnappers into custody?"

A well-modulated voice answered them. "Sadly, I think the tragedies point to the glaring incompetence in our judicial system. If by some stroke of luck the hapless detectives are able to bring in a suspect, we have only a fifty-fifty chance that the current D.A.'s department will get a conviction." The rest of his statement was lost as his opponent vehemently denounced his claim.

Michele used her elbows to move through the edge of the crowd. The last thing she wanted right now was to appear on the nightly news in front of police headquarters, and she was relieved to note that the cameras and reporters were focused on the two well-dressed men in front of them. She hurried across the street toward the parking ramp where she had left her car.

When she was able to sink gratefully into the plush leather interior, she expelled a tremulous breath. With both hands at the top of the steering wheel, she rested her forehead against them to still their shaking.

Going to the police had been more traumatic than she had feared. She had debated with herself for days before deciding to come here. It had taken even longer to gather her courage to actually make the trip. She hadn't let herself consider the humiliation of having the police think she was a crazy busybody, a psychic rubbernecker intent on becoming part of the tragedy.

She moved her hands to her temples, trying to still the throbbing there by rubbing in circular motions. Her head felt much as it did when she awoke from one of her dreams, full and pounding. She knew from painful experience that the symptoms pointed to a migraine coming on. She fumbled with her keys and managed to place the correct one in the ignition.

As Michele backed her car up carefully, she bit her bottom lip. She had done her best. She had acted on the nightmarish terror of the dreams. Maybe now there would be peace in her sleeping hours. Perhaps she would no longer be revisited by the dark drama unfolding in those children's lives, an unwilling voyeur of their terrible suffering. And hopefully no one she knew would ever find out about her going to the police.

Because she couldn't bear it if the ability that had cursed her since childhood was ever made public again.

Chapter 2

Cruz Martinez knocked jauntily at the office door and entered at Connor's brusque command. Closing the door behind him, Cruz sauntered over to Connor's desk, tossing a paper on it. "Read it and weep," he intoned theatrically. He dropped carelessly into one of the chairs. "Your mind-reader moll is as clean as my freshly laundered shirts."

Connor cast a wry look over Cruz's informal attire. "High praise, indeed," he mocked, before turning his attention to the information before him. His brow furrowed as he perused the background information Cruz had compiled on Michele Easton. As his friend read, Cruz summarized it, ticking each item off on his fingers.

"Born twenty-six years ago. She and her mother moved to Philadelphia when Michele was eleven. She graduated high school and went to Penn State, majored in psychology, received her M.A. degree in same. Invited by James H. Ryan, Ph.D., to join Counseling and Psychological Associates two years ago. Pictured in the newspapers occasionally at fund-raisers for the homeless. Volunteers at a battered-victims' shelter weekly. None of the parents of the kids know her, and she's had no arrests—not even a parking ticket to mar her spotless record. Pure enough for you?"

Connor raised a jaundiced eye. "Nobody's that pure," he declared. "So don't canonize her just yet." He was less than impressed with her social efforts. He was too familiar with high-society women who enjoyed playing Lady Bountiful. Some of them even dabbled with a career, like Michele Easton. Their highbrow actions couldn't hide the fact that they had no real feeling for the people they were helping. Their only thrill was the accompanying publicity for their actions.

Connor tapped his index finger against the paper in his hand. There was nothing in it that pointed to a relationship between Miss Easton and any of the missing children, but then, he hadn't really expected there to be. That would have been too obvious, too easy. Something linked them, though. Of that he was reasonably certain. He could think of no other way to explain her knowledge of the jacket. Unless, of course, he gave credence to her explanation that she had dreamed about it.

His mouth hardened. He didn't believe in crystal-ball hocus-pocus. There had to be a real explanation for her knowledge. If she wasn't directly involved in the kidnappings, then she must have learned about the jacket from someone in the department. A leak could be extremely damaging to the case, especially since it had become a political juggernaut for the mayor and his running opponent.

Connor stood up and grabbed his leather jacket, thrusting his arms through the sleeves.

"Was it something I said?" Cruz inquired, watching his friend with lazy interest.

"I'm going to pay Miss Easton a visit."

Cruz's dark eyebrows rose comically. "I thought you said she didn't want anyone to know she'd been talking to us. I doubt she's going to be thrilled with you showing up at her place of business."

"That's the point," Connor retorted calmly. "Maybe seeing me there will put enough pressure on her to make her give me more information."

"You don't believe her story?"

The look Connor shot his partner would have withered grapes on the vine. "Do you?"

"Well," explained Cruz loftily, "as you know, I do make it a policy to keep an open mind." He accompanied his statement with a wicked grin as he added, "Especially with gorgeous blue-eyed brunettes."

"Gray-eyed," Connor corrected him unthinkingly.

"So you *were* paying attention," Cruz teased as he rose and followed Connor from the small office. "I knew even you couldn't be completely unmoved by a creature that beautiful." He clapped Connor on the shoulder. "There's hope for you yet, m'boy."

"Unfortunately, there's none for you," Connor said dryly. "I assume that report was merely preliminary?"

Cruz nodded. "If you still want me to dig further."

"I do," Connor affirmed. "Don't stop digging until you find something we can use."

Michele sat cross-legged on the floor of her office, watching intently. Erica, her four-year-old client, sat next to her in front of a dollhouse, positioning dolls and readjusting them to her satisfaction. When she paused, Michele asked softly, "Can you tell me about the doll family?"

A negative shake of a dark head was her only answer.

Michele waited, but the child remained silent. "The daddy doll is in the car," Michele observed. "How does the little girl doll feel when daddy leaves?"

A melodious tinkling was her only answer, and Michele sighed frustratedly. The signal to end the session seemed to have come more rapidly than usual, and she had made little headway with Erica.

She lowered her gaze to the dark eyes watching her solemnly. "That's all for today, Erica. When you come back on Thursday we'll play with the dolls again. Would you like that?" The small head nodded vigorously.

Michele helped Erica put her coat on, and they opened the door and stepped into the waiting room. Erica walked straight to her mother and, after murmuring her goodbye, they left the small room.

Michele watched them go, already busily planning her strategy for the next session. She had turned to return to her office when her eyes collided with the narrowed green gaze of Lieutenant Connor McLain, leaning against the far wall.

She felt as though her breath were trapped inside her chest, one hand going unconsciously to that area. Her surprise kept her momentarily deaf to what her secretary, Julie, was saying to her.

She had never expected to have to see him again, and he looked totally incongruous in the soft pastel room in his light-colored chinos and brown leather bomber jacket. She noted for the first time that he was barely taller than she was in her high heels. His shoulders were so broad, his persona so intimidating, that she had expected him to be taller.

Her emotional distress the first time she had met him had prevented her from fully registering his fatal impact. He was a compelling man. He wasn't conventionally handsome; his face was too hard, too unyielding, for that. But he was dangerously attractive, nonetheless. His mouth was chiseled perfection, his full bottom lip unashamedly sensual.

The two slashes at the sides of his mouth attested to deep masculine dimples.

Michele studied them bemusedly. She had seen his mouth curve into a derisive curl, but little humor had crossed his face in her presence. His expression was as impassive as granite, and she couldn't envision this man smiling. She shivered. Detective Lieutenant Connor McLain was dangerously sexy; he would be arrestingly attractive under other circumstances. But with his "cop face" on, he was icily stolid.

"Miss Easton? I'm sorry for buzzing you a little early. But Mr. McLain was quite adamant about speaking to you immediately."

With difficulty, Michele tore her gaze away from his burning one to lower her eyes to Julie's wheelchair and smile weakly at her. "Mr. McLain?" she questioned, as much for his benefit as for her own.

Connor pushed himself away from his position against the wall and approached them lazily. "I told Miss Lawson that I was a...friend of yours. She agreed to let me talk to you, even though I don't have an appointment."

Michele's gaze narrowed at the thread of sarcasm she detected in his voice. "I really don't have much time, Lieu—Mr. McLain."

Connor cupped her elbow in his hand and walked her back to her office. "Your secretary said you have twenty minutes before your next appointment. I'll only take ten." He guided her into her office and shut the door on Julie's curious gaze.

Michele pulled her arm away from him and whirled around furiously. "What do you think you're doing? How dare you come here, lie to my secretary and barge into my office like this?"

Connor said nothing as his eyes wandered over her. When she had come out of her office, it had taken him a minute to recognize her. Gone was the polished professional woman who had come to headquarters. In her place was a gypsy. Michele was wearing a scarlet blouse with a wildly patterned skirt. Her hair had been left down to fall like a thick silk curtain around her shoulders. Large hoop earrings completed the outfit. He marveled that she could simply, by the change of attire, appear so totally different. The wildness of her dress failed to mar her porcelain prettiness, however. If anything, it highlighted it. He ignored the sharp thrust of desire he'd experienced at seeing her. He could handle that. He concentrated instead on the ease with which she seemed to have changed persona since last he'd seen her. He answered her question sardonically. "Would you have preferred it if I had told your secretary I was a detective?"

Michele flushed. "I would have preferred it if you had never come here at all. What else could you possibly want from me? Unless..."

Her mouth went dry. "There hasn't been another abduction, has there?" Her knees went weak at the thought. She hadn't had another dream since she had gone to the police, and instant guilt flooded her at the relief she had felt when they had come to a halt.

Connor scowled at the color draining from her face. "Sit down," he commanded brusquely. Pushing her none-too-gently into a chair, he sat also. "No, there hasn't been another. Why? Did you expect one?"

Michele let out a sigh of relief at his negative reply. As her mind registered his question, her eyes bounced back to him. "What's that supposed to mean?" she asked stiffly.

Connor's laconic shrug was at marked odds with the intent look on his face. "I just wondered if you'd had any more...dreams."

"No, not since I last talked to you," murmured Michele. So far it had been as she had hoped. The dreams had come more and more frequently before she had gone to the police, each more vivid than the last. After she had told what she knew, she hadn't been disturbed again. It was too soon to tell if they were gone for good.

She eyed Connor squarely as she sat up straighter and crossed her legs. "Somehow I had received the impression from you, Lieutenant, that you didn't put much stock in what I told you. I find it difficult to believe that you came to me for more clues." She cocked her head. "Why don't you tell me what really brings you here?"

"How long has your secretary worked for you?" Connor asked lazily.

"Julie?" Michele was disoriented at his non sequitur. "Ever since I started here. Why?"

"How about that fellow I saw in the hallway? The janitor. How well do you know him?"

"Scott Jansma has also worked here since I started."

"You really are an equal-opportunity employer."

Michele's eyes darkened to charcoal, and when she spoke her tone was precise. "Julie's handicap in no way hinders her mind, her personality or her ability to do a superb job. The same is true for Scott."

"He appears to be slow," observed Connor.

"He may not be as mentally alert as most people, but he is able to think and feel and reason," Michele informed him. "We've never had any complaints about his work. Do you have a reason for asking, or are you just naturally prejudiced against people with different abilities?"

Connor watched the woman before him with interest. He wasn't biased, of course. But he had wanted to talk to the real Michele Easton, not the polished professional who had shown up in his office the other day. From her spirited return he had obviously hit on a subject guaranteed to make her lose that cool composure of hers. He took his time before answering her.

"Just interested. I wanted to see where you work, who you spend your time with."

Michele's eyes narrowed. "This sounds suspiciously like you're checking me out. I don't like that, Detective. I don't like it at all. Are you so hard up for clues that you're now clutching at straws?"

Connor rose during her tirade and moved around her office, studying the framed diplomas and licenses on the wall. "What's James Ryan like?" he drawled with studied casualness. At Michele's silence, he turned his head to look back across his shoulder at her.

At the question, his presence in her office took on a more threatening cast. Why the sudden interest in her employer? Her heart sank. Unless...he had come here today expressly to meet James, to perhaps tell him about Michele's visit to the station. He'd agreed to protect her privacy, but it wouldn't be the first time an officer of the law had broken that particular promise to her. "You told me earlier that no one would know of my involvement in the case." She met his gaze directly. "Is that why you came here today? Are you going back on your word?"

Connor looked wounded. "Are you accusing me of lying, Miss Easton? I just asked a simple question. If you don't want to answer it, I suppose I can always make an appointment and introduce myself to him."

The tenseness in her features almost made him feel sorry for her for a minute, but he shrugged the feeling away. Michele wasn't going to sway him by hysterics or tears. But the imminent possibility of either from this woman discomfited him in some way.

Michele engaged in neither. Imperceptibly, her face smoothed, and when she spoke, her voice was calm. "I can assure you that won't be necessary. I can tell you anything you want to know. James Ryan is a brilliant clinical psychologist. He was on staff at St. Mercy Hospital for twelve years before leaving to go into private practice. After five years he decided to take on a partner. He hired me, and I've worked with him for two years. What else would you like to know?"

Connor listened and then crossed over to stand in front of her. "Why don't you tell me why you're so afraid that he may find out you came to us with information?"

Michele's voice was scathing. "Use your head, Lieutenant. James is a highly principled professional. He expects his colleagues to be the same. He certainly wouldn't be at ease knowing..." She trailed off, her eyes fluttering away.

"Knowing that his 'highly respected' colleague dreams of things happening to other people?" he asked softly. At her silence, he asked, "Who does know, Michele? Who else have you told about these extraordinary things that happen in your sleep?"

Michele's face was a smooth mask. "No one." That wasn't strictly true, of course. Her mother was achingly aware of the trauma her dreams had always caused her. Neighbors in West Virginia had also known of her abilities.

Her mind skittered away from thinking about West Virginia. Because of what had happened there, she had always obeyed her mother's wishes to never share her secret with anyone after they had moved to Philadelphia. And she hadn't. Not until she had gone to the police.

"Why not? Because I may not be the only person who is incredulous about a person who claims to 'see' things in her dreams? Are you afraid others would also disbelieve you?"

"Or treat me like a freak?" Michele finished frigidly. "Yes, Lieutenant, I'm sure of it. I think they'd see me just as you do. Do you think I relish that kind of treatment? That I would seek it out?"

"Yet you did," he continued inexorably. "When you came to us."

Michele stood up and paced agitatedly around the office. "Only when I felt I had no choice. You are free to do what you wish with the information I gave you. The choice is yours. I don't need to have any more to do with you. I've told you all I know."

"But you think I should act on your information, don't you? Otherwise you wouldn't have come. You do believe your information to be accurate?"

"I know it is," Michele whispered rawly. She turned to meet his gaze with her own tortured one. "Lieutenant, please don't let your own bias keep you from making every effort to find those children, even if you have to use information that comes to you in an unconventional manner. If you disqualify what I told you, you may well be sentencing those children to a lifetime of horror, or death. Could you live with the fact that while you were pursuing leads from more conventional sources, something even more terrible happened to them?"

Connor's mouth tightened. He couldn't, of course. In his line of work he was too aware of the sick reasons people had for kidnapping children. As much as he derided her profession, as little stock as he put in people who claimed psychic powers, the truth was that they were desperate for information. There were few reliable witnesses to the abductions. No consistent firsthand accounts, no description of the person seen approaching the children. Be that as it may, he had no intention of being strung along by a nut case.

"You look very different today," he drawled, gesturing at her outfit. "So tell me. Which is the real you, the gypsy or the princess?"

"I beg your pardon?" Michele's voice dripped ice.

Connor allowed some of his derision to show on his granite features. "When you came to headquarters you gussied up like my great-aunt," he announced. "Now..." He gestured to her. "Well, now you look much different."

"So?"

"So, which is the real Michele Easton, the gypsy or the prim professional?"

"Personality, Lieutenant, is determined by much more than clothes," Michele lectured him. "One's inner self does not alter with each different article of clothing one wears." She cocked her head at him. "Or would you have me believe that in your closet I would find an endless supply of chinos and leather coats?"

"What you would find in my closet," Connor drawled softly, "might embarrass you. But if you'd like to come by and check it out, feel free."

Michele refused to allow herself to respond to his intentionally provocative remark, instead retaining eye contact steadily and silently. She didn't feel the need to justify her changed appearance. She often wore bright clothing when working with young children like Erica. Some of her clients responded to color with an increased level of trust. However, it seemed to have affected the detective much more than it had Erica, she thought wryly. And not in a positive way. He seemed to regard her changed appearance as a method of deception or disguise.

She was good, Connor admitted silently. He knew damn well he'd just embarrassed her, that she had come close to collapse earlier, but she masked her emotions well. Right now her eyes were blank pools of gray, reflecting nothing of what she might be feeling. He damned that ability of hers even as he grudgingly admired it. A psychologist knew all the tricks he was capable of using to intimidate people, to make them ill at ease and more inclined to babble. He was obviously going to get nowhere using those kinds of tactics with her.

Michele shook her head. "Is your suspicious nature natural, or a by-product of your job?" she inquired.

"It does come in handy in my line of work," he conceded, without really answering her.

"I'm sure a working knowledge of human nature also comes in handy, Lieutenant. So you should be aware that no one is one-dimensional. There are no black-whites, good-bads. Every person is multifaceted."

Connor faced her impassively. "That's what makes it so hard to tell the good guys from the bad guys, Miss Easton."

Michele looked at the gold watch on her wrist. "I'm afraid I really am running out of time for you, Lieutenant. My next client will be here shortly, and I have to prepare."

Connor rose and allowed her to usher him to the door. His visit here had been interesting but had provided him with very little information he didn't already have. At the door he asked with deceptive evenness, "The little girl the jacket belonged to is named Lucy. Did those dreams of yours tell you what happened to get it in such a state?" He turned to face Michele more fully, in order to closely watch her reaction to his question, but he needn't have bothered. It would have been impossible for her to hide. At his words, she looked as if she had been slapped. She stared at him silently, her lips slightly parted, visibly trembling.

Michele felt an actual physical shock jolt through her body at his abrupt question. She could recall each dream with excruciating accuracy. She'd learned long ago the futility of trying to bury the visions away. As she stared silently at him, her memory supplied her with the horrible details he'd asked for. Remembering was like watching a movie being played at extreme speed, the frames appearing in Michele's mind, into and out of focus, one followed immediately by another. Flash. Eyes round with terror, terrified screams emanating from the little girl's throat. Flash. Lucy being pulled toward something or someone unseen, before breaking away and throwing herself toward a car handle. Flash. The child being yanked back with force, screams of horror changing to screams of pain. Flash. Blood pouring down her arm, and the screaming, screaming, screaming...

"Michele!"

Michele's eyes fluttered several times before she looked up to find her shoulders held in Connor McLain's hard grasp, his face close to hers. She freed herself slowly, awkwardly, still reeling emotionally from the horrible memories. She turned away to give herself some time to regroup and strove to find her voice.

"Her upper left arm was hurt as she struggled to get away," Michele stated, striving for but not quite achieving an even tone. "It was caught on something in the kidnapper's car, perhaps a spring or wire." A shudder passed through her, and she turned awkwardly, feeling suddenly old and slow. She walked stiffly past him and opened the door, standing aside, clearly inviting his exit.

Connor studied her for an instant. Either this woman was crazier than a bedbug or the best damn actress he'd ever seen. What she had told him could have been true. Certainly the jacket had been torn in the area she'd mentioned. Someone had obviously taken the jacket off the child to get a closer look at the wound. The Dumpster it had been found in was only a few blocks from where she had been taken. But he was no closer now than he had been before to deciding by what means Michele had come by that information.

Michele, tiring of his inactivity, stalked out of the office. After a moment Connor followed her. Julie looked up as they entered the outer office. "Your next appointment just called and canceled, Michele. I rescheduled it for tomorrow. That was the last one of the day, so if you need more time..." Her eyes slid suggestively to Connor.

"We won't be needing any more time, Julie." Michele spoke distantly. "Mr. McLain was just leaving."

Connor nodded laconically to Julie as he passed her desk. "Nice meeting you."

The secretary sighed audibly as she watched Michele accompany his departing figure. "You too," she murmured appreciatively, before returning to her work.

They stepped into the hallway, and Michele reached to pull the door closed behind them. "I don't want to see you again," she informed him stiffly. "There's no need for us to have any more to do with each other."

Connor's mouth twisted at her words. She was at her haughtiest, her princess mask firmly in place. When he spoke, his tone was derisive. "What if you dream some more, Miss Easton? Surely you'll let us know."

Michele's chin rose even higher at his gibing tone, but before she could answer with a blistering retort, the doorway opposite them opened and a tall slim man dressed impeccably in a double-breasted suit appeared in the hallway.

"Good afternoon, James." Michele addressed the man in resignation, mentally cursing his timing. She felt rather than saw Connor come to attention and knew he had figured out the identity of the man before him. With an inward sigh, Michele introduced the two. "Dr. James Ryan, this is Connor McLain, a...friend of mine." She hated the deception, hated the man beside her for making it necessary by his presence here.

Connor reached to take the well-manicured hand extended to him. So this was the famous James H. Ryan, Ph.D., he thought derisively. The man resembled a banker more than anything else, both in his bearing and in his appearance. He and Michele suited each other perfectly:

the princess and the prince, both civil and proper and devoid of expression.

He glanced at the woman beside him and found more than warmth in her eyes; there were obvious sparks shooting at him. He almost grinned. "I've heard a lot about you from Michele." His tone was openly intimate, as was the gaze he shot her. "Nice to finally meet you."

Michele stiffened at his words. She had to get him out of here before he said or did something she would regret. "Connor was just leaving."

"Very pleasant to have met you," James said in cultured tones, and Connor frowned at Michele.

"I'll be in touch." He knew he had scored a hit by the startled look she shot him before he sauntered away.

Michele watched him go with mingled relief and anxiety at his final words. Her attention was torn from him when she heard her associate observe, "An interesting character, Michele. Is he a client?"

"No, just an acquaintance," she explained hastily, and changed the subject before he could inquire further. She spoke to James for only a few minutes before excusing herself and returning to her office. She tried unsuccessfully to force Connor McLain from her mind for the rest of the day, but she met with a decided lack of success.

It was with a heartfelt sigh of relief that Michele entered her duplex that evening. The tense muscles in her neck and shoulders were mute testimony to the stress she had endured that day.

A prowling feline appeared instantly at her entrance and wound enticingly around her ankles, demanding attention. Michele reached down to scoop up her white Persian cat. "Did you miss me, Sammy? Hmm?" she murmured, rubbing the cat's soft fur against her cheek. She set her pet down and continued through the apartment, dropping her purse and her clothes in disarray on the way to the bathroom.

Totally nude by the time she entered the bathroom, Michele adjusted the shower, then stepped in when it reached a cool temperature. She raised her face to the spray, smoothing her hair back as the water cascaded around her. She wished she could wash the day's distressing events away as easily as the water sluiced off her.

After stepping out of the shower she dried off vigorously, then slipped into a floor-length terry robe hanging on the back of the door. Padding barefoot to the kitchen, she found Sammy there, angrily demanding his dinner. After feeding him, Michele looked disinterestedly at the contents of her refrigerator before forcing herself to fix and eat most of a salad.

Afterward she curled up on the sofa and turned on the TV. Flipping through the channels, she finally stopped at the local daily news and watched with more interest than usual. The anchorwoman's face turned serious as she said, "And back to the disappearances of four Philadelphia children. Mayor McIntire denied today that he is trying to turn the public's attention from the investigation."

The mayor's face filled the screen, and Michele heard his voice as if from a distance, talking about the progression of the case. She hit the power button on the remote, and the silence in the room seemed to reverberate.

Pulling her knees up to her chin, Michele wrapped both arms around them and laid her forehead dizzily down. The disappearances again. It was impossible to escape the news and seemingly impossible to escape Lieutenant McLain. The last thing in the world she had expected today was to see him in her office, to have to watch horrified as he introduced himself to her co-workers. She recognized the hidden threat in his unexpected appearance very well. He knew how reluctant she was to have her visit to the police become public. By showing up when she least expected him, he had been trying to intimidate her. Michele knew he didn't believe her, but she couldn't imagine what he had intended to gain by speaking to her again, either.

She raised blank eyes to the wall, silently reliving what had passed between them that day. This whole thing had been a nightmare from the beginning, in more than just the usual way. She had been so sure, so desperate for peace, that she had convinced herself that the only way she would be released from her nightly horror was to go to the police with what she knew.

And it had seemed as if she were right, at least for a time. The trip to headquarters had been unpleasant and embarrassing, but it had cured her, at least for now, of dreaming of those children. But she was becoming grimly certain that she had made a terrible mistake by going to the police, though she didn't know how she could have lived with herself if she hadn't.

Michele looked at the telephone longingly. How she wished she dared to call her mother, just to hear her loving, calm voice. But she couldn't. She doubted her ability to keep the anxiety from her voice right now, and the last thing her mother needed was to detect what was really bothering her daughter. She had finally gotten remarried, to a man Michele heartily approved of. No one deserved happiness more than Sabrina Easton Griffen, and Michele was loath to destroy that with a phone call.

She clasped her knees tighter and began to rock a little. She would like nothing more than to crawl into bed and sink into sleep, escaping all that had happened today. But she feared sleep after her fresh encounter with the detective, afraid that the tension of the day could result in a return of the dreams. So, unable to face sleep, unable to talk to anyone about her terrors, Michele rocked slowly, watching the clock blankly as it ticked away the minutes of the night.

Chapter 3

It was late afternoon the following Saturday when Michele left the battered-victims' shelter. She bounced jauntily down the steps in her faded jeans and T-shirt, ponytail swinging. She felt surprisingly lighthearted. The people she worked with at the shelter often changed from week to week, but their plight never did. There were times, however, such as today, when she actually felt as though she could help make a difference, and those times were gratifying. She knew that she received as much as she gave, working with the women and children there.

She drove home, already busily planning the rest of her afternoon. Michele entered her home absently, scooping up Sammy in one hand and her mail in the other. She made her way through the living area, absently petting his soft fur. In the kitchen she dropped her pet, who promptly yowled his protest and wrapped himself around her ankles, batting at a shoelace. Michele sat down at the tiny table and automatically began to sort through the mail. She threw the useless junk mail into the trash without more than a glance.

She frowned as she picked up the last envelope. It had no name on it, nor did it bear a postmark or stamp. That was odd. She turned it over curiously, then ripped it open and drew out the single sheet of white paper.

Her stomach did a slow roll as she read the brief message. Crookedly cut letters from the newspaper were glued to the paper to form a single line of print. *Stay away from cops* was crudely but effectively glued to the sheet. Under the message was attached a picture of herself, one that had appeared in the newspaper several months ago, concerning her committee's work for the homeless. A red bull's-eye had been drawn over her face.

Michele dropped the sheet as if she'd been scalded. What kind of warped mind would think of this? she wondered sickly. Could it have been a joke by one of the neighborhood kids? A product of an elaborate game of cops and robbers? She discounted the notion almost as soon as she thought of it. She was on good terms with all the neighborhood children and often talked to them. Some of them were mischievous, certainly, but they lacked the inherent cruelty intended by the letter.

So if not kids, who? Michele asked herself. Her chair tilted back wildly as she stood abruptly, wrapping her arms around herself, suddenly cold. No one she knew had knowledge of the fact that she had gone to the police with information. There was no way anyone could have found out, either, unless... Michele's mouth tightened.

McLain! He or one of his men must have given the information to someone. She slid weakly back into her chair at the thought. Surely the information hadn't been released to the media, she prayed sickly.

She forced herself to think more rationally. Her involvement in the case hadn't been made public, she decided after a few moments. There had been no phone calls from the media, nor had she been the recipient of any sidelong looks or whispered conversations of the sort that she remembered from when she was a child. She wasn't being vain; she knew that if it had gotten out that a *psychic*—she cringed at the word—had gone to the police, it would have made the headlines. The media had been complaining for weeks that the police department was withholding evidence the public had a right to know. The department's standard reply was that all information that could be prudently released had been.

But even if the press hadn't been notified, the department, McLain specifically, had to be responsible for this information being leaked. There was no other way to explain how this crackpot had gotten hold of her name. Michele felt her ire rise rapidly. McLain was in charge of this case, and as the ranking officer, he should be held accountable, regardless of which of his officers was the source of the leak.

This did it. She had endured McLain's harassment tactics without comment, but this was going to stop. As of now. Michele got up and grabbed her purse, reaching distastefully for the paper and envelope. She shoved both inside her purse and left the house.

Connor McLain had a lot to answer for.

The district headquarters was no less chaotic when Michele entered it than it had been on her last visit, but she gave the atmosphere little notice. As she had driven over, her fury had mounted until she was ready to grab McLain and shake him. She made her way purposefully to his office. She rapped on the door once before trying the knob. Locked.

Michele sighed with frustration. Once she stopped for a moment she noticed that the office was dark. Wonderful. Obviously the great detective had weekends off. Michele turned away from the door in exasperation. The thought of having to wait until Monday to berate McLain made her want to grind her teeth with frustration. She made her way slowly through the sea of desks, lost in her own thoughts.

"Hey! What brings you here again, Miss Easton?"

Michele's head jerked up at the friendly greeting. Michael Riley was coming toward her, a wide smile on his cheerful face.

Michele smiled slightly. It was impossible not to respond to the officer's infectious grin. "I was just here to speak to Lieutenant McLain, but it appears he's not here."

Riley shook his head. "Nope. He's off all weekend. Did you have some more information for us?"

"No, nothing like that," Michele explained hastily. "It's...personal. I haven't seen him recently, and I needed to talk to him about a different matter."

Michael looked surprised, then delighted, as he misinterpreted her meaning. "You and the lieutenant have been seeing each other? That's neat, really neat. Since you checked out all right, he must have felt okay about asking you out, right? I feel kind of responsible for bringing you two together, in that case."

Michele stood still in shock, as much from his misunderstanding as from what he had just revealed. "Yes, I guess I 'checked out' just fine," she responded slowly.

"I knew you would," the younger man boasted. "I'm pretty good at sizing people up, and I could tell you were okay. I was kind of surprised that the lieutenant ordered a background check on you, but that's how he is, you know. Real thorough. Did you know he was the youngest man this department has ever made detective lieutenant?"

Michele was inwardly reeling. A background check! On her! How dare he! she seethed. When she found Connor McLain, he was going to be very sorry indeed. What rank came after lieutenant? she wondered. Whatever it was, he was never going to have to worry about making it. When she got done with him, he would be known as the youngest *dead* detective lieutenant this department had ever seen. She realized belatedly that Mike was looking at her expectantly, and her mind scurried to come up with the answer he so obviously expected. "Uh, yes, that is, I mean, no, I didn't know."

"I guess the lieutenant wouldn't talk about it. He's a pretty modest guy," Mike continued.

It was painfully obvious that Officer Michael Riley suffered from a bad case of hero worship for the soon-to-be-deceased Connor McLain. "I'm sure he is," Michele answered stiffly.

"I'm sorta surprised, though," continued Mike chattily. "You're not really the lieutenant's type. I mean," he went on hastily, "what used to be his type. What I mean is, you're classier than his usual dates."

I'll just bet, she thought darkly. She attempted to answer normally. "Well, I have to admit, I've never met anyone like *him* either." And hope never to again, she added silently. She extricated herself from the conversation with some difficulty, finding that Mike was eager to expound on McLain's sterling character. Pleading a prior appointment, she excused herself and left the building.

She was even more furious with the lieutenant now, after Mike's disclosure, and less inclined to wait until Monday to confront him. She tapped the steering wheel in frustration as she waited for a light to turn green. Struck with an idea, she drove to the nearest service station and asked to see a phone book. Flipping through the thick book quickly, she found the right page and ran a finger down the listings until she found the name she was looking for.

C. McLain.

With a quick burst of hope she jotted down the address on a slip of paper from her purse. She consulted the city map in the back of the book, added directions to the paper and returned to her car. She crossed her fingers as she drove, hoping fervently that the address she'd found did, indeed, belong to the lieutenant.

Twenty minutes later Michele was getting out of her car in front of a small white house with green shutters. She looked it over carefully. The front door was standing partially open to let in the cool June breeze. She braced herself. Now, Detective Lieutenant McLain, she thought grimly as she started up the walk, I hope I give you the jolt of your life.

Connor McLain's forearms bulged as he lifted the barbell for the fiftieth time. Sweat ran profusely from his face and dampened his back and chest. Fifty-one. Fifty-two. Fifty—*Rrrring.* He cursed out loud as he brought the barbell down with a crash against the stand. The doorbell sounded again. He sat up and grabbed a towel, wiping his face as he made his way up the stairs from the basement.

"Yeah, yeah," he shouted, as the buzzer sounded persistently again. "What's your damn hur—" His final words were bitten off as he pulled the door completely open and saw who was standing there.

Well, well, well, he thought bemusedly as he stared back at the woman before him. The porcelain princess has come down from her throne to visit the peasants. Then his flight of fancy hardened.

"What the hell are you doing here?" he demanded brusque-ly.

"Aren't you going to ask me in?" she inquired brazenly.

Connor stared at her for a moment before shrugging and pushing open the screen door for her to walk through. He turned and led the way through the small living room to an even smaller kitchen. "Did you decide to come and check out the contents of my closet after all?" he threw over his shoulder.

Michele knew she shouldn't be surprised at his rudeness. She gritted her teeth and followed him to the kitchen where he held a glass under the faucet before raising it to down the contents in one long swallow. He ran another glassful before shutting off the faucet and turning to face her.

"To what do I owe the honor of this visit?" he asked sardonically.

"To several things, actually," Michele began, feeling her fury rise again as she thought of the events that had led her here. "Let's start with your incredible stupidity, for one. And your utter gall," she bit off, glaring at him.

He gazed silently at the obviously angry woman in front of him. With those long legs sheathed in jeans and her hair pulled back with a barrette, she looked like a high schooler. He took another long drink of water. Those gorgeous gray eyes that she usually schooled to a silvery blankness were anything but blank now. They were actually spitting fire. He smiled slightly. He much preferred them shooting darts at him than devoid of any emotion at all. "Let's narrow this down a little," he drawled. "Just what have I done that you disagree with?"

Michele wasn't fooled by his innocent act. "You—" she came forward and stabbed him in the chest with her forefinger "—had me checked out! Me! Would you like to explain just what you hoped to find by running a background check on me?"

Connor's eyes narrowed. "Where did you get that information?" he bit out.

"Never mind!" Michele snarled at him, her face close to his. "I'm not answering any more of your questions. It's time you answered a few of mine. Just what the heck do you hope to find out by snooping around in my life?"

"What is it you're so eager to hide?" Connor countered, before taking another long drink of water.

Michele ground her teeth in frustration. He was being deliberately obtuse. She inhaled and exhaled slowly, trying to regain her calm. She stared at him mutely, attempting to give herself some time before she reached out and strangled him. For the first time she looked, really looked, at him.

Slow heat suffused her body. He was very bare. He wore running shoes with no socks, brief shorts and a gray tank top. Perspiration had stained his shirt and tangled his dark blond hair. She had obviously interrupted him in the midst of some sort of exercise.

Suddenly Michele felt smothered. Needing some space between them, she turned and moved away before facing him again. This time she kept her eyes trained strictly on his face. "Tell me why you ordered a background check on me," she demanded with forced calmness.

Connor surveyed her silently for long moments. He hadn't really expected that Michele would learn of the discreet inquiries Cruz had made, but it was possible. What interested him more was the fact that she was so agitated about it. Was that an indication of her duplicity in the case, or the honest indignation of an average citizen?

His mouth twisted. *Honest* was the last word he would apply to a woman like her. It was obvious she was upset. She was probably unused to being treated with suspicion, her being such a high-society professional and all.

It was that thought more than anything else that made him abruptly throw his normal caution to the wind. If she wanted answers, she would damn well get them. And he was certain the lovely princess wouldn't like them.

"It's standard procedure to run a check on someone who has information about a crime," Connor explained soberly. "Especially when you suspect that the person might have been involved herself."

Michele's mouth opened in shock, but nothing came out. She felt as though she were reeling from an invisible blow. "Me?" she questioned faintly, still unable to believe it. "You suspected I might have been involved in the kidnappings?" Taking Connor's silence for agreement, she shook her head in disbelief before swinging her gaze back to him. "But why?" she asked, unaware of the almost plaintive note in her voice.

Connor watched her through hooded eyes. Whatever else this woman was, she was one hell of an actress. If she was acting, which she had to be, he corrected himself grimly. He didn't believe her lame story about dreaming about that jacket. Nobody outside the few men working on the case and Connor's superiors knew of it. Nor had Connor been able to find a leak among those officers. As far as he had been able to ascertain, Michele Easton had never had any contact with any of his men until she came to the police with her information.

She had been at several of the same fund-raising functions as the mayor and Brad Jacobs, the current D.A. But neither man was a fool; neither would spread such information. Connor had even checked—discreetly, of course—to see if there was possibly a closer connection between Michele and Jacobs, McIntire or even the police commissioner. It wouldn't have been the first time that, in the midst of an illicit affair, pillow talk ensued.

But he had been unsuccessful following that line, as well. Most likely someone had made a slip about the jacket to a third party, who had in turn mentioned it to Michele. Unless, of course, his original suspicion was correct and Michele Easton was in on this up to her pretty white neck. In that case, it made her voluntary involvement in the case even harder to fathom.

"Why not you?" he asked brusquely. "You come to us with some cock-and-bull story about dreaming up this information. You beg us not to tell anyone else. You get defensive when I show up at your office."

Michele had partially recovered from her shock. She could feel her anger rising again. "I don't believe this!" she exclaimed, throwing her hands in the air. She paced several steps before twirling back to him. "Is this how you treat every citizen who comes to you with information? You insult them—no, don't deny it," she said sarcastically as he appeared ready to interrupt. "You've treated me from the beginning like a lunatic. That's fine. I'd half expected that. I believed that doing what was right would make up for the very real possibility that the police would laugh at me, or worse. But you have absolutely no reason, *none,* to suspect me. If this is the way you run your investigations, Lieutenant McLain—" her voice was scathing "—it's certainly no wonder you've made little headway on this case."

Connor listened to her tirade emotionlessly, until she appeared to have finished. He carefully set his glass next to the sink, then turned back to her and said with deceptive mildness, "Why shouldn't we consider you a suspect in this case? After all, you did come to us with information that hadn't been released to the media, knowledge that you couldn't have obtained unless it was leaked to you by someone in the department. Unless," he added with a hard edge to his voice, "you were there yourself."

Michele gazed at him in amazement. She felt as though she were Alice in Wonderland, conversing with one of the illogical, nonsensical creatures encountered behind the looking glass. "What," she asked, her voice rising despite every attempt to stay calm, "are you talking about?"

Connor's own patience snapped. He smacked the counter beside him, and the sharp crack reverberated through the small area. "I'm talking, Miss Easton, about your knowledge of the jacket. The media was never told about our finding it, or the state it was in. Even the parents weren't told. So would you mind telling me how the hell you knew? Either someone told you, or you're involved in some way." His voice was even, but as cold and deadly as a blade. "Which is it?"

Michele stood watching him without comment, their gazes enmeshed. She had been too kind in her first assessment of him, she decided. She had assumed he was hard, somewhat unfeeling, but she had never suspected that he was so bullheaded and blind. There was no arguing with this man; he quite simply refused to believe her. She might as well save her breath.

"I've already told you how I came by that knowledge," she replied simply. "It's not my problem if you refuse to believe me, it's yours." She started for his front door, unable to stand one more minute, one more second, in his exasperating presence. Her hand was on the knob before she suddenly remembered what had sent her looking for him in the first place. She turned around suddenly and almost collided with his hard body, he was following her so closely. As it was, she shrank back self-protectively against the door.

He certainly was...big, she thought inanely, feeling suffocated by his closeness. Not that he was especially tall, he was only a few inches taller than she was with both of them in sneakers. It was more than that. His shoulders were so broad, they blocked her view of the room. His arms bulged with muscles, as did his chest, which the damp tank top clung to revealingly. The power was echoed in the long ropes of muscles in his legs and calves. She fidgeted in spite of herself. Something about this man made her uneasy. He exuded power, both physical and from the force of his presence.

Connor watched with interest the rapid rise and fall of the T-shirt before him. If he hadn't known better he would have misinterpreted that visual raking of his body for interest. He noted her imperceptible movement away from him, closer to the door, and something inside him tightened. No doubt the princess was repulsed by a male body that wasn't freshly showered and cologned.

That knowledge, that he repelled her physically, made him want to do something shocking. Something like close the small distance between them and press her pretty body against the door. Press so close that the feel of them, their smells, their tastes, would intermingle. Press close enough to stamp her with his touch, so that when she left she would be unable to forget the feel of his body against hers.

Hell! Connor pulled away abruptly in disgust. What was he thinking? This woman spelled nothing but trouble for any man, himself especially. He'd had enough of pampered society sweethearts to last him six lifetimes. This one was even worse than most of the shallow empty-headed debutantes; she might even be involved in a crime. He widened the distance between them by several more steps, overcome with self-recrimination. What was it about this woman that made him lose his cool?

Michele let out a long shaky breath she hadn't been aware of holding. Surreptitiously she wiped her palms on her jeans, wiping away the inexplicable moisture his nearness had caused.

"What else do you want, Princess?" Connor's voice was taut with self-restraint, the name she brought to mind slipping out before he could stop it. "You want me to apologize for doing my job? Do you expect me to say I'm sorry for not believing your farfetched stargazing abilities?"

Michele felt her unease evaporate in the face of his attack. "What I expect is for you to act like the professional you're supposed to be and do your job to the best of your ability...." She trailed off as he walked away from her. "Where are you going?" she asked in frustration.

"To take a shower, which I'm sure I badly need, so as not to offend your delicate sensibilities," was his sarcastic reply. He turned and invited, "You can come along if you wish. I'll bet a mind picker can tell even more about a man's psyche from the items in his bathroom than those in his closet." He disappeared into a hallway, and Michele heard a door close firmly.

She felt like following him to the door and giving it a hard kick. Instead, when she heard water running, she threw herself furiously into an easy chair. That man was the most insufferable human being she had ever had the misfortune to meet, she fumed silently. But she darn well was going to wait until he finished with his shower. She hadn't told him about the letter yet, an omission she could hardly believe. But with the stupefying news that he considered her a suspect, she had forgotten everything but her own anger.

Michele sat motionless for a few minutes, silently rehearsing just what she was going to tell the almighty detective. Her eyes roamed the room vacantly, then returned to peruse it with more interest. Somehow she wouldn't have expected this man to live in a house. A sterile, impersonal apartment seemed more his style. She allowed her gaze to sweep the small living room in which she sat. She was forced to admit it was anything but impersonal.

A cream, brown and navy color scheme had been used to match the carpeting, furniture and blinds. The colors were tied together by the wallpaper covering one wall of the room. Michele rose to examine it more closely. Though the room was somewhat stark, with little hanging on the walls, a man's stamp was apparent. Michelle stopped in front of one shelf, which bore a group of pictures. The people in the photos were strangers to her, but one man in a picture with McLain looked familiar. Michele looked more closely. The two men were in uniform and looked younger. Both were laughing, and Michele was arrested by the fact that Connor McLain did indeed have deep masculine dimples. She looked fixedly at the other man in the picture before remembering abruptly that he had been in Connor's office the first time she had gone there.

"Find anything interesting?" a low voice drawled behind her.

Michele forced herself to turn slowly, though in truth he had startled her. He'd changed into a different pair of running shorts and another tank top. His feet were bare, and his hair was brushed back wetly from his face. She raked his figure with her gaze before returning it to his face and retorting pointedly, "Absolutely nothing."

The brief flare of his nostrils was her only indication that she had scored a hit. His voice, when he spoke again, held its usual sardonic tone. "There must have been something compelling to keep you here. Why don't you get it out so you can be on your way? You're messing up my day off."

That ignited Michele's usually even temper like a spark to prairie grass. "Well, that's just too bad, Detective. Because my day was already ruined." She dug in her purse to find the note she had received and held it up to his face.

Connor read the message quickly, his gut clenching as he took in the words and the defaced picture. "When did you get this?" he demanded. He tried to force down the immediate leap of excitement he felt. But if this linked Michele to the case, it might be the break they'd been looking for.

"It was with the rest of my mail this afternoon." She fumbled in her purse and pulled out the envelope it had arrived in. She held out both the letter and envelope, but when McLain made no move to take them, her arm dropped. "Somebody obviously slipped it through the mail slot, no doubt thanks to you." Her voice was caustic.

Connor's eyes sharpened. "Me? What do I have to do with this?"

Michele was incensed. "You're obviously guilty of the same thing you've been accusing me of. Despite your promise to keep our conversations private, you've blabbed it to someone. Someone," she said thickly, "with a sick mind."

Connor's gaze sharpened at her accusation. "You're blaming me for this?"

"Damn right I am." Michele spoke emphatically. "Nobody knew I'd gone to see you. I certainly didn't tell anybody. Either you or one of your men let it out. I suppose it's only a matter of time before this is splashed all over the press," she bit out. "So much for your word."

He scowled at her. This note tied her to the case in a way he couldn't deny. It also gave him the sinking feeling that she might be in danger. The immediate protective instincts that arose at the thought made him uncomfortable, then angry. "I can assure you, Miss Easton, that neither my men nor I would have told anyone about you. We have nothing to gain by it. You must have inadvertently let it slip to someone you know," Connor said bitingly. "For all I know, you..." He trailed off, raking his hand through his wet hair exasperatedly. This woman could set him off faster than a firecracker. He didn't like her, he thought frustratedly. And it was becoming damn hard to hide that.

But Michele seized on his unfinished sentence and drew her own conclusion. "For all you know, I what? What were you going to accuse me of now, oh mighty detective? Writing the sick thing myself?" When he didn't answer, her fury mounted. "You are the limit," she snapped. She shoved the note back in her purse. It gave her something to do with her hand, which itched to slap his hard cheek. "I give up. You're right. You were right from the start. I masterminded the kidnappings. I came to you because I couldn't stand being ignored. I manufactured this note for the same reason. There you go, Lieutenant, case solved. Now you can go back to playing kindergarten cop."

Her eyes, those usually calm gray eyes, were blazing up at Connor. His mouth twitched with a tiny smile. Her face wasn't as beautifully serene as it usually was, but he preferred it as he saw it now. More emotion was displayed on it now than he would bet normally crossed it in a month. "You have quite a sarcastic streak in you," he mocked. "Very uncharacteristic in a professional lady such as yourself."

Michele closed her eyes and strove for calm. "I will not even begin to catalogue your unattractive personality traits, Lieutenant McLain. Except to tell you that you are the most incredibly obtuse man I've ever met. From what I've seen so far, you are to police work what Mr. Ed is to Thoroughbred racing."

Far from annoying him as she had intended, her remark seemed to entertain Connor. He threw his head back and laughed out loud. Michele stood transfixed for a moment as she witnessed firsthand the fatally masculine dimples at the sides of that well-formed mouth. They were just as devastating as she had feared.

When Connor finally stopped chuckling, he eyed Michele with amusement. "You really should cut loose more often," he gibed. "Keeping it pent-up inside for too long makes you really vicious. Let me see the note again."

"Why?" Michele snapped. "So you can use it to somehow show my involvement in the case? Forget it."

"It would appear that you *are* involved in the case, Michele. Too involved for your own good. I'll need to take the note down to headquarters and have it checked out." His eyebrows came together as he watched her pull the paper out of her purse. "Not much reason to dust it for prints, if that's how you've been handling it."

Michele flushed guiltily. She hadn't even thought about the possibility that she might be destroying evidence by her careless handling of the letter. She watched as Connor went to the kitchen and returned with a plastic bag. He returned and opened it, and Michele dropped the note inside.

"I don't suppose you saw anybody around your house who shouldn't have been there?" he inquired.

"I was out all day."

"I'll have the lab take a look at this," Connor said. "We'll talk to your neighbors, the mailman, see if anyone saw someone near your house." Then he warned her, "But don't expect too much."

"Where you're concerned," Michele responded loftily, "I'm learning to expect very little."

"Good," Connor responded imperturbably, his light green eyes watching her soberly. "Then you won't be disappointed."

Michele returned his gaze silently, wondering why she had the feeling that she had just received a warning on a personal, rather than a professional, level.

Chapter 4

At the knock on his office door, Connor sat back in his chair and turned over the papers he had been perusing. "Come on in," he invited, fully expecting to see Cruz or one of the other men come through the door. Instead his eyebrows rose comically when Dave Lanthrop walked in.

"I've got the lab results you were asking for, Connor," the other man said, handing over the written reports. "I was on my way home and had to pass this way, so I thought I'd drop it off myself."

"That was sure fast," Connor observed. "You guys in the lab must not be as busy as usual."

That remark got a rise, as he'd intended. The lab worker good-naturedly invited Connor to take a scenic route to the devil's headquarters. "You said it was a rush job," Dave replied. "You also reminded me that I owed you one. How you figure that, I don't know, but we're even now, after this."

Connor grinned as he listened to the older balding man in front of him grouse. "We'll never be even, Dave," he said wickedly. "I saved your rear that night, and you know it." Connor was referring to a poker game the two of them had attended years ago. Dave had lost much more money than he could afford to and had been white with fear at the prospect of facing his wife. Connor had staked him for the rest of the night until he had won most of it back.

Dave rolled his eyes comically. "I do know it, believe me. Especially after you read those results. They won't be much help, I'm afraid."

Connor grimaced as he quickly read through the short report. "You're telling me," he agreed. "Not that I really expected anything different."

"There's one set of clear prints all over the paper and envelope. I assume they belong to whoever received the letter?"

Connor nodded.

Dave continued. "There are a few other smears on the paper, but no other clear prints. The envelope and paper are both mass-produced, low-grade types, sold in any department store. The picture had been drawn on with a red marker—nothing special there, I'm afraid, unless you come up with one belonging to a suspect for a match."

Connor's expression told Dave the chances of that were minute.

Dave went on. "There was some human hair caught in the adhesive used to hold the letters on the paper. I'll need more time if you want a breakdown on that."

Connor nodded decisively. "Go ahead and run the tests, Dave. Somehow we have to establish the link between the kidnapper and Michele Easton. The letter shows that he knows who she is, maybe even knows her personally."

The other man gave a low whistle, recalling the message evident in both the letters and picture. "Well, I hope for her sake, as well as the department's, we find something that will lead you to him. We'll get on it right away."

Connor was well aware how backed up the workers in the lab were, but this investigation had been granted preferred treatment by the police commissioner. "Thanks, Dave."

Lanthrop rose. "Since that's all I have for now, I'll leave you to more important things."

"Yeah." Connor heaved a sigh as he walked the lab worker to his office door. "Which is a meeting with the top brass, starting in—" he checked the gold watch on his wrist "—exactly seven minutes. I wouldn't want to be late, especially since the mayor himself will be there to chew my butt for what he sees as a plodding investigation."

Dave grinned in commiseration. "Sorry, my man. But better you than me."

Thirty minutes later, Connor was not inclined to agree with Dave's estimate. The mayor and his entourage had been late, as usual, keeping the police commissioner, the chief of detectives and Connor waiting for over fifteen minutes. Once there, McIntire had proceeded to chew each of them up and spit them out for the way the investigation was proceeding. Connor waited impassively, arms crossed, for his turn to come, as it surely would. As the supervisor overseeing the case, he would be held directly responsible for its outcome.

Relying on years of practice, Connor tuned out the mayor's booming voice. He had been at loggerheads with McIntire before today and was sure he would be again. There was no love lost between the two men, stemming from McIntire's days as a defense attorney. In Connor's estimation he had strayed over the line a time or two in his zeal for acquittals. He'd once all but accused Connor on the stand of falsifying evidence against his client. Which made his subsequent winning mayoral campaigns based on being tough on crime laughable. McIntire was an inveterate politician. He had the glib words and phony sincere attitude to tell the public what they wanted to hear.

Connor had no sympathy for the tough race the mayor was currently involved in. His opponent was a minister, for God's sake, who had a local radio show. He apparently had quite a following, because the two men were running neck and neck. Recent allegations of bribe taking by members of the mayor's staff, selling his time for meetings with prominent businessmen and special interest groups, were hurting him, although the evidence had yet to be made public. But McIntire was being kept on the defensive for once, with less time to spend on his usual campaign speeches. And the gist of this meeting was that the lack of progress in the kidnappings was being regarded as a personal affront to the mayor, another black spot on his record.

"Well, McLain, what about it?"

Connor's bored gaze rose slowly to meet the mayor's belligerent one. Oh, good, he thought wearily. It was obviously his turn to be raked over the coals.

"What about what, Mayor?" he asked with mock politeness, causing McIntire to turn almost apoplectic.

"I was just telling the mayor that you had your men following up every available lead," Nick Kincannon, the police commissioner, put in smoothly.

Connor's gaze slid back to the mayor. Nick and Bob Lovitt, the chief of detectives, seemed to be waiting with almost held breath. Connor was amused to note that neither seemed to trust him not to start a war. He shook his head. He didn't know where he got a reputation like that. He wasn't a yes man, but he knew how to play the department games when they were called for. And now they were clearly called for.

Connor took his time answering, aware that during his silence the mayor was turning purple. "I'm sure the mayor is aware of that, Commissioner. After all, that's what he's run his campaigns on all these years, isn't it? A police department that's tough on crime. And he's certainly fulfilled his campaign promises. If I were to sit here and tell him that not all was going well, that would reflect back on the mayor's office, wouldn't it? And we wouldn't want that. Not with the election so close and all."

The three men looked at each other, carefully avoiding looking at the mayor. All were aware of the truth of Connor's statement, but neither of his superiors could believe he'd said it. They waited for an explosion.

It wasn't forthcoming. Larry McIntire leaned forward and asked through gritted teeth, "Is that what you're telling me, Lieutenant? You've got leads that are panning out, you're seeing progress in the case?" His tone was almost pleading.

Connor looked at him stonily. "We're progressing, Mayor. It's going to take time. In some of those neighborhoods people don't see anything, you know what I mean? We found a car abandoned last night that fits a description of the one used in the last kidnapping. The lab workers are going over it now."

Larry McIntire leaned back in his chair, suddenly expansive. "Well, that *is* good news, isn't it? I'm sure you'll have something to report later on that. Fine, fine."

Connor endured the hearty slap on the shoulder and the mayor's insincere flattery stonily. He was well aware that if the car hadn't been found yesterday, leaving him with nothing new to report, his head would have been on the chopping block. For now, he was the fair-haired boy. He almost snorted out loud. God save him from politicians.

The mayor and his people filed out of the office, followed by the police commissioner. When the door closed after them, Bob Lovitt looked at him soberly. "You almost walked too close to the line that time, Connor."

Connor heaved a sigh. He liked Bob Lovitt, and he respected him. He went to the line for his detectives. That meant a lot to Connor. The last thing he wanted was for Bob to take more heat because of him.

"What was I supposed to say, Chief? I can only report on what we've got, and I'm not about to apologize if the clues don't come in at times that correspond with his latest press conference. Hell, you and I both know that the only reason the FBI hasn't been called in on this is because McIntire wants the glory when the department cracks the case."

"Maybe so. But that doesn't make the politics disappear." Lovitt shook his head. "I know that you and McIntire aren't best friends. But unless you want to be tossed off the case, you'd better toe the mark when you talk to him about this. The race is heating up, tempers are short. I was shocked when the mayor requested that you be put on the case, given your run-ins with him in the past. And I doubt he'd hesitate to remove you if you ticked him off. So watch it."

"Yeah," Connor muttered, getting up to leave.

"Connor?"

Connor turned his head quizzically.

The chief was surveying him shrewdly. "You look like you could use some sleep. Why don't you get out of here on time for once and go home?"

"Good idea," Connor said, as he headed out the door. "I have one stop to make first, though." It was time he put aside this aversion he seemed to have to Michele Easton. As reluctant as he was at the idea, he planned to drop by her place on his way home to tell her the results of the lab tests. She deserved to be kept abreast of the developments stemming from the note, so he was going to have to get beyond the instant antagonism he felt in her presence. And while he was there, he would hold his tongue, even if he had to bite it in half. All he needed right now was some high-society princess screaming police harassment.

It was actually almost three hours before Connor reached Michele's address. The lab results had come in on the car they had found abandoned. Since it had been reported stolen shortly before the kidnapping, the owner wouldn't be much help. They were able to find some samples of hair and fibers and were working on linking them to the victims or the sender of Michele's note. Connor was exhausted but confident that finally they had a real lead.

He knocked on Michele's door and frowned as the force of his rap sent the door open several inches. She didn't even have the door latched tightly, never mind locked. You would think after the scare she'd had, the woman would be more careful.

Even as he thought it, Connor's hand went to the butt of his revolver. In his profession it was second nature to be prepared when things didn't appear quite right.

"Miss Easton!" he barked loudly, even as he entered the home carefully. His observant gaze saw nothing out of the ordinary. Michele's purse and suit jacket lay across the top of a small desk in the entryway. Receiving no answer, he made his way slowly into the living room, where the scene that met his eyes made his mouth flatten in disapproval.

Michele was asleep on the couch in front of the television, which was still on. A cat was curled at her feet, and it yawned delicately as it blinked at Connor. A more mundane scene he couldn't imagine, and Connor's hand dropped from his gun. His arrival and shouting hadn't even roused Michele, and he ground his teeth. His first instinct was to shake her awake, hard, and give her a tongue-lashing about safety. He mentally counted to ten. He had promised himself that this was going to be a purely professional visit, and he was going to remain calm, no matter what it cost him.

He reached out to shake her, but his hand jerked as if he had been scalded. "God Almighty," he whispered reverently. His mind hadn't even registered what she was wearing until he had reached out to touch her shoulder. Her bare shoulder, he corrected himself mentally. Somewhere on her trip to the couch she had managed to shed all her clothes except for the lacy peach slip and filmy nylons.

Sweat broke out on Connor's forehead, and when he swallowed, his tongue felt thick. The damn knot she had scraped her hair back into was coming loose, and tendrils of ebony curled enticingly across one cheek and shoulder. He allowed himself one sweeping glance to ascertain that her legs were as gorgeous as he had feared. Long and smooth, they seemed to go on forever.

Connor pulled his eyes firmly back to Michele's face and forced himself to keep them there. As a result of his resolve, his hand was rougher than he had intended, his voice harsher.

"Miss Easton? Michele? Wake up!"

He frowned as he peered down at the still-sleeping woman. She must have been exhausted to sleep this soundly, and as if to attest to that fact, he noted the faint mauve shadows beneath the sooty fans of her lashes. But this was not, as he had imagined, a restful sleep. Her eye movements were rapid beneath the delicate lids, her breathing quick.

Connor picked up her wrist and whistled soundlessly at the racing pulse he found beating beneath the fragile tracing of veins. She must be having a granddaddy of a nightmare.

Even as he thought it, Michele began to tremble, soundlessly shaking her head in mute appeal. The whole couch moved with the force of her quaking, and Connor decided he had stood motionless long enough. He sat down on the couch next to her and grasped both shoulders, pulling her to a sitting position. He shook her slightly, repeating her name over and over.

Michele felt as if she were being pulled down a dark vortex. As always, she was a helpless spectator to another's suffering, the agony intensified by her inability to speak, to move. She wanted to cry out, to plead with someone to stop it, to help these children, to help them, help them....

"Michele! Wake up! Michele!"

Her eyes fluttered open, then fixed on the stern face so close to her own. She didn't even acknowledge the incongruity of finding Connor McLain in her dreams. Still in the grip of the nightmare that had overcome her, she grasped his face in both hands. "You have to help them. You have to find them. Time is running out."

Connor felt a flash of cold fear in the pit of his stomach at her words. Her flat statement, delivered so devoid of emotion, accompanied by the silvery, almost metallic sheen of her eyes, was eerie. Even as he was recovering, Michele seemed to visibly crumple, her hands falling away from him, the shaking intensifying.

He pulled her onto his lap, his hard arms coming tightly around her. "It's all right, Michele, it's all right. It's over." His crooning voice continued, providing her with a lullaby with which to slowly return to from her nightmare.

Michele wasn't aware of how long they sat like that, with her shielded in his arms, before she became completely aware. The pounding in her temples, which always accompanied the end of one of her dreams, was hammering away inside. The trembling in her limbs made even conversation difficult but still she tried. "What are you doing here?" she muttered, trying to strain away from him. In the aftermath of the nightmare, she wasn't even surprised by his presence.

Connor tightened his arms, making escape impossible. "I pushed open the door. You didn't even have it closed," he informed her, some of his annoyance creeping back into his voice. "Anyone could have come in and found you like this."

"Anyone did," she returned, but the shaking in her limbs made even sarcasm impossible. She raised one hand to rub her temple, but the trembling made her attempts ineffectual.

Connor stared down at her hard. "You have a headache?"

"Stop screaming," Michele pleaded querulously. "I always have a headache when I wake from one of those dreams."

Though his arms still automatically tightened as her body continued its furious trembling, Connor was frozen. This was it, then, a recurrence of what he had ridiculed as psychic claptrap, had dismissed as her imagination or, worse, a cover-up for her involvement. No one had ever claimed that Connor McLain was easy to fool, and he would eat his gun if this scene tonight had been faked. There was no way she could have known he was coming, for one thing. And the shape she was in was a statement in and of itself.

He became aware then of her faint attempts to free herself from his arms. He gathered her even closer. "Stop it," he muttered. "You're in no shape to fight with me or anyone else tonight."

"I don't need your help," Michele retorted through the hammering inside her head.

"You need someone's help, and I'm here," Connor announced flatly. "No wonder you have a headache, the way you keep your hair pulled back like that." Michele felt him pull the remaining pins from her hair, and then it spilled down her back. Her protests were faint and easily ignored by him. His hands went next to her temples, massaging so gently that a surprised sigh came from her.

Michele felt herself go limp, leaning more heavily into him. He was the last person she should trust, the last one she could afford to let her guard down around, but she couldn't bring herself to care. It had been so long since someone had been there to calm her in the aftermath of her dreams.

Connor's gentle massage managed what aspirin couldn't. The loud clanging inside her head dulled to a tolerable throbbing. She was unable to control her shaking, though, and Connor seemed to sense that and moved his hands from her temples to pull her closer into his embrace, trying to still the shock-induced shaking.

But he was unable to stop her trembling, no matter how tightly he held her. He had seen enough shock victims to be fairly certain of what was afflicting her. God, if those dreams were vivid enough to cause this kind of physical response, he wondered grimly, what kind of emotional cost would they bring? He'd had little experience calming people down; his was usually the kind of personality that riled them up. But he instinctively knew that Michele needed something, anything, to take her mind off the events of her sleep.

He began to talk to her, softly, and without much purpose, just a way of letting her know she wasn't alone, to give her something else to focus her attention on. He wasn't even aware of what he talked about—innocuous things, events from his childhood, from his work as a detective. He told her about his family, his parents and sister. His voice went on and on into the night.

Michele gradually calmed in his hard grasp. She focused rigidly on his voice at first, welcoming his attempt to divert her attention. But at some point things began to change. She began to listen more to what he was saying than to the sound of his voice. She smiled to herself as she heard him recount some funny tale from his childhood. And slowly, gradually, the tension eased from her limbs. The shaking lessened and gradually stopped. His voice lulled her into a semiconscious state, one where she was warm, safe. Who would ever have thought, she wondered drowsily, that Connor McLain could be so consoling?

As the aftermath receded, however, the events of the dream became clearer, more focused. Michele hated to interrupt the unlikely truce that had developed between them for the time being, but she was forced to speak. She moved her head slightly, wincing at the renewed pain her action brought. "Two of them are gone now, Connor," she whispered, unconsciously using his first name. "The youngest boy and Lucy are both gone, the others are still there. You have to find them, you have to, before the others..."

Her words brought on renewed trembling, and Connor's mouth tightened. "Shhh," he soothed gruffly. "Let it go for now. You're in no shape for this discussion." He looked down into her pleading gaze, and something indefinable twisted his insides. He wasn't much good at consoling people, especially women. He lowered his lips to hers and gave her the only kind of consolation he knew.

Michele froze in disbelief when those warm lips touched her own. What was he doing? This wasn't... Her mouth softened even as her mental argument grew fuzzier. His mouth was chiseled perfection, alluringly soft over her own, enticingly sensual. He brushed his lips over hers softly, until unconsciously she followed their movement with her own.

Connor's mouth came down on her more firmly, and Michele's senses careened wildly. Her own mouth opened of its own volition, and his tongue pushed surely, strongly, into the sweet chamber. Even as she reveled in his sensual mastery, something inside cried out achingly. She'd been able to keep him at arm's length before, but tasting him like this, sharing this with him, was going to make it impossible to go back to their previous footing. But, oh, the taste of him was so warm, and she had been so long in the cold. Something inside her was beckoned to the flame burning in Connor. Even knowing that, like a moth tempted too close to the flames, she, too, would be singed. She allowed conscious thought to drift away and gave herself up to the magic of his kiss.

Connor was seared immediately by a heat so intense that he couldn't believe he'd hardly touched her. Her lips were sweeter than any wine and just as addicting. He returned to them again and again, mindlessly drugging himself with their sweetness. When Michele's lips opened under his, he felt his last rational thought swept away against the tide of need flooding him to taste, to sample, the sweet nectar within.

Michele's head arched beneath the sensual onslaught, and Connor mindlessly followed her movement, lowering her so she rested on the couch, one hip pressed intimately against him. Connor shifted uncomfortably, moving to lie half over her. Michele's eyes fluttered open, and the gray orbs looked faintly surprised to find him so close, looming above her. Connor noted with purely masculine satisfaction that they had lost that cool blankness she strove for around him. They were a smoky charcoal now, darkened with passion. He lowered his lips to her again, and Michele's neck arched under the tender bites he placed there, up and down the cords of her throat. Her hands slid from his shoulders to tangle in his thick golden hair, guiding him back to the lips invitingly parted for him.

Connor sealed their mouths again but soon found it wasn't enough. One hand slid up her slim arm and across the delicate lace adorning the slip's bodice. She wasn't wearing a bra, and that discovery set fire to his insides. He deliberately skirted her breasts, aware with his last remnant of sanity that if he touched her like that he would be lost. Instead he tortured them both for long moments by tracing the lace lightly, his touch leaving a path of fire in its wake.

Connor finally forced himself away from temptation, but it wasn't long before his wandering hand had him in trouble again. He reached to stroke her silky leg, mentally damning the nylon sheathing it. Again and again he swept his palm up and down her thigh, each time pushing her slip a fraction higher, as their lips twisted together.

Michele had lost what little rational thought she had. Under his compelling tutelage their tongues dueled intimately. She had never been kissed like this before, but she reveled in the unashamedly sensual sensation. Connor's chest came down closer to hers, and she pulled at his shoulders, mutely pleading for a firmer contact. He obliged at the same time that she became aware of his hand sweeping beneath her slip and touching her bare thigh where her nylons ended.

They both reacted as if they had been scalded, she jerking away and Connor sitting upright. He raised one shaking hand to rake through the tumbled mass that only minutes ago her hands had been buried in. His chest heaved in and out in gigantic breaths as he struggled for control. Looking at Michele sprawled wantonly half under him almost made him lose what little grip he had on his straining libido.

Michele stared up at Connor, stunned at his sudden departure. Gradually, passion cleared from her mind, and she took in the tight control he was trying to maintain. Her gaze dropped to their bodies, and she gasped as she became belatedly aware of her state of dishabille. Their legs were still tangled intimately, and one smooth thigh was almost totally exposed. Her hand moved quickly to pull her slip down to a more discreet level. At the same time Connor reached to smooth it down for her, and their hands met, scorching at the simple contact.

Connor mentally cursed and extricated his body from hers, turning his back as she sat up and arranged her disheveled clothing. When he turned back to her, Michele was standing, face averted. "I'll be right back," she murmured. She quickly walked to her bedroom for a robe, which she slipped on quickly. Afraid that Connor would simply come after her if she was gone too long, she reentered the living room. He was standing where she had left him, staring hard at her.

Michele swallowed, one hand automatically going to the vee neckline of the robe to close it more securely. She easily read the expression that crossed his face at her belated modesty and blushed.

"You should go," she told him, her voice soft but firm.

Connor looked at her steadily. Far from donning her ice princess mask as he had half feared, half hoped for, she looked far too vulnerable. The evidence of their passion was apparent in her kiss-swollen lips and the faint red marks on her neck, where his evening whiskers had abraded.

Michele flushed at the direction of his gaze and walked jerkily to the hallway, hoping that he would take the hint and leave gracefully. And indeed, it seemed as though he was going to take her cue at first. He followed her, but he didn't go out the door. Instead, he watched as she backed up against the wall rather than get too close to him. A week—hell, an hour—ago he would have taken that backing away as an affront, interpreting it as an unwillingness to touch such a commoner. But now he knew better. A few minutes ago she had not only been touching him, she'd been writhing under his touch. She'd desired it; she'd invited it. He was able to interpret her withdrawal for what it was, an unwillingness for any contact that would reignite the embers of their passion. He knew he was correct, because he felt the same damn way.

He watched her fidgeting soberly. "Don't look so scared," he said finally. "This doesn't have to mean anything. You needed comforting, and I was here. We stopped. It's not the end of the world."

"You couldn't begin to understand," Michele muttered. "I can't believe I let you...of all people... You don't even trust me!"

She saw the truth of her words sap the mockery from his face, to be replaced by his familiar guardedness. Even though she had known the truth, hurt slammed into her at having it verified. She wrapped her arms around herself and leaned her head wearily against the wall. "Please leave."

Connor made no movement toward the door. "I came over here tonight to tell you about the lab results," he said.

Michele put one hand to her head, where her headache was threatening to return full force. "Not tonight, Connor," she pleaded. "No more tonight."

He made a sudden decision. "You're right," he agreed and reached in front of her to lock the door.

"What are you...?"

He turned and swept her up in his arms, then followed the path to her bedroom that he had seen her take earlier. "I'm putting you to bed," he announced flatly. He laid her down in the middle of her brass bed but didn't spare more than a glance for the white wicker furniture and soft pastels. "You need sleep. Go ahead," he invited as he swept her under the covers. "I'll stay tonight. At least until you're asleep. You shouldn't be left alone right now."

Michele sputtered at his audacity. "I've told you..."

"And I've told *you*," he stated imperturbably. His light green eyes were full of promise. "If you want to try and throw me out, this could end up in a wrestling match. And while I certainly wouldn't mind, I was under the impression that you didn't crave my touch."

Michele grabbed the sheet and pulled it up to her neck, glaring impotently at him.

"That's the way," he said mockingly. He sat down in a wicker rocker near her bed. "Nighty-night, Michele."

Miraculously, Michele slept soundly, deeply, all night.

Chapter 5

Michele awoke the next morning without the lingering effects of a poor night's sleep that usually accompanied one of her dreams. Her head had the usual muzziness, though, that attested to the headache she had battled all night.

As she remembered the events of last night, her eyes jerked to the wicker rocker near her bed, where she had last seen Connor. It was empty, nothing about it suggesting that just hours ago it had been occupied by the most enigmatic man she had ever met. Michele released a breath she hadn't been aware she was holding. He must have left after she had fallen asleep. She was profoundly grateful that she didn't have to face him this morning.

A glance at the alarm clock told her that she had plenty of time before she was due at her office, so she planned a leisurely bath to soak all last night's trauma away.

As she headed to the bathroom she reflected that more than a little of last night's trauma was due to Lieutenant Connor McLain's unexpected appearance. What a strange man, she mused, so antagonistic and yet so inexplicably gentle when she had needed someone last night. He had certainly proven to be a mass of contradictions.

As Michele reached for the bathroom door, it opened inward suddenly and she found herself unexpectedly facing the mass of contradictions himself. Almost all of him, in fact.

Even as she stood, stupefied at his presence, her eyes wandered over his broad shoulders and well-developed biceps, down his wide bare chest, covered with whorls of hair several shades darker than that on his head. It narrowed at his waist and arrowed suggestively below the knot in his towel.

His towel! Her eyes bounced back up to his face. He had spent the night here. Her shock must have been apparent, because his face, his freshly shaven face, she noted unconsciously, took on a quizzical look. "You seem better this morning," he noted, "although somewhat surprised to see me. I slept on the couch last night. I hope that's okay."

She couldn't very well say otherwise, after all he'd done for her, so she responded stiffly, "That's fine."

Connor watched the expressions come and go across her face and would have laughed out loud if he hadn't had such a lousy night's sleep. There was shock there, then embarrassment and unease. Unfortunately, her couch had not been the most comfortable of beds, made even less so by his body's magnificent memory of who lay sleeping only steps away. Some of his ill temper prompted him to gibe, "I used a spare toothbrush and razor you had. However, I had to make do with the shaving cream in the shower."

Michele looked at him, taken aback. He had certainly made himself at home.

Connor returned her look soberly. "It was pink," he said in a pained tone.

Michele's mouth turned up slightly. This tough Philadelphia police detective with his face covered with pink foam would have been a worthwhile sight. Her smile quickly flickered away, however, as she was visually reminded that seeing him clad in only a towel was proving very worthwhile, too.

"Do you mind?" Connor asked with feigned politeness. Michele went blank for a moment before she became aware that she was blocking his exit from the bathroom.

"Excuse me," she said as she stood aside and let him pass. She followed him into the living room mindlessly, still wondering at his continued presence in her house. What was the usual protocol in a situation like this? she wondered wildly. Should she fix him breakfast?

Connor looked up to find Michele standing near and still staring at him. With a casual shrug, one hand went to the knot in his towel. He didn't have time to play games this morning; he was due at work. If the lady was interested in seeing if he was wearing his gun, he would oblige her.

Michele's shocked gasp and quickly turned back told him that she wasn't interested in that after all. Connor chuckled aloud as she marched stiffly into the small kitchen and, for lack of anything better to do, started the coffeemaker. As her ears attuned themselves to hear the subtle sounds of him dressing, she hurriedly opened cupboards and took out two coffee mugs. She slammed them on the counter with more force than was necessary.

Having him here in her apartment this morning was too intimate, she decided. As intimate as what had almost happened last night. It was as if they had gone through with what had begun between them and were engaged in an awkward morning-after scene.

She poured the coffee after it finished dripping and turned to find Connor standing a few feet away, regarding her fixedly. He was just finishing buckling his belt, and Michele flushed. She thrust a steaming mug toward him and said, "I hope black is okay."

"It's fine."

Unable to stay still beneath his intent gaze, she turned back to the refrigerator. "I think I have some eggs. I could fix you an omelet."

"Don't bother." At his abrupt response Michele turned to regard him quizzically. He sipped cautiously from the mug before going on. "Don't you think that would be straining the thin veneer of civility between us just a little too far?"

Michele's chin went up. "Yours has apparently snapped already."

He clarified. "I have to be at work in about twenty minutes, so I'm going to have to leave right away." He drained his cup, wincing as the hot liquid scorched a passage down his throat. Then he put the mug down and looked at her. Michele returned his gaze but said nothing. He turned and walked back to her living room, grabbed his jacket and headed for the door. She followed him, not knowing what else to do or say.

When he reached the door, Connor turned back. "Look, I need to talk to you about those lab results. I've got a full day scheduled, but I could probably break around six. Do you think you could come by headquarters about then?"

Michele was thankful she had a reason to say no. "I have late appointments tonight. I won't be done until seven-thirty or so."

Rather than giving up as she had hoped, he nodded curtly. "I'll meet you at eight, then. We can grab something to eat at the same time. Do you know Ricardo's?"

Michele nodded bemusedly at the name of a well-known Mexican restaurant.

"See you there at eight." And with that he walked out the door.

Michele stood stupefied for several moments before closing the door slowly. What had just happened here? she wondered dazedly. Far from putting him off as she had hoped, she'd just agreed to meet him later. For supper, for heaven's sake. As if she could swallow a thing sitting across from that man.

Suddenly noticing the time, she realized she had to hurry to get to work. In the end she settled for a quick shower rather than the leisurely bath she had counted on. Damn Connor McLain!

She was out of breath when she entered Psychological Associates. Julie was already typing and called out a cheerful greeting when Michele entered.

"Hi, I was just about to call and see if you were sick."

Michele flushed when she thought about what would have happened if someone had called an hour earlier. She wouldn't trust Connor McLain not to have answered her phone!

"I'm not late, am I?"

"Silly question," retorted Julie, wheeling her chair around expertly to flip open the appointment book. "I'm so used to you beating me here, though, that it seemed odd for me to open the office without you. Dr. Ryan has been looking for you already."

Before Michele had a chance to answer, the door opened and James came in. "Michele," he greeted her in his cultured voice. "I was hoping to schedule some time today to consult with you on the Howard boy. Do you have anything open?"

Michele looked questioningly at Julie, who pursed her lips as she perused the calendar. "It doesn't look like it, Michele. You have that luncheon at eleven-thirty to address the PTA. That will last until mid-afternoon. Then we have you scheduled until seven-thirty."

"Excellent," James said heartily. "We could have a late dinner. If that's all right with you, of course?" he asked Michele politely.

She smiled weakly. This wasn't the first time she had gotten the uneasy feeling that James would like them to be more than working associates. Somehow their working dinners and lunches rarely turned out to be such. Usually by the time they arrived at the restaurant James no longer wished to discuss business.

She briefly contemplated calling and leaving a message for Connor, canceling, but she quickly decided against that. She couldn't be sure that he wouldn't come here again to talk to her, and she wanted to avoid that at all costs. Finally she shook her head, and when she spoke, her voice was regretful. "I'm sorry, James, I already have plans for dinner. Perhaps tomorrow?" She looked at Julie, who busily searched for free time during the next day.

"All right," James said graciously. He studied her for a moment. "A date tonight, Michele?"

Michele hoped her face didn't give her away. By no stretch of the imagination could this meeting with Connor qualify as a date. "Not at all." She laughed nervously. "Just an acquaintance. We have some things to discuss."

James nodded and told Julie to call him with the list of times for tomorrow and left the office.

Michele met Julie's quizzical look but said, "Oh, look at the time. Have you pulled the first file for me, Julie?" Julie handed her the file before she even finished speaking.

"Thanks." Michele stepped into her office and closed the door on Julie's bemused gaze. Though she was usually thankful that she had such a super secretary, right now she would be grateful to have one who was a little less observant.

Connor hadn't been exaggerating when he had told Michele he had a full day planned. With some leads finally coming in on the investigation he was swamped with work. But he made time during the day to knock on the door of Bruce Casel, the police psychologist.

Bruce's face when he saw Connor was comical. "Lieutenant..." His voice was wary when he stood to greet Connor. "I'm...surprised to see you here, to say the least. No one told me you had been involved in a shooting."

Connor waved him back to his seat and sat down in a chair in front of the psychologist's desk. "I haven't been. That's not why I'm here." He stopped then, mentally weighing his words. He wasn't sure how best to ask Bruce what he wanted to know, especially since the last time they parted it hadn't been congenially—at least, not on Connor's part.

Bruce's wide face expressed confusion. "Then exactly why are you here, Lieutenant?"

What the hell, Connor thought in disgust. He might as well just come right out and ask him about Michele. He was no good at subterfuge. "I came for some information, Bruce. I'm hoping you can help me." He stopped then.

"You need information from me?" Bruce's tone was pleased. "About a case? What can I do for you?"

"Actually, it's a little complicated. How much do you know

about..." Connor hesitated, unsure how to proceed. "Psychics, I guess you'd call them."

"You mean people who claim extrasensory powers?" Bruce clarified, and Connor nodded. "Actually, I had a little experience with them when I was a grad student. I worked for a short time in the parapsychology laboratory at Duke University. What sort of information are you looking for?"

"Well, what's your opinion? Is it all a scam? Hocus-pocus?"

"That's certainly the opinion of much of the scientific community," Bruce said, nodding.

Connor didn't know whether to be angry or relieved.

"However," the psychologist continued, "there are some very renowned scientists who do believe that some people have such powers. Many well-known universities have departments researching the phenomenon. The field of parapsychology is fully recognized by some and regarded by others as having possibilities."

"How about you?" pressed Connor. "What do you think?"

Bruce took off his horn-rimmed glasses and polished them reflectively before answering. "Well, I'm not really sure, Connor. I'd like to say that I know without any doubt that such things can't exist." He replaced his glasses and returned Connor's impatient gaze imperturbably. "But I saw a few things at the university that defied easy explanation. I guess I feel that there are indeed people—relatively few people, but some—who do have inexplicable powers of perception." He shrugged. "Why do you ask?"

Connor proceeded to give Bruce a brief description of how Michele had come to them with information, and her story of how she had gotten it. "I know it sounds nuts—believe me, I agree—but she did have some information she shouldn't have had any way of knowing."

Bruce frowned. "How often does she have these dreams?"

Connor felt hunted. "How the hell should I know? She just had another last night, and whatever it was, it was real to her, you know what I mean? Her pulse was pounding, her heart was racing and she was shaking afterward like a freight train."

"Shock, I'd guess," mused Bruce, and Connor nodded. Bruce watched Connor curiously. "How many other times have you witnessed this happening to her?"

Connor glared at him. "None. Why would I? I just went over there to give her some information. It was official police business."

Bruce was silent.

"I'm certainly not dating her. You can get that idea out of your head. Hell, she's practically a suspect."

"Practically a suspect." The way Bruce delivered the statement demanded an answer.

"Like I said, she shouldn't have had the information she gave us. I thought she had come by it by more devious means, but now it looks as though she might be in danger, and after seeing her last night..." Connor's voice drifted off.

"After witnessing her dream, you believe she may have extrasensory powers."

"Hell no! I don't believe in that crap. But I'm beginning to believe that *she* believes it. I saw what it did to her. I just wanted to know if you could give me some more information about it." Connor was rapidly becoming convinced that he had made a mistake in coming here. He should have remembered how difficult it was to get straight answers out of Casel.

"She sounds like someone who may have clairvoyant powers. That's the ability to be aware of an event happening far away," Casel clarified. He looked soberly at Connor. "What about you, Lieutenant? *Do* you believe her?" he repeated.

Connor looked surprised at the question. Did he believe Michele? He didn't know what to believe anymore. Except that, as hard as he had tried to hold on to his original suspicions about her, they were rapidly slipping away from him. Though he still doubted the reality of clairvoyants and psychics and the rest of that nonsense, he could no longer doubt the reality of the experience for her. He had seen firsthand how it shook her. No, whatever else, he didn't doubt that something happened to Michele Easton when she slept. But more than that he was unable to give her.

He became belatedly aware that Bruce was regarding him quizzically and realized he hadn't answered. "I don't know," he finally said honestly. "I'm not sure what to think. Thanks for the help, Bruce." He turned to leave the room, but Bruce's voice stopped him.

"Lieutenant?" Connor turned to the psychologist.

"Whatever you might believe or disbelieve about this woman, I want you to keep one thing in mind. If, in fact, she is clairvoyant, those dreams are more than deeply disturbing to her. They're probably best described as the equivalent of a psychological mugging." He noted with interest the savage expression in Connor's eyes as he digested that last bit of information before turning silently and leaving the room.

Michele was running late when she finally locked up her office. She never would have dreamed that she would be thankful for such a busy day, but it had served to keep disturbing thoughts of Connor McLain at bay. And now she was still in a rush, her schedule threatening to make her late for her meeting with him.

Her heels clicked loudly on the tile floor as she passed through the shadowy corridors of the darkened office building. She steadfastly refused to consider this appointment with him as anything as intimate as dinner out. In fact, the less time she spent thinking about it, the better off she was. Once she had this out of the way, she fervently hoped that she would never have to see the man again.

As she rounded the corner of the hallway, she banged her shin painfully on an unseen obstacle.

"Ouch!" she gasped loudly. What the heck? She peered more closely in the dimness and recognized the culprit. She had gracefully run into the wheeled bucket the janitor used to mop the floors. Even as she recognized it, Scott appeared from a nearby doorway.

"M-m-m-miss Easton. You h-h-h-hurt?" he stuttered in solicitous inquiry.

Michele gave a tight smile as the young man hurried over. "Only my pride, Scott. I should have watched where I was going."

"I sh-sh-shouldn't have left the b-b-bucket there," he apologized.

Michele shook her head. She would have to reassure Scott or he would berate himself about this for days. He was, as Lieutenant McLain had so crudely put it, somewhat slow. But he was an extremely conscientious employee. "It wasn't your fault, Scott, really. I wasn't paying attention. I'm all right, though. No harm done."

"I d-d-didn't know anyone was st-st-still here."

"I was working late. I'm on my way out now, and I'm late." She laid a gentle hand on the anxious young man's arm. "It's all right, really. I appreciate your concern, but I'm okay."

"R-r-r-right, M-m-miss Easton. S-s-s-see you tomorrow."

Michele waved and smiled as she hurried away. Now she was really going to be late, and no doubt the detective would have something appropriately sarcastic to say about her tardiness. Oh, well, she thought. If he didn't believe her, she was sure she was going to have quite a bruise on her leg to prove how she had hurried.

On her way to the little restaurant she thought of her encounter with Scott. His stutter had seemed worse than usual tonight, but it got that way when he was nervous, she knew. James, in an unusual pique one day, had suggested that it was Michele who made Scott nervous, indicating that the boy had a crush on her.

James. Michele's mouth turned down at the corners as she thought of him as she pulled up in front of the restaurant. Perhaps she had been too imaginative. His dinner invitation might have been exactly what he said, a collaboration between professionals. She certainly hoped so. She didn't want to have to extricate herself from a sticky situation.

As she entered the restaurant, Michele spotted Connor right away and strode toward him. Despite her best intentions, her mouth went dry at the sight of him, and she mentally damned her nervousness.

She slid into the booth across from him and murmured, "I hope you haven't been waiting too long, Lieutenant."

His mouth quirked up on one side. "I think we've gone a little past formalities, haven't we, *Michele?*" He stressed her first name. "After last night, I would certainly expect you to call me by my first name."

Michele gritted her teeth, but said saccharinely, "All right, Connor. I hope you haven't been waiting too long."

"I'm used to waiting for women like you," he said cryptically.

Michele frowned. She didn't know exactly what he meant, but she was sure it wasn't a compliment.

Connor handed her a menu, and Michele snapped it open, already annoyed, and she had only been in his presence a few seconds. After less than a minute she closed it and gave her order to the waitress Connor had summoned. The waitress had turned away with their orders when Connor said, "Oh, and bring us two margaritas, would you?"

The woman nodded and walked away even as Michele protested, "I don't really want one, Lieu—Connor."

Connor made no attempt to call the waitress back. "You could use one," he announced. "Looks like you had a rough day. And we know you had a rough night last night."

Michele drew in her breath. Did he have to keep referring to last night? It was embarrassing enough for her to have to remember it. She cringed every time she thought of how she had let him touch her, kiss her. She responded in the only way she knew, the way she had practiced as a child to hide her feelings from the rest of the world. She deliberately blanked her expression.

Connor's brows lowered as he watched the lovely cool mask descend over Michele's perfect features. It was unbelievable, he thought bitterly, how she could do that, don her porcelain mask at will, like a princess at her most haughty. Well, that was too damn bad. She was going to sit here with him until he was finished talking to her, and she'd better hope that what few better instincts he had took hold. Because when she looked like that, something inside him wanted to shake her up, mar that cool composure, and he wasn't too concerned about how he did it.

The waitress returned then with two huge glasses filled with icy frothing margaritas. Michele looked at the glass in astonishment as it was placed before her, then raised her eyes to Connor's sardonic gaze. "Am I supposed to drink this?" she inquired mischievously. "Or bathe in it?"

Connor said nothing. He wasn't able to. Her unexpected humor had caught him off guard, especially when he saw how it transformed her face. He'd never seen her smile before, he realized in amazement. Really smile, with her pretty eyes all crinkled up and her face alight with amusement. Some of his belligerence drained from him, leaving him momentarily disarmed.

"Feel free to do whichever you prefer," he invited.

Michele shook her head. "I wouldn't want to get thrown in jail for indecent exposure." She ducked her head and peeked up at him wickedly. "I've heard the Philadelphia police are real sticklers about things like that."

One side of Connor's well-formed mouth kicked up in a lopsided smile. "I happen to know one cop who would smooth things over for you," he murmured. "And I doubt very much that anything you exposed could be called indecent." Tempting, maybe. Seductive. Erotic. But never indecent.

Michele blushed but was unable to lower her eyes from his. This was a very different kind of conversation than she ever would have dreamed of having with this man, but she was unwilling to shatter the shaky truce they seemed to have reached in the past few moments. She leaned forward to sip from the icy drink, and Connor did the same. For a few minutes they sat in silence, enjoying the frosty beverage.

Finally Michele interrupted their peaceful silence. "You said you were going to tell me about the lab results on that letter I received."

Connor took a long time answering. "I'm afraid there isn't much to tell," he said finally. He briefly relayed what little information Dave had been able to give him.

Michele felt her heart sink. "Well, you warned me of this," she responded.

"We're not done yet," he added.

Michele looked at him inquisitively, and he went on. "They did find some hair follicles in the adhesive. I told them to go ahead with the tests on those."

"What would that tell you?" asked Michele.

"It could tell us quite a lot, especially when we have a suspect to match the samples with. We can also see if they match other samples we've found in the case. But don't get your hopes up. The lab's so backed up it will probably be a while."

In spite of his warning, Michele felt her heart warm. "Thank you," she said, impulsively reaching across the table to touch his hard arm. "Maybe I overreacted, but it...it frightened me," she admitted.

Connor shifted uneasily in his seat. He was unused to gratitude from this woman. Hell, make that any woman. Most of his intimate relationships started out with blatant physical interest and invariably ended with bitter acrimony when the women found how little he had to give them emotionally. Reflexively he drew away, both physically and mentally, from the woman in front of him. He had to remember, for his own sake, just what she was. He might no longer consider her a suspect, but she was still far too high-society for his comfort. He would do best to remember that and not let her get too close. He'd been put through an emotional wringer by a woman just like her, and he would be damned if he'd let that happen again.

Michele recognized his withdrawal and was inexplicably hurt by it. She drew her hand back and busied herself stirring her drink, sipping cautiously. Connor McLain was an impossible person to read, she thought. No sooner did she think she had reached him on some level than he withdrew and the distance between them grew wider than ever.

The waitress placed steaming plates of food in front of them then, and Michele gratefully occupied her hands with something else for a while. The silence stretched between them, and she watched Connor as she fiddled with the food on her plate. His strong white teeth showed briefly as he took each bite, and she watched the column of his throat hypnotically as he swallowed.

Connor became aware of her interest, and it inspired instant irritation. "What's the matter?" he asked testily. "Am I eating with the wrong fork or something?"

Michele flushed at being caught staring at him, but she responded acerbically. "You certainly have a gigantic chip on your shoulder, do you know that, Lieutenant McLain?"

He grunted. "Well, if I do, my wife put it there."

Michele looked appalled. His wife? He was married?

"My ex-wife," he corrected himself. Connor read the amazement on her face and didn't know whether or not to be insulted. "Yeah, I was married a long time ago, for a blessedly brief duration. Don't look so astounded," he said dryly. "Believe it or not, I do have a personal life."

Michele didn't doubt it for a minute. With that face and body, she was willing to bet that his after-hours were very personal indeed. She only had difficulty figuring out how he fit his women into his work schedule. "You sound bitter," she managed lightly.

"Hardly," came his response. "That's gratitude you read in my voice, not bitterness."

"What happened?" Michele dared to ask.

Connor looked at her silently, but her face was sympathetic. She didn't seem to have any morbid interest but genuine empathy. He decided to show her that she shouldn't bother expending any such emotion on him.

"She decided that being the wife of a Philadelphia policeman wasn't going to be as exciting as she had imagined. That it was going to be, in fact, lonely, boring and poor. She wanted out." He shrugged. "I can't really blame her. There's a high incidence of divorce in the department, and Tricia was less willing to work at a marriage than most."

"Why do you say that?"

"Because she went into it for the excitement, because it was as far removed—*I* was as far removed—from what her family wanted for her, as she could get. But her period of rebellion was as short as her usual attention span."

Connor picked up his fork again, intent on finishing his meal, already regretting his uncustomary freedom of speech around her. What was it about this woman that made his tongue loosen? He certainly didn't have a reputation for being especially forthcoming about himself. Last night he could excuse; Michele had just needed something else to focus on for a while. He doubted she'd heard or remembered anything he had said to her. But he certainly couldn't say the same about just now. And because he was feeling touchy about exposing this much of himself to her, he allowed his usual sardonic tone to creep back into his voice as he pointed his fork at the woman sitting across from him, silently watching him with calm gray eyes.

"Actually," he drawled, meeting her gaze, "she was a lot like you."

Chapter 6

Michele reacted startledly to his bombshell. "Like *me?*" she demanded. "How so?"

She wasn't too sure she wanted to pursue this line of questioning. In fact, she was almost positive she would regret it. Most assuredly it would be unflattering. But she was helpless to keep from learning more about him, anything about him. He was usually so guarded that before last night she had doubted he experienced any real emotions. But his unexpected gentleness with her the previous evening had made him seem more approachable, more human, and she found herself curious about what made this man tick.

Connor began naming all the similarities between the two women that he had noticed since the first time he had met her. "You both obviously shared privileged upbringings. No doubt your family is just as careful as Tricia's about who you associate with." He ignored Michele's dumbfounded expression and went on. "You fill your time working on society's latest issue of the moment, incidentally receiving the spotlight and public acknowledgment for your bountifulness."

Tricia had also shared that touch-me-not air that surrounded Michele, the same one that made a man long to be the one to turn the ice-cold goddess into a writhing passionate woman. He had obviously failed with Tricia; he tried to keep from remembering how close he had come to succeeding with Michele. He stopped himself from listing their further similar attributes. From the look on the lady's face, she was already about to blow.

But Michele did nothing of the sort. She smiled almost sadly and said, "You know, for a police lieutenant, you are incredibly close-minded. Your background check must not have been very accurate if that's an example of the conclusions you were able to draw from it."

Connor stubbornly remained silent as he finished his margarita and signaled the waitress to bring him another. She could deny it all she wanted, but he didn't need the scanty information from the check to tell him what she was. He had been able to tell the moment she walked into his office. His short time with Tricia had taught him to assess expensive clothing, which Michele wore, but it was more than that. Michele had the same walk, the same aristocratic air of breeding, that had him grinding his teeth in moments, unconsciously longing to do something shockingly crude, unspeakably uncouth, just to jolt some real emotion from her.

God knew his in-laws had always had that affect on him, so some of their dislike of him had been deserved. And ultimately Tricia had shared their view that he was a common low-life cop, with low standards and even lower manners. When he had returned to his apartment on that day to find Tricia gone, he'd been downright relieved.

Michele knew it wouldn't do her any good to take offense at his remarks. Whether he had meant to insult her or not, he actually seemed to believe his assessment of her. It was comical, really, that someone had mistaken her hillbilly roots for origins of wealth. She laughed. "I guess I ought to be flattered. I have to admit, no one has ever mistaken me for a debutante before."

Connor looked at her sharply, but her humor seemed genuine. "And you're so different?" he mocked, obviously not believing it.

Michele's eyes were alight with amusement. "I was, believe it or not, Lieutenant, a coal miner's daughter in the hills of West Virginia. My father died when I was four, in a mining accident. My mother and I..." Here Michele hesitated, as unwelcome memories intruded. "Well, we had a hard time making ends meet." She cocked her head and baited him. "Surely you uncovered all this in the background check you ran on me."

Connor studied her silently. Cruz hadn't completed the more in-depth check he had ordered. For some reason, a few days ago Connor had told him he could put it aside and concentrate on other things. Because the investigation was heating up, he told himself uncomfortably. That was the only reason. At any rate, he had only the preliminary report that Cruz had done. No doubt he could shock her with some of the personal things he *did* know, but for some reason he wouldn't name, he wanted her to volunteer information about herself.

Okay, so he was curious, he admitted to himself savagely. That didn't mean a damn thing, did it? It certainly didn't mean that he was about to let his guard down around her or let her get close to him. He only needed to be burned once to learn to stay away from fire. And Michele Easton was definitely scorcher material. Despite her very different background, she was still cut from the same cloth as his ex-wife, or close enough that it didn't matter. He wasn't about to make the same mistake again.

"Okay, if I'm so wrong, correct me," dared Connor.

Michele watched him warily. She would have liked nothing better than to prove to him just how wrong he was about her. But something told her that it would be beyond her powers to do so. Something—or more likely someone—had hurt this man, had burned him so badly that he had built a fortress around himself to avoid getting hurt again. Or maybe she was giving him too much credit. It was just as likely that it was this exact attitude that had cost him his wife to begin with. Heaven knew he had tried her patience to the limit on countless occasions, and she didn't have to live with him.

Live with him. She sat back abruptly, stunned at the sensations curling in the pit of her stomach at the thought. He would be a difficult man emotionally, but physically she was certain that living with him would be very easy indeed. She was aghast at the direction her thoughts were taking, but she blamed it on her uncharacteristic drinking tonight.

She studied the man seated across from her. She couldn't afford to open herself too much to this man; she didn't trust him not to use what he learned against her somehow. But what did she have to lose? He could learn anything he wanted to about her whenever he wished, just by picking up a phone. Suddenly she felt her old anger at this power he had over her life, this ability to pry into her background at will.

"If I've learned one thing about you, Lieutenant," her voice was acid, "it's that you are capable of learning anything about me that you wish. You've already proven that." Michele gathered her things and slipped out of the booth. She'd suddenly had enough for one day. She doubted her ability to last one more moment in his presence without losing her cool completely.

She turned to face him and reached in her purse for some money. "Here's my half of the check—" she began, but his sudden movement interrupted her. Connor grasped her wrist and tugged with just enough strength to pull her down into the booth beside him. He leaned closer then, and Michele felt a flash of panic. He was too close, and after last night she never wanted to allow him so near again. His pale green gaze was shooting sparks, and she swallowed hard in the face of his dangerous attractiveness.

"What's your hurry, Michele, hmm?" he murmured, keeping a firm grip on the wrist she was trying to retrieve. "Things getting a little too personal for you?"

Michele's chin went up at his gibing tone. "I hardly think you'll miss my company. You said yourself that I bring back unpleasant memories."

Connor considered that. "I don't believe that's exactly what I said," he countered. "I said you have a lot in common with my ex-wife. But the joke's on me, not you, Princess." He bared his teeth savagely. "You know why? Because that similarity doesn't make me want you any less. It doesn't stop me from wanting to touch you, to feel your silky skin against my own. It doesn't keep me from wanting to feel your mouth crushed under mine."

Michele's eyes were shocked and wide open, and her breath came in short bursts. She was aghast at the suddenness of his attack as well as the light burning in his eyes. "I'm leaving," she said breathlessly, and, miraculously, her wrist was released. She rose shakily and laid her money on the table before she turned to flee.

Connor rose, too, and threw some bills on the table and followed her quickly out the door. She slipped away from him, intent on getting into her car without further conversation. But her trembling hands refused to fit the key into the lock properly. She cursed mentally as she tried again and again before she heard the click signaling the lock's release. Her sigh of relief was short-lived when she felt his hard body in back of hers.

"Michele," he whispered, drawing her back against him. His mouth went to the sensitive area below her ear, and she shivered as he pressed a light kiss there. Both his hands were cupping her shoulders, his fingers kneading lightly. "Don't run away from me."

"Stop it," she whispered agonizedly. "What's the point of this? You don't like me, and you certainly don't trust me. I'm not about to get involved with anyone who feels about me as you do." What was she saying? she thought aghast. She wouldn't get involved with Connor McLain under any circumstances. Every ounce of self-preservation she had screamed at her that he could be the biggest mistake of her life. And she had made a couple of huge ones.

Connor turned her around then and moved closer until she was pinned between the car and his hard body. "Why shouldn't you be as tortured as I've been?" he demanded, his tone harsh. "Why shouldn't you relive the memories of being in my arms? I spent all last night and today wanting to touch you again. It's only fair that you be tortured by it, too.'' His mouth swooped down then and captured her own, and Michele was lost. She felt herself spinning out of control, her senses careening madly. She gave herself up for lost and returned his kiss.

Connor felt her capitulation and urged her closer. In some region of his mind he marveled at how well she fit him. Only a couple of inches shorter, her legs were an almost perfect match for his own. When he pulled her close like this his aching groin was pressed where it wanted to be, against the warm juncture between her thighs. He tried not to torment himself further by imagining the perfection of their fit if neither of them was clothed.

His mouth slanted over hers. His tongue just skimmed her lips, barely entering her mouth, and Michele moaned unconsciously. Desire slammed through Connor at the sound. He parted her lips and swept the recesses of her mouth surely, as if he had the right. And he did have some rights, he thought savagely. Last night had forged a bond between them, one she was anxious to deny, one he was just as anxious not to let her forget. He wasn't sure of his own thoughts where she was concerned, didn't know what he wanted from her, other than the obvious, of course. But he was damn sure he was unwilling to let her run away before he was ready to let her go.

He gentled his touch, his kiss becoming less demanding and more wooing. What he had forced on her a moment ago he asked of her now. He cupped her head with one large palm, his thumb keeping her chin raised to him.

Michele found his gentleness as compelling as his fierceness a moment ago. His heated breath was coming in short spurts, caressing her cheek warmly. He had her crowded against her car, her body caught between cold metal and warm, very warm masculine heat. Her body slackened against his, and he used the opportunity to gather her closer, until she felt as though they were imprinted upon each other's flesh. And still it wasn't close enough. His lips were nibbling at hers now, coaxing the response he wanted from her.

Michele slid her hands up his strong arms and tangled her fingers in the longer hair at his nape. She had never suspected that such a hard man could be capable of such smoldering passion, that he could evoke a similar response from her. She shuddered as the tip of his tongue traced the shell-like cavity of her ear before he moved to take the lobe in his gentle teeth.

Connor's mouth covered hers again, and his tongue stroked her velvet heat. Their tongues danced intimately with each other, stabbing in delightful pleasure before waltzing away again, only to return for a longer taste.

Michele's head whirled with the sensations he could evoke with a simple kiss. Never had she experienced such passion; never had she evoked such passion in a man, she realized dimly. The proximity of their bodies made her fully aware of how aroused he was, and it was that fact that made her pull her mouth away from his, avoiding the lips that followed to coax her back.

"No, Connor, I don't want this," she whispered. She didn't want to get close enough to anyone to allow herself to be vulnerable, and this man especially was a danger to her. What he could do to her emotionally as well as physically frightened her, and she had to call a stop to this madness now, before both of them were too far-gone to stop at all.

"Your body is calling you a liar," Connor mocked, arousal making him grit his teeth with the effort it took to stop.

Michele looked askance at him. "You can't possibly want a complication like this to jeopardize the case. Or are you telling me that, despite all the wonderful things you believe about me, you're willing to believe that the one thing I may not be guilty of is kidnapping?"

Connor didn't answer. He was pretty sure that she couldn't be involved in that, but it still didn't explain how she had come by the information about the jacket. Hell, he supposed it was possible that she had overheard it somewhere, maybe even at one of those society functions she was so involved in. Perhaps she didn't even remember she had heard it until it had figured in one of her dreams.

Listening to his own thoughts, he loosened his grip on her and turned half away, disgusted with himself. Was he making excuses for her now, he asked himself derisively, because he really believed her, or to excuse his own interest in her?

Michele felt an inexplicable lump in her throat at his silence. The answer to her question seemed clear enough, she thought bitterly. And it made her long to hurt him in return. She lashed out. "Apparently your libido dictates your professionalism. How convenient for you, but it doesn't bode too well for the safety of this city."

Because her words so closely paralleled his own thoughts, Connor bared his teeth in return. "And what's your excuse, Miss Easton?"

Michele blanched at his renewed antagonism. It merely highlighted the ludicrousness of the feelings that had begun to creep into her thoughts. "Stay away from me," she commanded him shakily. "I don't want to have anything more to do with you, understand?" She turned away then and yanked her car door open.

"I have a feeling, Princess, that neither of us is going to be able to control that," he said cryptically.

Michele started the engine and threw the car into gear, leaving him standing in the parking lot staring pensively after her.

Too uptight to face going home to an empty house, Michele drove around the city for over two hours, using the skill she needed to maneuver the busy freeways to keep her mind off Connor McLain and her confusing attraction to him. Finally she was unable to delay the inevitable any longer and drove home. She unlocked the door, then closed and locked it behind her. Connor's warning had sunk in, if for no other reason than the ease with which he'd entered her apartment the other night.

Michele flicked on a light and put her purse away. "Here Sammy," she called. "Kitty, kitty, kitty." She frowned when there was no answering meow of welcome. Sammy almost always met her at the door, welcoming her in the same breath he used to demand his dinner.

She entered the living room. Sometimes the cat hid after he'd done something wrong, like the time he'd shredded several pairs of her nylons. Her eyes scanned the room, but she saw no mess he might have made there.

She stopped, her eyes going around again more slowly. That was odd. She turned in a complete circle, looking more closely. She felt a presence...as if someone had been here. She shivered, barely realizing when Sammy came out from behind the couch to leap into her arms. Michele walked slowly through the house, her senses humming. Nothing was disturbed, there was no sign of an intruder, but she couldn't shake the feeling that someone had been in her home.

Of course, she thought, relief spilling through her. Connor had spent the night there. That would explain the aura of another presence in her house. She unconsciously relaxed. Obviously her house found it just as difficult to shake off his stamp as her body did.

She hurriedly changed into a nightgown, turned on a bedside lamp and pulled the covers back. She padded out to the kitchen to feed the cat and listen to her answering machine. It whirred softly as it replayed two clicks and finally one message from her mother, asking her to call back when she had time.

Michele smiled fondly as she turned off all the lights and slipped into bed. Although it was too late tonight, she would make time to call her mother before she went to work tomorrow. It had been over a week since she had talked to her, and that was longer than usual.

There was a strong bond between them; there had been for as long as Michele could remember. They had been alone for so long, dependent on each other, that it was normal that they would be close. But Michele knew it was more than that, more than the usual closeness a mother and her child shared. The adversity they had gone through before they had moved to Philadelphia was at the root of it, and force of habit had Michele trying to push those memories from her mind. But like an insidious fire they spread, ignoring her conscious desire to forget.

Her father had died when Michele was four, but she thought she remembered him. She had inherited her straight dark hair from him, although her features favored her mother. She remembered laughter from that time in her life, and a feeling of safety, of wanting for nothing.

A feeling that had turned out to be just an illusion, one that had shattered at her father's death. There hadn't been any insurance, and it wasn't long before they had lost the house. Bit by bit they had slid closer and closer to the edge of poverty. Michele's mother had taken in sewing and stayed busy during the day, but at least she had been able to stay at home with Michele when she was young. When Michele had entered school, her mother had gone to work in a textile factory.

But even in those times, when they often had but one meal a day, and that likely a sandwich, Michele remembered being loved. She had never doubted that her mother would take care of her. Until Bill Strought had come into their lives.

She closed her eyes tightly, trying to shut out the sight of him, but his likeness swam before her mind. Michele had never understood then how her mother could have married him, but after her work in the battered-victims' shelter, she thought she understood it at least a little. Her mother had been desperate to lift Michele from the cycle of poverty that was fast swallowing them both.

Michele buried her face in her pillow, vainly wishing her thoughts away. Maybe Bill Strought hadn't been a bad man, maybe things beyond his comprehension had caused him to react in a way he normally would not have. She had long tried to feel forgiveness for him, to try to understand what had motivated him, but the most she was able to feel was relief. Relief that they had finally escaped him.

Michele had only been seven when her mother had remarried, but even at that young age, she had recognized that this was not a man she would ever run to, not a man she would call Daddy. He had tolerated her, she supposed, until she had made it impossible for him to ignore her any longer. Then he had made sure that she regretted his attention with all her young heart.

Michele didn't remember the first time she'd had one of the dreams that plagued her. She knew that she had always had the nightmares, as her mother and father had called them. She remembered awakening screaming at night, but mostly she remembered being cradled in someone's arms, being comforted until she slept again.

She had been eight years old the first time her mother had admitted that what afflicted Michele was more than just bad dreams. Over and over for several days Michele had awakened sobbing, babbling about an old woman lying bleeding in a cabin. Michele's mother had comforted her as best she could. Bill had loudly proclaimed it childish nonsense and warned Sabrina that Michele was just doing it for attention.

But there had come a day when they were shaken by the fact that it was more. Bill had come home from his job in town with the news that old man Bislow had hacked his wife up with an ax and left her in the cabin to bleed to death. He'd been liquored up with whiskey, probably out of his mind with rotgut moonshine. They said when he had realized what he had done he had taken off for the woods. It had taken one of the neighbors better than two weeks to come around looking for the Bislows and find the body.

The similarities between the incident and Michele's dreams were too numerous to miss. Bill had been out of his mind after hearing about it in town. He had grabbed Michele and shaken her long and hard, calling her a witch and a changeling. That had been the beginning of the longest nightmare in Michele's life.

For the dreams were nothing compared to the daily terror of watching Bill's uncaring attitude change to one of mistrust, then fear and hostility and finally abuse. Sabrina had tried to shield Michele as much as she could. She begged Michele to say nothing of her dreams anymore, to do nothing that would set the man off. That meant that Michele now woke from those dreams alone, swallowing her screams, choking back sobs. There was no one there to comfort her anymore, no one to chase the demons back into the night.

And Michele had tried to keep the dreams a secret, she really had. But it had been a big load for a little girl to carry. Even at that age she was aware that the folks in her region were a superstitious lot, and many of them didn't trust people who were different. She had wanted to fit in as much as any other child would have. But it was difficult to keep some things to herself. One day she was playing with a group of friends who wanted to play in the woods. Michele had told them, "I'm not going. Rachel's cat is in there. It was killed by a wild boar." And when in fact that turned out to be true, the children had gradually begun to shun her, too.

That time Bill had taken her to a pond nearby, and she had been terrified at the look on his face. He had looked as if he hated her, and she had known he meant her harm. He had ignored her struggles and dragged her into the pond, holding her head underwater for long minutes, letting her catch a tortured breath, then doing it again. Her throat had been raw, her lungs ready to burst, when her mother had arrived to save her. Michele never knew whether he had meant to kill her that day, but she remembered him telling her mother over and over again that it was the only way to deal with witches, and if Michele wasn't a witch, what was she?

Michele's mother had finally come to fear for her child's life. Beatings had been frequent—to get the devil out of her, Bill had said. Sabrina stopped him when she was there, but she couldn't protect Michele every second of every day, and Michele hadn't always been able to outrun him. She had felt that she had no one to go to, nowhere to turn. Sabrina had promised Michele that she would get them out somehow, but she needed some time to ferret some money away, and then they would run away from him.

Michele rolled over on her back, still in the grip of the bitter memories. Things had continued that way until she had dreamed of Tommy Hacknow. A little boy in the next town had been reported missing, and Michele dreamed about a boy facedown in a pond, tangled in some weeds. Only eleven years old, she had known what she had to do. She just hadn't recognized the publicity that her disclosure would bring.

She had marched into the sheriff's office one afternoon after school had let out for the day. She had demanded to talk to the sheriff, and she told him about her dream. He hadn't believed her, of course, especially when Michele had admitted she didn't even know the boy. But she had been able to describe him and the approximate location where he was found. She went home confident that the sheriff would check it out and no one would be the wiser. After all, she hadn't told anyone else, had she? The sheriff wouldn't tell; he had promised.

He had promised, she remembered silently, as a lone tear rolled down her cheek. But neither of them had reckoned with the deputy the sheriff had told. He told the story all over town, especially after they found the body exactly where Michele had told them they would.

Bill had been enraged, she remembered with a shiver. Even Sabrina hadn't been able to stop him. He had dragged Michele to the woodshed and locked the door. Michele remembered lying in a heap watching him unroll the strap he used to sharpen his razors. She could still hear the whistle it made when it came through the air, feel the agonizing cut of its sharp surface as it made contact. Still hear her own screams, feel the blood run freely down her open flesh...

Michele could feel her heart pounding just as it always did when she relived the memory. Sabrina had broken down the door with the ax from the woodpile, and then Bill had started on her. Michele didn't remember the trip to town, stumbling down the mountain paths, her mother half carrying her, both of them bloody and weary and out of their heads with pain.

The sheriff had found them, Michele remembered. She would never forget the look on his face when he picked her up and she stared up at him and whispered, "You lied."

It was probably guilt that made him take them all the way to Buffalo Springs to the hospital. He had put them in contact with a church that had helped them, given them enough money to board a bus and travel north. To Philadelphia. To freedom.

Michele wiped at the tears that had inexplicably appeared on her face. They had been lucky arriving here. There were other churches waiting to help them, and they had made it. Sabrina had found a job, they had found a small apartment and slowly the wounds had begun to heal. Michele didn't think her mother would ever get over the guilt of not finding a way out sooner—for both of them.

But Michele had learned a valuable lesson that night. Whatever it was that caused those dreams was not normal. Other people didn't have it, nor did they trust it. She had put up with enough ostracism from her peers to eagerly agree when her mother told her that she must not under any circumstances tell another soul about the dreams. And she never had.

Until Connor McLain.

Chapter 7

Connor winced at the hearty greeting and accompanying slam of his office door. He opened one bloodshot eye to recognize Cruz and groaned aloud. Just what he needed on this of all mornings, Cruz's unfailing cheerfulness.

He perused his good-natured friend sourly. After Michele had left, he had gone back inside the restaurant and tried to drink them out of margaritas. His headache today was proof of his attempt, if not his success.

"Connor, old boy, you look like hell," clucked Cruz. He rolled a chair closer to Connor's desk and dropped down in it, propping his feet on the edge of the desk. He peered a little closer at his friend. "Don't tell me you went out to tie one on and didn't even invite me?"

"You definitely would have made a crowd," Connor told him.

"Oh, a date!" Cruz crowed. He leaned forward with a grin. "Who was it, Connor? Marta, that little Spanish spitfire who can dance? Or was it Jill, the airline stewardess?" At Connor's pained expression, a new thought struck Cruz. "Don't tell me it was someone new? You met someone and didn't even bring her here to introduce her to Uncle Cruz? Shame on you, Connor," he complained reproachfully.

"It wasn't a date," Connor was goaded into revealing. "At least, not exactly."

"Do tell. And what is a 'not exactly' date?" quizzed Cruz, his handsome bronzed face alight with amusement. "I may want to try one sometime. No, wait, don't tell me." He held up a hand as he started to guess. "It starts with you drinking as much as you can, am I close?"

For not the first time in their friendship, Connor gave serious consideration to strangling his friend. Or shooting him. "Yeah, you're a real riot," he noted sourly. "What the hell do you want, anyway?"

Cruz whistled tunelessly. "You are in a good mood, aren't you? That must mean you also struck out on your 'not exactly' date. How many times do I have to offer, Connor? If you need some lessons in putting women in the mood, all you have to do is ask."

The command Connor gave Cruz would have been anatomically impossible even for a contortionist. He ground his teeth at the sound of his friend's laughter. Only the knowledge that he had given Cruz an equally hard time on more than one occasion and probably would again made this visit bearable.

After Cruz seemed to have recovered from his mirth, Connor growled, "Do you have any particular reason for coming in here and annoying me? Outside of your need for amusement, I mean? I've got work to do."

"I just came in to prove I did my job, Connor." At the lieutenant's blank gaze, Cruz went on. "You know, on Michele Easton. You wanted a more in-depth check on her. This is it." He nodded to the sheaf of papers he handed over to Connor. When his friend didn't immediately reach out and take them, he dropped them on the desktop.

Connor stared at the papers as if they would bite him. His eyes raised to his partner's. "I told you to hold off on this," he croaked.

Cruz frowned as he stared concernedly at his friend. He really was acting strangely, even for having a hangover. "You did tell me to concentrate on the investigation. But the inquiries I had made were already in the works. When the information came in anyway, I figured you would want to see it. Well," he said, as Connor made no move toward the papers, "aren't you even interested? I can assure you it's worth reading."

Connor swallowed and looked down at the papers on his desk. Michele's name seemed to scream up from the top sheet. He didn't know how to explain his reluctance to open the file. Except that he was already convinced that Michele wasn't personally involved in the kidnappings. And after her accusations last night, he was especially loath to read what was in the report.

Then he hardened his heart. For God's sake, he was acting like a lovesick fool. This was his job, and he wasn't going to let Michele's feelings stop him from doing it. Besides, he was curious. After their conversation last night he would very much like to see which of them was more accurate in their assessment of her.

He picked up the file decisively. As he read the pages, Cruz left and came back shortly with two steaming cups of coffee. He placed one on Connor's desk, but Connor took no notice of it. Cruz settled back in his seat to wait.

Connor felt stunned as he kept turning the pages like an automaton. Everything Michele had told him had been true. But she had left so much unsaid. Like the fact that she had probably been abused for years by a stepfather who was more than a little unbalanced. That she and her mother had fled for their lives. That far from being raised in the lap of luxury, they had only some church organizations to thank for not joining the ranks of the homeless at one point. He read the last page slowly, then reread it again. He lifted his eyes slowly to Cruz, who was blissfully sipping his coffee.

"Where in the world did you come up with this information?" Connor demanded, his voice tight as he indicated the last page of the report.

Cruz looked smug. "It wasn't easy, my friend," he said. "To say that the people in those parts are closemouthed is putting it mildly. But I got lucky."

"Do tell."

"Yep. I was on the phone to the sheriff's office and got hold of some deputy who had been on the force at the time Michele and her mother left West Virginia. He was quite verbose on the subject. In fact, he said it was the 'dangedest thing' he ever did see," Cruz quoted with an accent. "According to him, Michele and her mother were lucky they got out when they did. Bill Strought wasn't the only one in town being spooked by her dreams."

Connor felt a chill run down his back. It wasn't that he had been so wrong about her upbringing. Her disclosures last night had revealed his error. No, it was the last fact that Cruz had alluded to that made the shiver of unease skate up and down his spine. This report verified that Michele Easton had a long history of these dreams. And that she had been found right on more than one occasion.

Connor rose agitatedly from his chair to pace across the small office. This was nonsense, he told himself sternly. A bunch of superstitious hillbillies had read a lot more into it than there actually was. But it would explain how she knew about the jacket, an inner voice reminded him slyly.

Cruz said as much. Connor wheeled on him. "Don't tell me you believe that psychic crap?"

Cruz shrugged. "Although there's not much I don't know about women, my friend—'' he grinned and winked at Connor ''—I admit there are a few gaps in my knowledge of science. I don't see why you're so dead set against believing her. What can it hurt to check out what she tells us?''

''Anything we obtained from her wouldn't be admissible in court, you know that. Besides, what has she told us besides the fact that the children are being held in what *might be,*'' he stressed, ''an abandoned building? Do you know how many buildings that would encompass in Philadelphia?'' Cruz's grimace indicated that he could guess. ''We don't have the kind of manpower to check them all out. Even assuming it's in Philadelphia. And assuming she's even right.'' He didn't reveal the content of Michele's more recent dream. He was definitely not in the mood to discuss that scene with his friend.

''Let's just assume, for the sake of argument—'' Cruz held up his hand to stem Connor's words ''—just suppose Michele is right about the children being alive. She told you they're all being held together, right?'' Without waiting for an agreement, he went on. ''So if they are still alive, what's the motive of the kidnapper?''

Connor sighed but went along with his friend. They'd been worrying this same question ever since the case started. ''Ransom's out. There still have been no demands, no attempts to contact the families.''

''We can discount murder if Michele is right about what she dreamed.''

''A big if,'' Connor muttered.

''But no bodies have been found, so she could be right,'' Cruz reasoned.

''Possibly,'' Connor stated.

''What's left?''

''Child pornography?'' Connor suggested distastefully.

Cruz grimaced. ''God, I hope not.'' The two men were gloomily silent for several minutes. Trying to attach reasons to the bizarre happenings was one of the most frustrating aspects of the case.

Finally Cruz spoke again. ''Well, if we're ever going to answer that question, I'd better get back to work, and you can get back to your hangover. And, hey, this report should certainly clear Michele as a suspect, even in your mind. Right?'' He didn't wait for Connor's answer before he went on. ''So there'd be no hint of impropriety if I asked her out, would there?''

Connor glared at his friend. ''Stay the hell away from her,'' he snarled, ''if you know what's good for you.''

Cruz looked taken aback. ''That's being a little hard-nosed, even for you, Connor,'' he finally said mildly. ''I don't see the harm in...'' A light obviously went on for him. "Of course." He sat forward and snapped his fingers. "Michele Easton was your 'not exactly' a date last night." He chuckled as he put the whole thing together, and the pained look on Connor's face verified everything for him. "Why didn't you just say so?"

"Because there's nothing to say," growled Connor. "I spoke with her last night, that's all."

"Is she the reason you decided to drink yourself under the table?" inquired Cruz. "Or was that a way to console yourself when she turned you down?"

Connor gritted his teeth. "For the last time, I do not have anything going with Michele Easton. You should know better than anyone else that she's not my type."

"Yep, tall, gorgeous brunettes have always been my type, not yours," replied Cruz, pretending to misunderstand his friend. "Let me get this straight. She's no longer a suspect, she's the reason you tied one on last night, and she's not your type, but you're warning me to stay away from her." He cocked an eyebrow at his friend, who was by now glowering at him. "Did I get it all?"

"You have exactly two seconds to get the hell out of my office," crooned Connor dangerously.

Cruz knew that tone. Perhaps he had baited his friend a little more than was wise. "I'm going, I'm going." He used a hurt tone as he unwound his tall figure from the chair and ambled to the door. With one hand on the knob, he turned around and said, "Oh, and Connor...? Let me know when it would be all right for me to ask her out, okay?" He ducked out of the door just in time to avoid the file of papers that hurtled through the air toward his head.

Michele stared across the dinner table at James Ryan and smiled in reply to one of his quips. Instead of finding a time during the day to discuss the Howard boy with him, she had agreed to have dinner with him this evening. She had insisted to herself that it would be a business meeting, that she would not allow James to put off the original reason for their dinner. And she had enjoyed their discussion. Michele sometimes forgot how pleasant it could be to exchange methods and strategies with a colleague, how energizing the sharing of ideas could be.

James was a perfect dinner companion, she mused, as she studied him surreptitiously. Similar experiences in their jobs meant that they had enough in common to be at ease with each other. He was a charming man with an old-world manner that was subtly flattering to a woman. She could be utterly relaxed with him and not worry about having to be on her guard, constantly matching wits with him the way she did with Connor McLain.

Heat rose in her cheeks at the thought of Connor. Where had his image come from? she wondered with panic. She had managed to keep thoughts of him at bay all day. She had, she insisted. Because to think of him was to embroil herself all over again in that strange emotional quagmire she felt each time he came to mind. He was as different from James as it was possible for a man to be. Where James was cultured, refined, polished, Connor was crass, rude and arrogant. Where James was a gentleman, Connor... Well, Connor simply was not.

Why, then, she thought despairingly, as James signaled the waiter to bring the check, did James not elicit even a fraction of the interest Connor held for her? If she had to become emotionally entangled with someone, why couldn't it at least be with a person she understood, one who shared her values and trusted her on some level?

She wrestled with those questions all the way home, unaware of the concerned glances James was sending her way. The simple truth, she finally admitted with a sigh, was that for whatever reason James did not interest her at all on a more personal level and Connor did.

Connor scared her to death emotionally. He had already gotten closer to her in some ways than any other person besides her mother. And she was petrified to let him even closer, to open herself up to the kind of hurt he was sure to bring her. Two people could not be more different than they were. Physical attraction was not enough to build a relationship on, and that was all they shared, wasn't it?

"Michele?"

Her head snapped around at James's faintly chagrined tone. "Yes?"

"We're home."

Michele turned, stunned to see that they were in her driveway. She turned sheepish eyes back to the man at her side. "I guess the trip home was like riding with a zombie."

"Not quite that bad," James disavowed gallantly. "But I could certainly guess you had something on your mind. Why don't you invite me in for coffee, and we can talk about whatever it is."

Michele hesitated for a moment, a refusal on her lips. The last thing she wanted to discuss with James Ryan was her strange feelings for Connor McLain. But she reconsidered after a moment. Although she still had no intention of telling James who she had been thinking of, she thought perhaps she would welcome his presence for a while longer. Certainly conversing with James was preferable to the thoughts that had been troubling her.

"I will never understand," James said as they strolled up the sidewalk to her house, "why you insist on living in such an awful neighborhood. Surely you could find a more suitable place, perhaps one of the condominiums springing up along our skyline daily."

"This neighborhood isn't awful," Michele said defensively. "It has character. Where else could I enjoy having half a house to myself, with an upstairs and a downstairs?" Michele's home was in what had at one time been a single family dwelling. It had been converted to a duplex years ago. "Right now I don't even have neighbors, so I feel like I have the whole place to myself. Besides, most of those beloved condos of yours don't allow pets. With my fenced-in backyard, Sammy can even be outdoors some of the time."

James fleeting grimace was his only answer, and Michele sighed silently. She knew he had an aversion to animals, to cats and dogs in particular. She unlocked the front door and prepared to step in front of James to protect him from Sammy's usual welcome.

"That's odd," Michele murmured, looking this way and that around the room.

"What?" asked James politely as he entered her small living room and sat down.

"Oh, Sammy usually greets me at the door, but this makes the second night he's been hiding somewhere when I've gotten home." She shrugged and managed a smile. It was also the second night she had come home to an uncanny feeling of a presence in her apartment. Connor McLain's aura certainly was tenacious, she thought grimly as she went to brew some coffee.

As she reentered the living room with the two cups, James patted the couch next to him invitingly. "Come sit down, Michele," he suggested. Michele obeyed, handing him the cup. He sipped from it, then set it down on the table in front of him. Turning to face her, he said, "Why don't you tell me what was bothering you in the car this evening?"

Michele's startled gaze flew to his. She used the coffee mug as a shield, sipping from it as her mind searched frantically for something to say. She certainly wasn't about to disclose the real reason for her spaciness. She set the cup down carefully and said, "Oh, it was nothing really. I talked to my mother this morning, and I was just thinking about our conversation, that's all."

"Nothing wrong, I hope?" James asked smoothly, never taking his eyes off her.

"No." Michele smiled faintly. "There's nothing wrong." That was the same lie she had told her mother this morning, but James looked more satisfied with it than her mother had been. He shocked her then by picking up one of her hands and holding it in both of his.

"Michele, I'm sure you realize that I'm interested in you as far more than a colleague. I find you most...enchanting." His mouth came down to hers softly, and Michele sat frozen, her eyes fluttering shut as she accepted his kiss.

It was...nice, she realized sadly. Merely nice. It raised no answering feelings in her; instead it left her empty. She despaired even as she acknowledged that fact. It was unfair of her to make comparisons, but it would be even more unfair if she were to use James's attraction to her to shield her from Connor McLain.

"I'm sorry, James. I don't feel the same way."

James watched her keenly. "Perhaps in time, if we dated..."

Michele shook her head. "I think it could get a bit uncomfortable at work if things didn't work out," she averred gently.

James dropped her hand and inquired tightly, "There's someone else?"

"No!" Michele's surprise wasn't feigned. "No, there's no one. I'm just not very interested in developing a relationship right now."

The man at her side shook his head. "Whether you're interested in it or not isn't really the issue, Michele. It just happens. What about that McLain person who came to the office the other day?"

Michele felt horror wash over her as she imagined every aspect of her relationship with Connor becoming common knowledge. "What about him?"

"You're not dating him?"

"I told you, James, I'm not dating anyone. Certainly not Connor McLain." Her agitation was apparent as she rose and took her cup back to the kitchen. "I don't know where you got that impression."

"Just from observing the two of you that day, actually. There were some interesting undercurrents. I must have misinterpreted them."

"You must have," Michele said flatly. James took his cue from her tone and stood.

Michele walked him to the door. "I'll see you tomorrow. Thank you for dinner this evening, James."

He looked down at her. "Thank you for the company, Michele." And then he was gone.

Michele thankfully locked the door after him and leaned against it. Imagine James thinking he had read something into the brief time when he had been in the presence of her and Connor. All he'd read was her desire to crack him one, she thought waspishly and crossed to pick up his cup. She remembered once again that she hadn't seen Sammy yet tonight. She sighed and began a search for him.

She finally found him in her bedroom, the last place she looked and had to spend several long minutes coaxing him out from underneath her bed. When she finally had him in her arms, she stood up, lecturing him in a severe tone. "I suppose this means you've been really naughty, hmm, to have hidden yourself away for so long? I'm not sure you deserve supper tonight after all." She turned toward the door without hesitating in her scolding. As she started out of the room, her eyes opened wide.

Michele screamed involuntarily, then clapped one hand over her mouth as her eyes took in the large dead bird hanging from her dresser mirror. It hung from a noose fashioned with one of her own hair ribbons. Its head lay limply to the side, its neck obviously broken.

She felt bile rush up in her throat and looked around wildly, half expecting to see the person responsible for this cruel scene, before rushing out of the room. She had reached the front door before she stopped, reason slowly returning. Whoever had been here was obviously gone. She had been all over the house already, looking for her pet, and certainly she would have seen the intruder if he was still there.

Her skin crawled at the thought, and she dropped Sammy unceremoniously. Turning and leaning against the door, she took deep breaths, trying to still her racing heart. Her mind was whirling so madly that she failed to respond even when Sammy wound around her ankles, mewling querulously. Finally, after long moments, she drew a deep shuddering breath. Slowly, without even thinking about it, she walked to the kitchen and dialed the phone.

"McLain!"

Connor cocked an eye at the desk sergeant as he walked by. He had just finished more than twelve hours on the job, and he wasn't anxious to linger.

"Line three is for you."

Connor bit out a curse. The last thing he wanted to do right now was start on something new. He was burned-out. All he wanted was some sleep.

"Who is it?" he asked warily.

The desk sergeant rolled his eyes. "I'm not your answering service, McLain. Some broad."

Connor picked up the phone and punched the button. "Lieutenant McLain," he answered tersely.

"Connor." A soft voice trembled, then was quiet.

Connor could hear the other person on the line draw a shaky breath. "Who is this?" he demanded. A sudden, frightening thought struck him. "Michele? Is that you?" He barely waited for her affirmative reply before demanding, "What is it? What's happened?"

Michele drew a deep breath, striving for an even tone when all she really wanted was to scream and scream and scream. "Someone's been here," she managed, before her voice broke.

"Where are you? Are you at home?" His voice was tight. At her barely audible reply, his voice changed, got lower and more soothing. "Okay, Princess, here's what I want you to do. Do you have a neighbor you could call?"

Michele's hand went to her forehead. Why did he ask that? How would that help? "Yes, I suppose...."

"Okay, that's fine, that's okay. Listen to me." His voice was controlled and soothing. "I'll have a squad car at your place in five minutes, okay? You go to your neighbor's and wait for them to arrive. And I'll be there as soon as I can, all right? Hang on. Someone will be right there." Connor frowned as he heard the soft click.

He replaced the phone and turned to the desk sergeant. "Radio a squad car to go to 406½ Daley, will you? Tell them it's a possible intruder." He took off at a run.

"Yeah, okay, but where are you going?" yelled the sergeant at his departing figure.

"Tell them I'll meet them there," Connor shouted over his shoulder.

A uniformed police officer who Connor recognized answered the sharp rap on Michele's door. "Evening, Lieutenant," he said respectfully. Connor nodded as his sharp gaze traveled the room and found Michele seated on the couch with another officer. Relief flooded him at her apparent well-being. He didn't question the feeling, just as he didn't question the slow burning rage that was forming inside him.

"What happened?" he asked, turning his head to pin the officer with his gaze.

"Miss Easton was next door when we arrived, sir. She was pretty shaken up, but she took us to her bedroom, and that's where we found it."

"Found what?" Connor bit out.

"Dead bird, sir. Someone had shot it, with a pellet gun, probably, and then broke its neck. Found it hanging from the side of the dresser mirror. Kind of sick, huh?"

"Yeah," he murmured grimly. "Real sick."

"Oh, and, sir?"

Connor looked back impatiently.

The officer lowered his voice. "There was a note with it, the letters cut from a newspaper or something. It was stuck between the mirror and the frame. Just one word. *Remember.* That's all."

Connor turned this new information over in his mind. "Okay. I'll take care of Miss Easton. Question the neighbors. See if anyone saw someone around here today. And get rid of the mess in her bedroom."

The officer shrugged. "Sure thing, Lieutenant."

The other officer moved from the couch when Connor came in and sank down next to Michele. "How are you doing?" he asked gently.

"Fine," she replied tremulously. "I'm sorry I had to call you. I wasn't really thinking...."

"You did exactly the right thing," Connor soothed. "Lucky for me I worked late, so I was still there when you called." He gathered her up and pulled her into his arms as she bit her lip. "Hey, c'mere. It's all right, Princess. Everything's going to be all right."

Michele knew she should object to his holding her, object to that blasted name he kept calling her. But she was so weary of fighting. All she wanted was to shut out the cruelty she had witnessed tonight. And it felt so good to be held in his arms right now. Later she would pull herself back together; later she would focus on being strong. Right now she allowed herself to be comforted in Connor's hard arms. To be soothed by his strong heartbeat, which sounded steadily beneath her ear, where it was pressed against his chest.

Connor didn't put a name to the cold fear that had been with him since he'd taken her call and had accompanied him until he'd walked in her door and seen her unharmed. Wrapping her in his arms was as much for himself as for her.

"Lieutenant?"

Both Connor and Michele looked up as one of the officers summoned him. "Looks like that's how the intruder may have entered the premises." The officer indicated a window in the kitchen. "I found the screen outside in the bushes."

"It doesn't lock." Michele was shocked at the hoarseness of her voice. She cleared her throat and tried again. "It never has. The landlord always promises to fix it...." Her voice trailed off as she met Connor's hard gaze.

"We'll take care of it tomorrow," he promised tersely. "In the meantime, you're not staying here tonight. Get your things."

"I'll be all right," Michele began, but Connor was having none of it.

"The next time you might not be so lucky, Michele. He could be back. I am not going to allow you to spend the night here and that's final."

Michele found some of her strength returning in the face of his implacable attitude. "All right," she uttered as she acknowledged the sense he was making. "I'll find a motel to stay in."

"Not a motel." Connor rose and strode in the direction of her bedroom. "You can stay with me."

Michele didn't know who was more astounded at his assertion, her or the young officer who overheard him make it. She watched as the young man coughed and turned away, while she sat frozen. Stay with him? Like hell! She marched into her bedroom to see him rifling through her underwear drawer.

The sight infuriated her enough to take her mind off the last time she'd been in that room. "Get away from my clothes," she hissed at him.

He paid her no attention as he casually picked out a bra and added it to the pile of clothes in his hand.

She marched over to him and slammed the drawer, narrowly missing his fingers in the process. "I am perfectly capable of packing for myself," she told him.

"Good," he told her imperturbably. "Put everything you want in that bag over there." Michele swung her gaze to the overnighter he had obviously dragged from her closet. He brushed by her on his way to the bathroom. When she followed him, she saw him picking up shampoo and makeup and her curling iron, before he passed her again to go back and dump his armload into the open suitcase on the bed.

She followed him back to the bedroom, beginning to feel like an obedient puppy. "Will you stop messing around in my things?" she demanded.

Connor closed and zipped the bag, then turned and grabbed her elbow with his free hand, and guided her toward the door. "Let's go, Princess. I'm beat, and we can both use some rest tonight."

Michele dug in her heels. "I am not going anywhere with you," she insisted. At his glowering look, she added, "All right, I'll spend the night elsewhere, but not at your place! There are plenty of motels—"

"What you need tonight is to get out of this house. What you definitely do *not* need," Connor stressed, "is to be alone. And you will not be alone. You'll be with me." He attempted once again to guide her out the bedroom door.

Michele became belatedly aware of the two officers in the house, most likely within hearing distance. She kept her voice to a furious whisper. "If I need to be with someone tonight, I assure you that I can find better company than yours."

Connor lowered his voice to match hers, but his still managed to be sarcastic. "Oh, and who would you call? Dear James? I can't believe that you would choose to explain this whole ordeal to anyone else tonight. Whether you know it or not, you're teetering on the edge right now. You didn't call anyone else tonight, you called me! And you know what that tells me, Michele? It says that despite all your protests, you trust me. And I'm taking you home with me tonight, and that's final!" His last words were almost a growl.

Michele stared up at him mutinously. He was the last person on earth she wanted to spend the night with. But he was also right, damn him. She didn't really relish spending the night alone, starting at every little noise. And she certainly didn't want to recount the experience to any of her friends and face the questions that would inevitably arise. But that didn't mean she had to be happy with the situation.

She allowed herself to be walked to the front door, since Connor left no room for any further disagreement. "Stop pulling at me," she groused.

"Quit your bitching," he retorted. "After all, what could be safer than spending the night with a cop?" He exchanged a few terse words with the officers before gathering up her suitcase and, with a hand on her back, ushering her out the door, down the steps and to his car, which was parked illegally out front.

"Nice example you set," Michele sniped huffily at him as he put her in the car and set her overnight bag on the back seat. "How safe will I be with a policeman who ignores any law he likes?"

Connor slammed her door and walked quickly around to his own, then slid into the car and started the engine. Sparing only a glance in her direction, he replied, "You'll be as safe as you want to be, Princess."

Chapter 8

Connor slid a concerned glance to his couch, where Michele was sitting forlornly. She had gotten quieter and quieter in the car before falling into complete silence. He much preferred their quarreling to this winsome sorrow that had enveloped her like a shroud. At least when she had been sniping at him, she had been feeling real emotion. But that emotion had slipped away, to be replaced, he knew, with the memory of the sicko who was badgering her.

"I put your bags in the second bedroom," he said, startled at how loud his voice sounded in the semidarkness.

Michele nodded. What was she doing here? she wondered wearily. This was the last place in the world she should be, the last place she wanted to be.

But that wasn't exactly true, she realized in a flash. She wasn't thinking very clearly at the moment, and this probably wasn't a good idea. But she couldn't think of anyone else she would rather be with at this time. She didn't have to talk to Connor, didn't have to pretend that she was all right, or try to take his mind off what had happened to her tonight. Connor would have seen through that in a second. He was content to leave her with her own thoughts, and she knew that if those thoughts got to be too much for her to bear, he would be there for her. Strangely enough, she found the idea comforting.

She looked at him then, standing still and ill at ease in his own home, and she almost smiled. He obviously didn't know what to do with the stray he had just brought home. "Will you answer my questions?" she asked him quietly.

Connor looked wary. "I might."

"Do you think the same person responsible for that—" her voice shook slightly "—that bird is the one who sent the other note, too?"

Connor watched her soberly. "Probably," he conceded. "But I sure haven't figured out what the connection between the two of you is yet. The lab should have full results on that letter you received soon. It will be interesting to see if there's any kind of match with the clues picked up from tonight."

"What kind of clues do you think the officer may have found tonight?"

"The intruder had to take the screen off, and the window will show prints if he didn't wear gloves."

Michele watched him closely, half-amazed at how well she was beginning to be able to read him. "What else?" she asked flatly.

Connor returned her look but said nothing. Michele was certain that she was on to something, because she knew Connor wouldn't lie to her. If he didn't want her to know something, he might try to change the subject or stonewall her, but he wouldn't lie.

"There's something else. I can see it in your face. You may as well tell me. I'm not going to go into hysterics. I'm stronger than I look."

Connor had no difficulty believing that. Unfortunately, that wasn't much of a recommendation. She looked as fragile as spun glass, and just as breakable. This latest ordeal had drained most of the color from her face, and she looked strung as tautly as a wire. "We can discuss this tomorrow," he said, turning away.

"No!" Michele's vehement response surprised him into turning back to face her again. Her eyes were wide and shooting darts at him. A good sign, he silently acknowledged, but not on this subject. She had already dealt with enough tonight; she didn't need any more turmoil. But from the look on the lady's face, she wasn't going to give him the chance to protect her from it.

"Connor, if there's one thing I've learned about you, it's that you won't lie to me. Now, I want to know what else you learned about this thing tonight."

Connor was stunned at the warmth that stole into his chest at her words. She was right. He couldn't lie to her. Especially when she was aiming those gray eyes in his direction. He didn't want to bring her more pain, either, though. "Michele, wouldn't it be easier to let it go for now?"

"Let what go, Connor?" Michele rose from the couch and came to stand next to him.

The steady look in her eyes made him mutter a curse and rake his hand through his hair. Oh, what the hell. What was he trying to prove, anyway? That he was some sort of Sir Galahad who could rescue her from harm? She was going to find out sooner or later anyway. But the truth was, he did want to protect her from any more pain. From what he'd read in her file, she'd had much more to bear in her life than she should have. Was it a crime not to want to add to it?

He shot a look at her, and she was still regarding him steadily. Apparently it was, in her book. He sighed in resignation. "Whoever it was left another note for you."

Michele shook her head. "I didn't even notice. Did the officers find it?"

"Yeah. Same as last time. Letters cut out and glued to the paper."

Michele swallowed hard but forced her voice to remain calm. "What did it say?"

Connor watched her closely, but she didn't look like she was breaking. The events of the night had shocked her, sickened her, but she was still standing. Michele Easton was right. She was a lot stronger than she looked. That didn't make it any easier to tell her, though. "It just said one word. *Remember*. That's all."

"Well, he certainly enjoys being cryptic." Michele tried to joke and failed miserably. "What's that supposed to mean?"

Connor shrugged. "Remember me? Remember September? Remember the Alamo? Who the hell knows?"

"Or remember the last message," Michele said slowly. "Don't talk to cops, didn't it say? You don't have any violent ex-girlfriends who are into enacting scenes from *Fatal Attraction,* do you?" she asked, only half-jokingly.

Connor sent her a wry glance. "My ex-girlfriends are usually bitter, but any violence they'd initiate would be aimed at me, not you, rest assured. Probably something that would impair my social life for the next few years."

Michele's eyebrows rose, but she couldn't help the flash of jealousy his casual assertion caused. "Do you leave 'em crying, McLain, you big stud, you?" she inquired sweetly.

Connor's eyebrows lowered at her levity. "Not exactly. I just leave 'em."

Michele's attempt at humor left her. Because she had no doubt that his last statement was very true. Connor McLain loved them and then left them. No ties, no entanglements, no commitments. He had very little to give any woman, hadn't he told her that? She had every reason to believe that he was a man who wouldn't lack for female companionship. He was virile, compelling, dangerously attractive. Nothing seemed to attract women more than a man who couldn't be pinned down, one who was obviously intent on remaining unsnared. Such a man was even more challenging when he was as up-front as Connor McLain, telling a woman exactly what his intentions were. But Michele was sure his honesty wasn't appreciated when it came time for him to leave.

"Look," Connor said, his voice interrupting her reverie, "do you want to take a bath or something? It might relax you, and you probably want to go to bed." His remark was robbed of any sexual connotation by the obvious concern in his voice.

Michele shook her head. "I just want—" Her voice cracked, and she bit her lip. She just wanted this whole thing to be over. She wanted the children to be found. She wanted to stop being afraid in her own home. She wanted the torment of the dreams to cease, and most of all she wanted not to break down in front of this man.

Connor roughly enfolded her stiff body in his arms. He rocked her gently back and forth, then bent his head to whisper a kiss across her cheek. At the same moment Michele raised her face to his, and suddenly their lips were very close together. Her eyes flew to his questioningly, and what she read there made her swallow hard. His heavy-lidded gaze was focused on her parted lips, causing her to wet them nervously with the tip of her tongue. A muscle twitched in one hard cheek at her action. She wasn't sure who moved first, or if it was a simultaneous decision. The next moment their mouths were touching lightly, barely meeting, as if each was afraid the other would call a halt.

Their mouths parted then, before moving back together for more of a taste, more pressure, a closer contact. Connor gathered her nearer as he rubbed his mouth across hers, reveling in the sweetness he found there. Michele caught his chiseled lower lip gently in her teeth and worried it with her tongue. By mutual decision they stopped their tentative play and kissed in earnest, lips opening, tongues meshing, bodies straining together.

Michele could feel the effect of the kiss clear to bottom of her polished toenails. Heat spread in direct correlation to each plunge of his tongue. Her mouth twisted under his sweetly, giving back as much pleasure as she received. Connor relished her response and thanked her gently with more sensual delight, their mouths successfully communicating in a way they couldn't do with words.

They broke apart, his ragged breathing countering the short bursts of breath coming from her. Their eyes opened, and they surveyed each other solemnly. Michele recovered first, embarrassment filling her. He had brought her here to help, that was all, to give comfort. And here she was, throwing herself at him like one of his bimbos. She could barely look him in the eye, so ashamed was she of her unfamiliar actions. Until today she would have sturdily avowed that one had to like a man, had to respect him, to be able to feel such passion in his arms. She didn't know herself like this, and she was in a panic, hoping he wouldn't see how clearly out of her element she was.

"I believe I will take that shower now," Michele told him. She was unable to meet his eyes, but she was proud of the even tone she managed.

Connor's eyes narrowed. It was amazing how she could switch from a warm giving woman to ice princess in such a short space of time. But if that was the way she wanted to play it, that was fine with him. "Sure," he fairly snapped. "The bathroom's through there." He indicated with one hand. "I'll shower downstairs." A cold shower, he promised himself grimly as he strode away. One as icy as Michele Easton became each time he thought he had reached her on some level.

Michele entered the kitchen a half hour later to find Connor pensively staring into space. She stopped, heart in her mouth at the picture he made.

That he had showered was evident. His hair was still slightly damp, left to dry in ignored waves. He wore only jeans and a white ribbed undershirt, and her mouth went dry. Both hands were braced overhead as he leaned against the bottom of the cupboards. Michele noted with fascination the way his chest curls whimsically peeked out around the edges of the shirt. It clung to him like a glove, and she was able to discern the muscles of his chest through it. Then he turned his head to look at her, though she had made no sound. His look speared through her, seared her with his heated silent regard, and still he said nothing.

She became belatedly aware of the picture she made. "I'm sorry," she apologized. "You didn't pack anything for me to wear to bed. I called out, but you must not have heard. I hope it's okay," she continued more slowly in the face of his still silent scrutiny. "I raided your closet." She was fast becoming even more uncomfortable. Maybe this was his favorite shirt, she thought uneasily, or worse yet, maybe his ex-wife had bought it for him. She probably should have looked for a T-shirt instead, but something inside her had shied away from going through his dresser drawers. She had hoped that the tails of a dress shirt would cover more than a softer, more clinging cotton shirt. She just wished he would say something.

Connor was stunned at the fist of desire that slammed into his gut at the sight of her wearing his shirt. She shouldn't have been sexy, standing there barefoot wearing only his ruffled tux shirt. But she had to make the most sensually provocative picture he had ever imagined. Though she was fairly tall, she was small boned and small waisted. The shirttails trailed over her to cover her to smooth midthigh. The gaps on the side were as provocative as slits in a skirt, and her long, slim, pretty legs looked as elegant as if she had been wearing a cocktail dress. The shirt hung down off the shoulders, and she had rolled up the sleeves to reach just below her elbows.

His gaze wandered higher and fixed on the undone top two buttons, which only barely hinted at cleavage. He swallowed thickly. It shouldn't have been seductive, but it was. His shirt draped her enticing shape, hiding it and making him even more aware of what was inside it.

Michele almost turned and ran at the searing look Connor shot her. His blistering regard was frightening; she was sure she had made a grievous error. But something inside her wouldn't let her turn away; something womanly forced her to return his heated gaze. Michele found a strange portion of herself exhilarated at the look on his face.

Because Connor McLain wasn't angry; he wasn't framing a heated setdown at her audacity. He was a man trying to come to grips with his own passion. Michele wasn't so inexperienced that she was unable to read the signs in his taut skin and flared nostrils. She could also read the fact that he was not going to do anything about it.

Michele almost gasped at the knot of pain she felt with that realization. Connor didn't make a move toward her, although his eyes were devouring her hungrily. It wasn't the first time she had surprised that look on his face, and he was making no attempt to hide it. But Michele knew he wasn't going to act on his feelings. Whatever else he thought of her, Connor was too honorable in his own way to take advantage of what he saw as her vulnerability tonight. And she wasn't sure she knew how to change his mind.

Michele chewed her bottom lip as she considered the problem. And it *was* a problem, she acknowledged, because suddenly she realized that, more than anything else in the world, what she wanted from this man right now wasn't safety, wasn't comfort.

It was this realization that made Michele close the distance between the two of them. Connor shifted to face her as she drew closer to him, and she saw that he was gripping the countertop in back of him so tightly that his knuckles were white. Still he made no move toward her.

Michele came closer still until she was almost touching him. "Connor," she whispered, and stood on tiptoe to brush her mouth over his.

Keeping his hands from reaching out and touching her, from bringing her as close as he could get her, was like trying to lasso a runaway locomotive. Still, he tried. He wasn't big on chivalrous instincts, but this lady brought out the few he did have. "Michele..." His voice was raw. "What do you think you're doing?"

Michele's lips had drifted away from his and meandered up his freshly shaven jawline. "Seducing you," she answered before catching his earlobe in her teeth and giving it a nip, causing him to jump and then shudder. His head twisted sharply at her words, his mouth grazing her own as she spoke. "But I don't have a lot of experience at this," she whispered against his lips. "I'm not quite sure if I'm doing it right." Each word was spoken against his mouth like butterfly wings caressing it.

"Oh, yeah." Connor's voice spoke of the desire he was trying, and failing, to keep in check. "I'd say you're doing it exactly right." His arms came around her with lightning speed and pulled her closer to him even as his mouth crushed hers. Michele felt dizzy at the speed with which he moved, or maybe it was her natural feeling when his mouth was covering hers like this. She let her eyelids drift shut and gave herself up to the magic of his kiss.

Connor had no intention of taking what Michele was offering tonight. He wasn't that big a bastard. She was hurt and scared and feeling alone, and he wasn't going to mistake those feelings for any tender ones toward him. But he had overestimated his control, or underestimated her allure.

Just one kiss, he thought dizzily. And then he would let her go. Just one long, deep, hard, wet kiss and he would call a rational end to this. Just one. Or maybe two. His mind faded away as a more powerful feeling in his body took over. He pressed kiss after intoxicating kiss against her soft mouth and exulted in her response.

Michele was glad to lean into his powerful body, because she was suddenly unsure whether her legs were capable of holding her. It was sheer intoxication to give in to the attraction they held for each other. She allowed herself to be pulled down a sensual vortex, reveled in it as reason faded away. Connor thrust his tongue surely into her mouth, and Michele welcomed it gladly. Their tongues glided like velvet against velvet, dueling and playing before he abandoned such play for a more carnal caress. His intent was clear as his tongue speared her mouth over and over again, and Michele kissed him back with equal fervor.

One of Connor's hands dropped to her hips, and he pulled her even closer to him, rubbing her against his arousal. Michele gasped from excitement as much as surprise. She fit exactly, he thought fuzzily, perfection personified. His hand moved lower and swept her silky thigh. Up and down it slid, before it moved boldly under the shirttails. He didn't know whether to curse or give thanks when his hand encountered the barrier of her panties. Still his hand slid upward and cupped her silk-encased bottom, squeezing gently, lifting her into the cradle of his hips.

Michele moved at the feel of him, hard and ready, so close to where she was damp and aching. She moved again as Connor's mouth lowered and found her breast through the fine lawn shirt. One hand moved up to lift her flesh to his mouth, and he homed in unerringly on her nipple. She whimpered at the sensation of his warmth on her skin, separated only by cloth. The shirt grew damp as he coaxed the bud to tauten until it was a hard tip pressing against the shirt, begging for more of his attention.

Connor pulled himself away to regard his handiwork and lost his last thread of reason. He impatiently undid the buttons of the shirt and allowed it to drape around her partially nude form.

Michele felt her body heat under his smoldering regard, but she made no move to cover herself. Connor raked her with his gaze, noting the high round breasts, perfect for his hands, the narrow waist, curvy hips and the long sleek perfection of her thighs. He was barely conscious of his hands reaching into the open shirt, settling on her waist.

Michele gasped with surprise as he lifted her, her arms going automatically to his shoulders. He set her down on the edge of the counter and moved purposefully between her legs. Both hands slid up to the undersides of her breasts and plumped them, readying them for his lips. Her hands slid to his hair and held his mouth tightly against her as he suckled strongly from her breast. Jet streams of desire smoked through her, arrowing a straight pathway from her nipples to her womb. Connor suckled fervently, savoring one ivory breast before turning to feast on its twin. Michele pressed his head to her breasts mindlessly, forcing a deeper caress. "Connor," she whimpered. "Please."

Connor batted her nipples with his tongue, dueling with the tip of his tongue. He made wondrous swirls around her delicate areolae, always coming back to where she most wanted to feel his mouth. He moved slightly away to yank his own shirt over his head before grasping Michele's hips and pulling her toward him, lifting her off the counter and allowing her body to make a slow sensual descent along his own. He rubbed his chest against her throbbing breasts, and Michele gasped, reaching for his big shoulders, wanting more, needing a firmer contact. Connor stood firm, teasing her by lightly abrading her tender nipples with his rougher, scratchy chest hair. Soon the teasing was too much even for him, and he pulled her closer, as close as he had dreamed of having her for too long, but not close enough.

Enough reason was present in his desire-hazed mind to whisper to him to move, not to consummate their desire in his kitchen. And so he reached behind her and lifted her in his arms, sealing her mouth with his own as he made his way into his bedroom. He laid her down upon rumpled navy silk sheets and allowed himself one brief exultant look as he took in her partially nude figure on his bed. Then he followed her down on the mattress.

Michele heard one faint warning voice dimly in the back of her mind when her eyes fluttered open to see him gazing down at her, hard masculine intent stamped on his features. But before she could interpret the voice, he was on the bed with her, kissing her again, and the fire they had started became a conflagration. He rolled them both so they were on their sides facing each other, and somehow the shirt was lost. She delighted in the expanse of bare skin he was allowed access to.

Her hands were on an adventure of exploration as they roamed previously uncharted territory. Her long nails tangled teasingly in his chest hair, marveling at how much darker it was than that on his head. She touched his nipples and was pleased to find him as sensitive there as she was. She wiggled lower and put her lips to one, tugging gently, and was gratified to hear his breath hiss out between clenched lips. But when her fingers wandered lower, barely brushing the hard ridge behind his jeans, Connor once again took control of their play. Her wrists were grasped, and he shifted away from her, raising her body again so he could crush her to him.

Connor could feel his control rapidly spinning away and left his jeans on for just that reason. He swept her panties off with one hand, flinging them out of the way. He swallowed her moan as his hand settled on her mound, pressing gently. His mouth moved down the white column of her throat even as his exploring fingers found her slick dewy folds. His teeth lightly tasted her nipple at the same time that he entered her tight recesses with one long finger. She cried out at the dual assault, but Connor showed her no mercy. Again and again his finger thrust into her, his thumb pressing against the jewel of her desire. His mouth opened wider, swallowing more of her breast, and Michele felt the edges of reason cloud away.

Connor knew he wasn't going to be able to stand it much longer. He wanted it to go on forever, but blackness was swimming before his eyes, and heat was pooling in his groin. He forced himself to pull away from her, panting, as he dropped kisses in a random order across her delicate cheekbones. "Michele, Michele..." His voice was thick. "Are you protected, Princess?"

Michele's body stretched languorously under his, and she wondered how he could make the same nickname she so detested sound like a heated caress. "I...no..." she heard herself say as if from a distance and came fully conscious as she felt his weight leave the bed. "I'll take care of it," he murmured.

She sat up as he strode quickly from the room, and even as the sensations he evoked in her remained, she felt sanity resume. What was she doing? What would he think of her? Michele shook her head, for the first time becoming cognizant of the sensual abandon with which she had been sprawled against the silky sheets. She mustn't do this, a sane voice told her. She knew what Connor McLain was, and how he felt about her. She couldn't possibly hope to be able to compete with the hordes of other women in his past, and she knew suddenly that she wasn't going to try.

She slid her legs over the side of the bed and slipped out, amazed at their shakiness. Quickly she swept the room with her gaze and on the other side of the room saw the shirt she had been wearing. She had no sooner picked it up than she heard a sound and whirled around. Connor was standing in the doorway, gloriously naked, and Michele swallowed, even as she clutched the garment to her own form.

Her eyes wandered down the splendid length of him, and she closed her eyes dizzily. He was marvelously formed, lightly padded with muscle, and the turgid proof of his desire in the protective sheath made it rampantly plain that he found her completely desirable. He was magnificent, and Michele suddenly knew that she would not be leaving him this night. Everything she wanted was here; this man had the ability to give it to her. She pushed away questions of how she would recover when he left her and concentrated instead on the most intense physical desire she had ever experienced.

Even now, with all his senses screaming, Connor made no move toward her. It was her call. If she had changed her mind, he would not touch her, although one part of his body jeeringly asked how he would manage that heroic feat.

But it wasn't necessary. The shirt Michele clutched so tightly was released to fall forgotten between them as she reached out blindly to touch him. His arms came around her fiercely then, and his mouth ground against hers.

Suddenly it became too much. Connor lifted her, and she instinctively wrapped her long legs around his waist. He walked the few steps to the bed even as she was guiding his entrance, and he thrust into her before her back hit the mattress.

Michele gasped with the ferocity of his desire, and her eyes fluttered shut as his whispered words surrounded her. He groaned love words, sex words, into her ear, telling her how to move, what he wanted from her, how she was perfect, perfect, and then his voice broke and he lunged with even more strength into her tight moistness. Michele felt the world shatter and break away as the precipice whirled up and swept her over it in an infinite plunge into pleasure.

Chapter 9

"I hurt you."

His statement filtered through the sensual haze that enshrouded her in the aftermath of their lovemaking. With his body still partially covering hers, Michele continued to feel the fading eddies of sensation.

"No," she whispered, a slight smile tilting her lips. She reached out to cradle his hard jaw in her palm, guiding his mouth to hers. Their lips softly met, before Connor brushed a kiss on her neck. Then he moved to the side, pulling her with him, cradling her against his hard chest.

"I showed about as much finesse as a rutting bull, Princess." One hard finger lifted her chin so he could read the truth in her eyes. "I wanted you so badly that at the end I couldn't think at all. I should have been gentler." He looked down at her delicate features and felt a stab of remorse. "I was rough."

"You were...passionate," Michele corrected him gently, touched by his concern.

"Too fierce."

"Urgent."

Connor looked hard at her, but her soft gray eyes were guileless. He closed his eyes as he hugged her more tightly to his chest. When he had finally felt a flicker of reason return, regret had swiftly followed. He hadn't taken enough care of her, hadn't been gentle enough for the kind of woman Michele was. Tricia had hated it when passion had overcome him like that. She had accused him of acting like a caveman, and a selfish one at that. He had assumed that Michele would feel the same way. But one look at her face told him otherwise, even without her gentle corrections. She bore the look of a satisfied woman, her expression soft, her eyes still dreamy. And he felt a primordial satisfaction at being the man who had put that look on her face.

Michele couldn't have moved if her life had depended on it. A strange lethargy had stolen into her limbs, and she couldn't think of anywhere she would rather be than in Connor's arms. She rubbed her face against his crinkly chest hair and smiled bemusedly. She found his concern strangely touching, it contrasted so strongly with his usual self-confidence.

Not that she had fibbed. Making love with Connor had been like being caught in a tidal wave of sensation, making all thought rush away. Never had she been so supremely satisfied, not a little of that satisfaction stemming from the knowledge of how urgent his need for her had been. Michele hadn't had much experience, so it was heady to know that she affected this man as powerfully as he affected her.

Connor finally moved. He looked down at the woman in his arms and smiled a slow sensuous smile, one full of wicked promise in response to her own glowing face. "You're sure I didn't hurt you?" he questioned as he threaded his fingers through the soft fine ebony hair spilling across his chest.

"Positive. I keep telling you—" Michele broke off to receive the soft kiss he pressed to the corner of her mouth. She struggled to remember what she had been saying. "I'm not breakable."

Connor still wasn't sure about that, but the last thing he wanted to do with the woman in his arms was argue. "But that's so hard to remember, sweetheart," he whispered. "When you're so soft—" he dropped a kiss on one cheek "—so silky—" another was pressed against her shoulder "—and so wondrously tight around me." Michele shuddered, whether from his erotic whisper or the kiss beneath her ear, she didn't know. Connor rose on his elbows above her, carnal intent evident in his eyes. Michele helplessly returned his gaze, her arms reaching around his shoulders. And when he endeavored to prove his claim, she matched his every caress.

"What are your plans for today?"

Michele raised her eyebrows at the abrupt question. She had badgered Connor into allowing her to fix a breakfast of sorts for them. He had expressed other intentions this morning, until Michele had regretfully admitted to some lingering soreness from their leisurely night of love-making. At her confession, his amorous mood had evaporated quickly, to be replaced by an almost comical solicitude. His kitchen cupboards had yielded meager pickings, but she had managed to scrape together the ingredients for French toast.

They had been eating in amicable silence, each reading a section of the paper, with the television news in the background. "I usually go to the shelter on Saturdays. Why?"

Connor wiped his mouth on his napkin, but his attention was diverted to the TV screen as Mayor McIntire's familiar face filled it. They both listened in silence as he relayed to the citizens of Philadelphia the police commissioner's assurances that a break in the kidnapping investigation would soon be forthcoming.

Michele frowned slightly and cast a quick glance at Connor. He was watching the newscast impassively, and she grew curious at his silence. "Is it true?" she asked. Connor looked at her quizzically. "Are you close to solving the case?"

"We're getting there," he answered. "But that's not what's really going on here." He nodded at the screen, from which McIntire had faded, replaced by a picture of the Reverend Carlson. "It's all show with McIntire. If we don't solve the case before election time, he'll take it as a personal affront."

"You don't like him."

Connor shrugged. "I don't trust him, but then, I don't trust anybody who spends more time talking than doing." As the news moved on to another topic, he looked at her and went back to their previous conversation. "I have to go to work for a few hours today, and I don't want you going back to your apartment until I get off."

Michele's eyebrows rose regally. "May I ask why not?"

Connor's brows came together. "You shouldn't have to ask," he responded firmly. "I don't want you in that house again until the lock is fixed on your window, and I can check out all the rest of the locks. We really ought to check into a security system for you."

Michele knew she was gaping, but she couldn't help herself. His arrogant assumption that she would do as he said, that she would wait around until he had time for her, was dumbfounding. She strove to keep an even tone. "That certainly won't be necessary."

"It is necessary, Michele," he asserted. "As long as an intruder has easy access to your home, and to *you,*" he stressed, "there's no way in hell I'll allow you back in there."

His choice of words immediately raised Michele's ire. "You'll *allow* me? Since when do I need you to *allow* me to do anything?"

"Look, Michele..."

"No, you look!" she exclaimed, rising to her feet in agitation. "Don't think I'm going to let you run my life just because we...that is...we—" She stopped, suddenly flustered.

Connor rose, too, and approached her slowly. "Because we what, Princess? Just because we had sex last night? Because you let me get closer to you than I suspect any person has been in a long, long time? Because when I touched you, you melted all over me like the sweetest honey? Because holding you made me lose control faster than a randy youth, and I got harder quicker than I ever have before?" By this time he was crowding her retreating figure against the refrigerator, sliding a hand through her hair to cup the back of her head.

Michele slid both hands between them, palms against his chest. "What I mean," she started, and damned the breathless quality of her voice, "is that I won't take orders from you. I'm an adult. I'm perfectly capable of having that window fixed myself."

"Is that why it's been broken ever since you moved into the place?" Connor inquired smoothly. He made a quick dismissive gesture with one hand. "Michele, this is ridiculous. Are you actually going to tell me that you want to go back home before you know it's completely secure?" He bent his head to her.

"No," Michele murmured, her normally quick mind at a loss when his mouth was on her neck like this. That wasn't what she had meant. He was confusing the issue, confusing *her,* she thought fuzzily, as her neck arched under his ardent mouth. He had been giving her orders, he had tried to take over, hadn't he? And why did the importance of that fact seem to slip away when he was this close to her?

He made his way up the column of her throat then, and all thoughts went whirling away. Her lips parted to accept his hard, sure kiss and returned it with equal fervor. His mouth was hot and wild, calling to the most sensual side of her nature. Dimly she was aware of other sensations, of the cool unyielding surface at her back, the tensile muscles under her fingers, the equally unyielding hardness pressing against her. But most of her senses were focused on the man who was holding her, seducing her with his tongue.

Their lips parted, and their eyes fluttered open to survey each other, hers dazed and his regretful. Connor pulled himself away with a muttered curse and raked one hand through his tousled golden hair. "I didn't mean to do that," he said softly, taking a long shuddering breath.

He didn't know how this woman could keep doing this to him, but she got to him on a level he hadn't believed possible. He glanced at her, and it was all he could do to not take her in his arms again. Her eyes were smoky charcoal, the way they had been when he'd made love to her last night. He knew from experience that afterward they would be a wide, soft vulnerable dove gray. He took a few steps back from her. They made a combustible combination, the cop and the lady psychologist.

"Look," he tried reasonably. "You brought a change of clothes, so there's no reason why I can't drop you off at the shelter. What time do you usually leave?"

"Three," Michele murmured.

"Okay, so at three I'll pick you up, we'll make a stop at a hardware store, you can pick out the lock of *your* choice," he stressed humorously, "I'll take you home, install it. And all you'll have to pay for this service is a mere steak dinner."

"A steak dinner, hmm?" Michele pretended to consider. "I don't know. I've already cooked for you once today. I don't know if I want to set a precedent."

"Lady, you've already set a precedent," Connor crooned with a wicked glint in his eye, leaning one hard arm forward to set it next to her head. "And it has nothing to do with cooking."

Michele recognized the look in his eye and the intent on his face. Knowing that she didn't have a chance of thinking coherently in his arms, she agreed hastily as she ducked beneath his arm. "Okay, but if you want dinner, we're going to have to stop at the grocery store, as well. My cupboards are almost as bare as yours."

Connor recognized her diversionary tactic for what it was. But since he couldn't trust himself to keep his hands off her if he touched her again, he allowed her to get away with it. After all, he had made very important inroads here. Michele Easton was no longer questioning his involvement in her life.

When three o'clock rolled around, Michele couldn't help the feeling of relief that flooded her. She enjoyed volunteering at the shelter once a week. Something about these women and children touched a chord deep within her, reminding her all too vividly of the time of her life when she, too, had been a victim. Working here allowed her to give help to people, help of a sort that had been absent when she had needed it. But today had been different. She had watched the clock surreptitiously, waiting impatiently for three o'clock.

But when she exited the building, Connor was nowhere in sight. She frowned in confusion. He had been adamant about her not going home by herself, but the only man she saw was getting out of a beige car and strolling toward her.

He looked vaguely familiar. Where had she seen that dark head of hair and that swagger before? When he reached her, he swept off his sunglasses, and Michele started in recognition. He was the man she had seen in Connor's office the first day she'd gone to the police, the one who also appeared in some of the pictures in Connor's home.

She blinked. Somehow her memory, and the photos, had failed to do this man justice. He was movie-star handsome, with black hair and eyes, flashing white teeth and bronzed skin. Combined with that cocky strut, he was the embodiment of what every mother warned her daughter about.

"Cruz Martinez, at your service." He swept her a comical bow, ignoring her bemused look. "I'm Connor's friend," he explained. "You probably don't remember me, but I saw you at the station that day...."

"I remember you, Mr. Martinez," Michele said with a slight frown. "But I'm afraid I'm not sure why you're here."

"I'm doing Connor a favor," he explained easily. "He got roped into an emergency meeting with the police commissioner again, and he's going to be late. So I offered to come and get you." He held up a paper bag he was holding. "I've even picked up a lock for your window. I can probably have it on before Connor even gets there, and for that, he will owe me—big time."

Michele chewed her bottom lip unconsciously. She wished mightily that she had insisted on driving her own car. Then she would have been spared this embarrassing feeling of being at the mercy of someone else's schedule.

As if sensing her indecision, Cruz waggled his eyebrows. "I'm completely safe, I promise. I've had all my shots, and my mother still makes me go to confession every week."

Michele giggled in spite of herself. "I'm sure there's a real need for that, Mr. Martinez." At his look of mock insult, she relented. After all, she didn't have much choice in the matter. Soon she was seated next to him in his car and giving him directions to her home.

Cruz kept up a running commentary all the way. By the time they had arrived at Michele's place, he had regaled her with his family history. "It's true," he avowed, despite Michele's laughter. "My mother is Irish and my father is Mexican. I'm twice blessed—a Latin lover with the gift of the blarney."

Michele shook her head. He was an utterly charming man, with a ready wit and an easy sense of humor. He was also quite obviously a lady-killer, but he was so unabashed about it that there was something almost harmless about him.

Except for his eyes. Though his were dark where Connor's were green, they both shared a shrewd, assessing quality. They observed more than most people.

By the time Michele had found him a drill and a screwdriver, they were chatting like old friends. Even while Cruz worked on the window, he talked continuously. "I don't envy Connor his meeting today, that's for sure. The commissioner was hotter than, well..." Cruz continued with a quick look at her. "He was pretty hot. He's tired of being chewed out by the mayor, and I have a feeling he was going to do some chewing out in return."

Michele frowned. "But just this morning the mayor was on TV saying that the police were doing a fine job."

"Oh, yeah, we are. Just not as quickly as the politicians would like." He grimaced as he reached for the drill again. "But they don't always have a real good idea of what police work is all about, you know? They care about their image and their standing in the polls, and they forget that the rest of us are out there busting our butts to solve the case."

"He won't get into real trouble, will he?" Michele asked concernedly. "As long as progress is being made?"

"Who knows?" Cruz grunted in response as he screwed the lock into place. "With the mayoral race being so close right now, this case has turned into a hot potato."

"But no other children have disappeared," Michele argued. "You have a good chance of finding them, don't you think?" She was hoping for reassurance. Each time she tried to approach the topic of the investigation with Connor, he changed the subject. She was sadly aware that there was no way she could offer proof to Connor that what she had seen in the dream was indeed true. But she knew in her heart that it was. She had never been led wrong before, and she was certain that two of the children were no longer being kept with the others.

"There, all finished," Cruz said, turning to catch her faraway expression. "Hey, don't you worry," he said kindly. "We'll catch this guy. It's just a matter of time. And Connor will weather this meeting all right. He's been through it before, and he knows how to handle the overeager brass."

"Thanks a lot, Cruz," Michele said sincerely. "What can I get you? I don't have much in the fridge, but I do think I could find you a cold beer."

"That'd be great, thanks."

Michele reached in the refrigerator and found a lone beer for him, and a diet soda for herself. They drank in companionable silence for a few minutes before a knock on the door was followed by Connor walking in.

Michele's eyes went over him hungrily. After what Cruz had told her, she had been alarmed for him. But he didn't look any the worse for wear from his meeting, only a little out of sorts. Her body warmed as he returned her look tenfold.

"Sure. Now he shows up, after all the work is done," Cruz jeered good-naturedly. He pointed the half-empty bottle at his partner and addressed Michele. "He's the same way at work, Michele. Nothing but a laggard. I have to carry him every step of the way."

Connor approached and looked in the refrigerator, before turning a jaundiced eye on his friend.

"I see you commandeered the last beer for yourself in return for services rendered."

"Not at all," Cruz denied breezily. "Michele more than paid me back with that kiss she planted on me right before you came in. Wow, that mouth of hers ought to be registered at the station, buddy. Hey—" He broke off at the mask of ice that had settled over Connor's face. "I'm kidding, I'm kidding!"

Cruz took a long careful look at the two silent people and wisely decided to make an exit. If ever two people wanted to be alone, it was these two. "But you know, I was just leaving. As a matter of fact, I hear my mother calling me right now."

"I'll walk you to the door," Connor offered, and Cruz knew he had been right. He also couldn't resist baiting his friend one last time.

"I can sure see why you weren't too curious about the rest of the background check, old chum." He winked at Connor's still face as he went out the door. "Your taste is certainly improving. Bye, Michele," he called, barely getting the words out before the door was shut after him.

Connor was reluctant to turn around. It was too much to hope that Michele hadn't heard Cruz's remark. He turned slowly and mentally cursed. By the looks of her still face, not only had she heard, she had probably misunderstood. "Michele..."

"You son of a bitch," she whispered shakily. She wanted to scream; she wanted to throw something. But most of all she wanted to get away from him. She needed to hide, to pull herself back together, to regain her composure. She didn't want to have to face him like this, knowing that while she had been at her most vulnerable to him, learning to trust him, he had been coldly continuing to look into every avenue of her life. Which meant he still didn't believe her, of course.

That was hysterical, and she could almost feel laughter bubbling up inside her. She blinked tears away from her eyes. Please, God, no, she mentally prayed. That would be the final indignity, if she cried in front of him. "All the time—" her voice trembled despite her best efforts "—that you were gaining my trust, you never stopped suspecting me. Never."

Connor watched her while his gut split in two. He despised himself for putting that look on her face. "It wasn't like that," he tried.

"Oh, please!" Michele's voice dripped sarcasm. "You changed tactics to take me off guard, to keep an eye on me while you finished checking me out. Don't you think you went a little too far with that, Lieutenant?" she jeered. "Taking me to bed surely went above and beyond the call of duty."

"Taking you to bed had nothing to do with this," Connor said between clenched teeth.

"Oh, I'll bet not," Michele agreed caustically. "Is that what those medals are for on your shelf at home? How many dangerous female criminals you kept off the street by taking them home and—" She never finished the crude question, because Connor swiftly crossed the room and grabbed her by the shoulders.

"Stop it," he hissed.

Michele arched her head back to stare venomously up at him. "Why? You should be grateful to Cruz. You don't have to pretend anymore. Now your motives are out in the open—for once," she spat scathingly. "I assume that what you found out cleared me once and for all. After all, a great detective such as yourself would have cuffed me already if anything incriminating had shown up."

"I may not cuff you," Connor crooned, a dangerous glint in his eye, "but I'm giving serious consideration to gagging you." His grip tightened as Michele attempted to pull away from him. He shook her slightly, forcing her to meet his gaze. "Now you're going to quit jumping to conclusions and listen to me."

"There's no point," Michele stated dismissively. She welcomed the anger she was feeling now, but she knew it would be short-lived. When the numbing fury wore off, she knew it would leave pain in its wake. And she wanted Connor McLain long gone from here when that happened.

"You misunderstood what Cruz said."

"Oh, you mean you didn't order him to continue digging into my past?" Michele inquired saccharinely.

"I ordered it a long time ago, as you already knew."

"Then what was Cruz talking about?" Michele's eyes dared him. "He sounded like this was something quite recent."

Connor spun away, one hand raking angrily through his thick hair. "I told him to leave it, to concentrate on the investigation. He got some free time and followed up on it. The first I knew of it was when he placed the results on my desk a couple of days ago."

"And you read them."

Connor turned back to her, his gaze steady. "I read them."

"Well, since I'm not in a ball and chain, they must finally have convinced you that I'm above suspicion." Michele's hurt showed in her voice, and Connor nearly winced. "That's something, at least."

"You're not a suspect in this case," Connor said quietly.

"How nice to finally hear you admit that," Michele said sarcastically. "Not a suspect, just a fruitcake, right? You have exceedingly shaky standards, Lieutenant. You're not willing to sleep with a woman who might be involved in a crime, but one who might be nuts is fair game, is that it?"

Her sarcasm snapped Connor's tenuous hold on his temper. "I don't think you're nuts."

"Then you believe my dreams are real?"

Connor chose his words with care. "I believe that you believe them."

Michele's eyes closed in pain. How could she ever have allowed this man to get close to her? Usually her judgment was above reproach; if ever she erred it was on the side of caution. How had Connor gotten through her normally careful defenses so easily? The answer was glaringly apparent. Despite her careful machinations, he had barged through her defenses, and she had fallen in love with him. But that could be cured, she told herself bleakly. It had to be.

Michele opened her eyes to see Connor watching her steadily. She drew a deep breath, ignoring the stabbing pain it brought her. When she spoke, her voice was calm. "I want you out of here. Now."

At her words, Connor felt his own temper fray alarmingly. She was doing it again, donning her royalty mask, receding from him as surely as if he were already gone. So she wanted him gone, did she? he asked himself savagely. Well, that was just too damn bad. She wasn't going to kick him aside as easily as that. She was going to listen to him if he had to tie her up and gag her first. And from the look of the closed expression on her face, that might be necessary before he was done.

He tried anyway. "Michele, listen to me." He ignored her set expression. "This—none of it—has anything to do with you and me."

"It must be very convenient to be able to compartmentalize your life like that, Lieutenant. Very nice and neat. But I happen to believe that if a man can't be trusted professionally, he's likely to be untrustworthy personally, as well."

He took a deep breath, trying to hold on to his disintegrating temper. "I wanted you long before I read that damn report, as you well know. I would think knowing that would please you."

Michele's eyes widened incredulously. "Please me? Your ego is excruciatingly overblown. You grossly overestimate your reputation as a stud if you think that one night in bed makes up for the fact that you're a lying, untrustworthy, son of a—"

He moved so quickly that the rest of Michele's words were arrested. He grabbed her shoulders and pulled her so close that their faces were only centimeters apart. "That's enough, damn it," he growled. "You're going to listen to me whether you like it or not. You do know what listening means, don't you?" he sneered. "After all, that's supposed to be a psychologist's forte."

Michele's mouth snapped shut as she glared murderously at him. He was right, and of course he knew just what buttons to push. She would hear him out, and then she would kick him out the door.

"I ordered a background check on you," he began grimly, "because you came to us with information you should not have had. It was not inconceivable that you had arrived at that information criminally. It was my duty," he caught her expression and stressed, "yes, my *duty,* damn you, to have your credibility verified."

"That was impossible to do," Michele reminded him stiffly, "when you were—and are—incapable of believing I could come by the information in any other way."

"Ah, hell, Michele." His voice was bleak. "What can I say? No, I don't believe in psychics and dreams and all that. I'm too much of a pragmatist for that. But that doesn't mean I don't believe in you, the person."

Michele hardened her heart against the obvious despair in his voice. She mustn't let him get to her. She would hear him out, as she had promised. But she had to maintain the distance between them. For her own emotional equilibrium, she had to. "You've made it very clear on more than one occasion that I remind you of your ex-wife, who you do not hold in very high esteem. How am I supposed to believe that you suddenly overcame your antagonism toward me enough to want to..." Her voice trailed off as she searched for words to describe their unexpected attraction.

"Maybe I can't explain it, Michele, even to myself. Did you ever think of that?" he shot back. He let go of her to rake one hand through his burnished gold hair. "Hell, you've had me so tangled up in knots since we met that I don't even know myself anymore. Do you know what it did to me to find myself getting hard for a woman who stood for everything I've always steered clear of? I was burned by Tricia, and yeah, I've sworn off women like you. But worse than that, even before I was sure you had nothing to do with the kidnappings, I wanted you. I'm too good a cop not to be bothered by that."

She slanted a surprised glance at him. If he had wanted her from the beginning, he had managed to hide that fact very well. But despite herself, she felt herself warming at his words. At least the confusion and wanting weren't all one-sided.

He speared her with a look. "If you feel betrayed, I'm sorry. I never expected Cruz to go ahead with the rest of the check. But I wasn't able to pass up the chance to read it, either. And that seems to be what you can't forgive."

"Because you wanted further evidence of my innocence," Michele put in bitterly.

"Because I couldn't resist the opportunity to find out more about you," he corrected tersely. "Honey, I've been told I'm closemouthed, but you could give even me lessons. I was curious, okay? I already knew I had been wrong about you, but I wanted to see what was in the report about your life. If that's a crime, okay, sue me."

Michele's face was stiff. "And just where did this stimulating information come from?"

Connor watched her closely as he answered slowly, "From a deputy in West Virginia." He winced at the pain that showed briefly on her face before she turned away from him.

Michele was reeling from that information. She could well imagine the tale the deputy had shared. The story of how she and her mother had run away from Bill Strought was probably still being told from rocking chairs on porches all through town. But knowing that Connor knew about it made something inside her cringe.

She had never told another soul about that part of her life, and suddenly she realized that he was right about one thing. For a person who made her living getting other people to open up and share their experiences and feelings, she was remarkably reticent about her own.

"What's worse?" She jumped as his voice sounded in her ear. She had been so wrapped in her own thoughts that she hadn't been aware of his approach. "The fact that I read the rest of the report, or the fact that I learned about your life as a child? You're a psychologist, Michele. You know that none of what happened was your fault. The man was a lunatic."

"I know," she whispered around the lump in her throat. "But that doesn't make it easier to talk about."

His arms came around her, pulling her back against his chest. "If you want to, I'm here," he said quietly, surprising even himself. He wasn't exactly a man who invited confidences, but he figured he could return the favor. The night he had walked into her apartment when she had awakened from her dream, he had talked himself hoarse calming her, at the same time telling her more about himself than he had told his ex-wife in months of dating.

She shook her head silently but leaned back into him. She felt drained of her earlier pain, empty now, but no less confused. She knew that she was on exceedingly shaky ground here. Ever since she had moved to Philadelphia with her mother, she had played it safe. No more risks for Michele Easton. The last one had nearly cost her life, and that had been a hard lesson learned.

Maybe it was time for her to go out on a limb again. God knew she felt more emotion in Connor's presence than she had in years. While she was aware that this relationship would bring her nothing but heartache, she knew she was going to take the chance. She had lived in a cocoon for too long. "I don't know what we're doing together," she whispered, but he heard her and turned her around to face him.

"Neither do I," he admitted. "Gonna wait around and find out?"

"I'm sure this is not a good idea," she said with a sigh.

"Probably not," Connor agreed as he bent his head to her neck.

"I know I'll regret this," she murmured as she arched under his avid mouth.

"Likely we both will," he conceded as he nibbled his way up to her earlobe before taking it in his teeth and worrying it gently.

Michele felt her reservations fade further away at the feel of the muscled wall of his body pressing against hers. "This is police harassment," she charged feebly.

"So call a cop, sweetheart," he urged. His hand captured hers and pressed it against the hard ridge behind his zipper. "Dial 9-1-1. Make a cop come. You don't even need a directory," he added, as her fingers lingered to stroke gently. "Just let your fingers do the walking."

Michele gasped as he took a love bite from her shoulder that made her jump, before laving it soothingly with his tongue. "You are unspeakably crude."

"No, I'm unspeakably horny."

Michele giggled breathlessly. "That too," she agreed.

Chapter 10

Connor turned Michele around in his arms and pulled her close again. Tipping her chin up with one finger he gazed at her soberly. "You're sure that you want to go ahead with this?" he asked. "Because I'm not good at making promises. To be truthful, I don't have the slightest idea where we're going from here."

Michele's smile was slightly tinged with sadness. "Neither do I," she answered. Her gaze was steady as she added, "But I am sure." It was the only certainty in her life lately. She, too, had no indication that pursuing a relationship with Connor would bring her anything but heartache in the long run. But it was time for her to stop playing it safe and rejoin the human race. And if that meant feeling pain as well as pleasure, well, it would still mean she was experiencing more emotion than she had in years.

"We never got around to doing that grocery shopping," she reminded him.

"Well, since I didn't put the lock on your window, I guess I didn't really earn that steak you promised me."

"Aren't you hungry?" Michele asked ingenuously.

Even she was unable to ignore the predatory light in his eyes. "Not for steak, Princess," he whispered, before surprising a shriek from her by sweeping her up in his arms.

"What are you doing?" she demanded, laughing as he made his way toward her bedroom.

"If you can't figure that out, lady, you're even more naive than I thought," he teased. He dropped her over her bed and followed her down on it immediately.

All humor fled from his face as he surveyed her from above. "You really are exquisite," he murmured, one finger tracing her jawline.

Michele was embarrassed. "You've obviously been on the street too long, McLain," she replied awkwardly.

He was amused at her obvious embarrassment but declined to answer. He concentrated instead on dropping kisses lightly over her face, her forehead, her eyelids, her cheeks.

Michele was unaccustomed to allowing her natural wariness to recede completely, and now she reveled in the heightened pleasure her retreat from caution brought her. Connor's firm mouth was infinitely tender as he leisurely brushed his lips against her skin. Slow heat bloomed low in her abdomen. As much as she enjoyed his slow technique, the memory of his harder, almost desperate, kisses teased her, and she wanted them even as she enjoyed his languorous arousal.

She caressed his nape, fingers tangling in the dark gold curls twining enticingly around her fingers. Her throat arched under his questing mouth, her breathing jerky at the nibbling kisses he placed there.

Simultaneously they grew impatient with the gentle wooing. Connor raised his head and looked down at her, feeling an immediate tightening in his groin at the sight of her sprawled beneath him. He waited for her eyes to flutter open before taking her mouth in a deep, searing kiss.

Their tongues mated, their tastes meshed and their mouths twisted together, desperate for more. One kiss blurred into the next and the next, lips parting only to change the slant, to get closer, ever closer. This was the urgency she had wanted from him, needed from him. No one had ever desired her like this; she hadn't known she was capable of inspiring more than insipid passion from a man. But there was no mistaking the bucking of Connor's heart, the tensing of his muscles beneath her clutching fingers.

His tongue incited her own, searing her with his heat. It succeeded in igniting her passions, exciting her unbearably. She was used to wildness in nature; she recognized it in others. She was not familiar with feeling it herself.

He tunneled his fingers through her hair and held her still for the almost desperate quality of his kiss. Touching her was a fantasy. He couldn't get close enough, couldn't taste enough. He brought his jean-clad knee up between her slim thighs and swallowed her inarticulate moan.

Michele felt herself spinning in a vortex of sensations. Her hands began to roam restlessly, feeling the muscle and sinew through his shirt. He evoked electric pleasure with his mouth alone, and she felt as though she would shatter from his kiss.

Connor moved then, rolling them both so that they faced each other. Both hands skidded between them, touching her, moving over her figure restlessly. He unbuttoned her blouse, his fingers clumsy. His throat grew tight as her undergarments were revealed. She wore only a pristine white lace teddy beneath, and his hands faltered to a stop.

His chest heaved as he fought for control. At the rate he was going, this was going to be over too quickly, and he didn't want it to be that way. He needed to see her writhing and frantic beneath him. But he was going to have to exercise some control, somehow. He didn't want her ever to forget the taste of their passion, the tang of their desire. He wanted her always to remember how it had been between them, to somehow imprint himself on her mind and memory.

Michele felt slow heat suffuse her at his intense regard. Her hands went to his shirt, fingers quickly moving buttons through buttonholes, anxious to touch bare skin. When the shirt was loose, her hands moved up his torso slowly, savoring with almost sybaritic pleasure the feel of him. Her fingers kneaded his taut muscles testingly, loving the feel of sheathed strength there.

Both lost their breath at the first contact of hair-roughened skin against silk-encased breasts. Her blouse and his shirt were lost in a quest for freer movement. Michele sighed and arched her back, forcing a firmer contact. Behind the silk and lace, her nipples tautened into pebbled crests, unbearably sensitive, aching for his touch. She couldn't get close enough, couldn't feel enough. Her fingers slid to his sleek back, pressing him nearer. She wanted to press until they were absorbed together, a part of each other.

Shy hands stole to the waistband of his jeans and managed to undo the brass button before Connor's whole body jerked in instant, heated response. He pulled away from her, breath heaving in and out. His face had a light sheen of perspiration. Never had he looked as hard, as pagan, as intense.

He closed his eyes tightly. Every time he felt her sweet hands on him, he felt all his good intentions go up in smoke. He stripped her of her jeans and socks, even removed his own socks, but he left his jeans in place, hoping the barrier would prove an effective shield to her questing hands.

As Michele's lips were pursed to protest the inequity in their attire, he lay down next to her again, sealing her mouth with his until they both forgot all thought and concentrated instead only on sensation.

Connor peeled the straps down off her arms and then tortured Michele by going no further. Instead he brushed his lips along the lace border, kissing her shoulders and upper chest. He rubbed his face against her throat, and Michele shuddered, his whiskers abrading wonderfully.

Finally, when Michele thought she would go mad with longing, he hooked a finger in each strap and slowly brought the teddy low enough to expose her breasts. She arched toward him immediately, mutely pleading for his lips, but Connor took his time appeasing her. First his tongue had to draw tantalizing circles around her areolae, then bat playfully at the nipples. Then he drew one carefully into his mouth, laving it with his tongue, not touching her anywhere else.

Ribbons of desire unfurled deep inside Michele at his teasing, and her hands were frantic, eager to reciprocate. Connor withstood her petting and stroking of his muscled shoulders and chest until she began to pay particular attention to the brown masculine buttons hiding beneath the curling chest hair. At his indrawn breath, she was certain of a reaction, but her pleasure was short-lived. Her hands were captured in his own and drawn to his mouth so a kiss could be pressed into each palm. When he didn't release them, Michele's eyes opened quizzically.

Connor's searing regard was unmistakable, as was the meaning of his next words. "Such sweet, soft hands," he murmured, rubbing them against his cheek, "but so distracting. Now where can we put them to keep them out of trouble?"

"What are you doing...Connor...?" Her question ended on a moan as he used one hand to stretch both hers above her head, then ducked his head to take advantage of the breasts arched up toward his lips. She lost all sense of what she was saying while his mouth ravaged gently, teasing her nipples to bead more tightly, then suckling deeply from each one. Colors cascaded past her tightly closed eyelids, the colors of passion. Her breathing was jerky when she became aware of Connor placing her fingers around the headboard of the bed.

Immediately she let go and reached for him, but he captured her wrists and inexorably drew them up again and replaced them. "No," he murmured against her lips. "I can't think when you touch me, and I sure can't hold out. Now be good and leave your hands here." He paused to kiss her deeply before lowering his head to her neck. "Or I may have to use those handcuffs after all."

"I want to touch you, too," Michele gasped, but she didn't have the will to disobey his erotic command. "You're not being fair."

"There's nothing fair about your effect on me," he reminded her shakily, thrusting gently against her, so that she could feel his urgency held in check by the worn denim. "Or about your ability to turn me into a randy sixteen-year-old, with a bad case of raging hormones and an even shorter fuse."

"You must have been an extremely precocious sixteen-year-old."

"Not—" he paused to lightly nip, then lave one shoulder with his tongue "—as precocious as I intend to be right now." Then his teasing deserted him as he ground his mouth against hers, his tongue thrusting surely, signaling his intent. "I want to make this good for you," he continued, his voice a guttural rasp.

"You do," Michele moaned in response. "You are." But her body quivered in response to the promise implied in his words. And her hands stayed exactly where he had placed them.

Satisfied that his wishes would be carried out, Connor concentrated instead on baring the rest of her body to his avid gaze. As he removed the teddy, he kissed each inch of skin he bared until he pushed the fabric down her long legs and out of their way. Her skin was fair, her breasts high and firm, her waist sweetly indented, and her hips gently curved. He pressed a light kiss on the dark fleecy delta between her legs, and Michele jerked involuntarily.

Then he embarked on an erogenous journey of discovery, touching and kissing every inch of her. Michele twisted restlessly beneath his touch until the sensations produced by his skimming hands were indistinguishable from the desire humming through her veins. Tendrils of heat threatened to become a conflagration as each light kiss and touch sent shards of pleasure through her senses. His hands were questing, soothing her to his touch and inciting her to fever pitch. His mouth was hungry and untiring, leaving a trail of fire in its wake.

Then his touch went again to the softness between her thighs, and Michele's legs tightened reflexively, her eyes flying open. The sight of Connor's tousled golden head so near her body's most intimate secrets was devastating to her senses. His peridot eyes were glittering with passion and savage fire, and he held her gaze as he touched her again, his face tautening even further at her audible moan. But still she denied him, something inside her retreating from the intimacy. "No, Connor," she whispered, even as her back arched. His thumb had found the heart of her desire and started a rhythmic pressing, and his other hand kneaded her stomach lightly.

"Yes, Michele," he contradicted her gently. "Tell me yes."

But the power to speak, to concentrate at all, had quickly fled. Michele forgot her earlier reservations about the intimacy of his touch as his continued stroking and seeking hands worked their magic on her. Her thighs loosened without conscious decision, and Connor pressed them apart, adjusting them to suit himself. He lingered on her silky thighs, satin-smooth to the touch, before moving between them, slipping down on the bed and taking her in his mouth.

This time he used her body's involuntary bucking to grasp her hips and pull her closer to his mouth. Michele's hands came down to him, to push him away, to make him stop. Instead they stayed to linger, to rake through his hair, to press him even closer. Never had she experienced such razor-sharp pleasure, pleasure so intense it threatened to rob her of her sanity. She was buffeted by a storm of sensation, and Connor was at its center, pulling her into the vortex, forcing her to let go of reason and live only for her senses.

Connor's mouth caressed the secret core of her passion, his tongue stroking gently, driving her to maddening arousal. He drank of her body's nectar and forced her higher. Michele felt as if she were teetering on the brink of sanity. She fought the sensation, afraid she would shatter into a million pieces if she let go completely. She was unaware of her own voice keening, chanting his name, but Connor heard it. It drove him to push her further, higher, urging her to let go, let it happen, let it happen....

He tasted the wild heat of her while she spun out of control, his name on her lips, her fingers tangled in his hair. As gratifying as it was to hear her satisfaction, to taste it on his tongue, it had a more electric, immediate effect on his groin. Every muscle in his body was tensed with arousal, and his manhood was aching for the relief Michele had so recently enjoyed. But Connor couldn't help trying to stretch the anticipation out a little longer, and he silently cursed his own rampaging lust, trying to get it back under control.

"No more...Connor...I can't...." Michele's voice was trembling as she caressed his face, and he stopped his gentle stroking of her still quivering flesh. He rose to lie directly over her, his denim-clad legs lying between her own, his hips pressed directly over the part of her that had most recently been pleasured by his mouth. Michele gasped at the renewed fever that just the feel of his throbbing manhood could bring. She flushed at the sight of his partially clad body lying over her nude one. There was something slightly decadent in the sight.

But the eddies of sensation that were still rippling through her made her incapable of embarrassment. What she felt, remarkably enough, was impatience to feel that sleek, muscled body pressed completely against hers, with no barrier between them. And an overpowering need to see him shaking with satisfaction, as she was.

When her fingers brushed his burgeoning desire straining against the zipper of his jeans, Connor felt as though he would jump right out of his flesh. And when she tormented him by lowering the zipper slowly, tooth by tooth, he felt each fraction of descent along his entire rigid staff. His breath came out in a gust when finally his pants were loosened and her tender hands were caressing his throbbing manhood, pulsing painfully behind black cotton briefs. He closed his eyes tightly as she fondled him, fighting back the waves of satisfaction that threatened to overcome him.

Michele pushed the heavy denim from his hips, and Connor shimmied out of his jeans and kicked them off without leaving her. His briefs were next to go, and he groaned aloud when Michele touched his hot flesh for the first time. He ground his teeth when her fingers wandered the length of him, marveling at the velvety steel that was his desire. His manhood was as strong and bold as the rest of him, thrusting forth proudly from its nest of hair. But when she lowered her lips to him, his hands came up to thread through her hair, simultaneously cursing and praying at the rapturous feelings brought about by her curious tongue. Michele flicked her tongue over the velvety tip, licking away the drop of pearly liquid that had appeared there. And then she found herself in Connor's arms and flat on her back, with Connor pressed intimately against the cradle of her hips.

''No more teasing, Princess,'' he said, his voice throaty. He reached for his jeans and fumbled with the pocket until he pulled out a foil wrapper and impatiently moved away to protect her. Michele was unable to tear her eyes away. She was as surprised as he to see her hands push his aside and slowly roll the sheath over his throbbing shaft.

But when she would have lingered, Connor took her hands in his, threading their fingers together as he slowly rolled them so that she was again on her back, with his broad torso looming over her. Her hands still captured tightly in his own, he drew them over her head and brought his chest down and rubbed it over her breasts, driving them both crazy with the friction.

The assault on her senses was almost too much for Michele to bear. She wouldn't have believed it possible to want again, so soon, so much. The feel of him pressed so closely against her was heaven and agony. She wanted him closer, part of her, then wondered wildly if even that would be enough. The pressure of his hardness against her sent pleasure ricocheting down her spine.

Connor ground his mouth against hers fiercely, helpless against the hunger taking over inside him. It had never been like this, so fierce and hot and wild that he felt as if he would die if it ended and explode if it didn't. He wanted more of her, all of her, and he let go of her hands to race his own down her sides. But her hands went on their own adventure, touching him, stroking him, until his skin was like wildfire, his passion raised to a fever pitch.

He shifted so that he was pressed against her sweet softness, clenching his teeth against the need to lunge into her like a savage. He needed to regain control. But opening his eyes to look at her was the last thing he should have done. Her eyes were dark charcoal, and the slumberous passion he read in them ignited him even more. A wild hungry groan was pulled from his throat, and he kissed her hungrily, cupping her hips in his palms. His mouth went to her breast even as he surged into her, urged on by her slim thighs wrapping around his waist.

Michele was burning with need, a writhing mass of nerve endings. She welcomed the heavy rolling of his hips, bucking beneath him, sobbing in her quest for fulfillment. Connor gave one last powerful surge, and then her cries of satisfaction mingled with his own hoarse groan. In the aftermath of their passion they clung to one another, shaking from the fury of the storm that had swept them to oblivion.

It was a long time before either of them was able to think about moving. Connor finally became aware of Michele's choppy breathing and rolled them both to the side, unwilling to let her go completely. He had never experienced such heady pleasure with any other woman, and he stared at the ceiling bleakly, wondering what the hell that meant.

He couldn't afford to let Michele Easton too close; he knew she was poison for him. And he was no good for her. His short marriage to Tricia had proven just how little he had to offer a woman, especially one as elegant as Michele. Even though he now knew that she hadn't grown up wealthy, hadn't had the privileged background he'd assumed, he was still right about the kind of woman she was.

Classy. Refined. Cultured. Much too high-class to get caught in the revolving door of Connor McLain's social life. She was better suited to a man with a life like hers, a white-collar professional who could afford to shower her with all the things she deserved. Someone like James Ryan.

Connor's mouth flattened even as he thought of it. Something primitively savage in him wanted to shout a vehement denial to that claim, to assert that she was in his arms right now, by God, and no other man would ever lay a hand on her. But that was treacherous thinking that used all his body parts other than his head.

He closed his eyes as his arms tightened around her. He wasn't going to kid himself here; he knew there was no future for them. Michele was wrapped up in his life right now. She needed him for the moment, with some nut on the loose threatening her. As long as he kept in mind that she would be gone from his life when hers got back to normal, he could handle this. He could, he asserted surely. There was no reason why they couldn't enjoy each other until that happened.

Michele's heartbeat and breathing gradually returned to normal, but in some way she felt she would never be the same again. This wild experience was probably common for Connor; she had the feeling that he rarely lacked for female companions only too happy to share this with him. But it wasn't normal for her.

Even now, with her hunger twice satisfied, it was curiously seductive to be held so close to his hard body. With his gold coloring he resembled a lion, she suddenly thought whimsically. He certainly moved with a feline grace, and his body, with its sleek padded muscles, had the same leashed power. She moved her hands over his powerful torso now, finally able to fulfill her desire to touch him without restraint. The hair on his chest was several shades darker than that on his head. It spread luxuriously, becoming scarcer on his stomach, only a ribbon of hair arrowing down below his navel. She explored that area now, too, regretful that she had neglected it on her previous explorations. One adventurous finger twirled teasingly in the mysterious indentation.

Connor felt his newly regained ability to breathe endangered once again. He was astounded at his body's insatiable appetite for this woman, who currently seemed embarked on a dangerous journey. Already he could feel himself hardening in instant response, and he didn't know whether to be pleased or to groan in dismay.

He caught her wandering hands and laced his fingers through hers. "Do you know you can get in serious trouble doing that?" he asked.

"Oh, do go on," Michele answered interestedly. "What, pray tell, could happen to me?"

Connor pushed his hardness gently against her in answer. "You are in danger of becoming a victim of a sex-crazed maniac."

Michele's voice was demure, but the glance she gave him from beneath her lashes made his eyes widen in delight. "Thanks for the warning, Detective, but I think I'll take my chances."

"More than you know," he muttered, thinking of the solitary foil-wrapped package he had taken from his pocket. He kept a firm grip on her hands. "Do you like pizza?" he asked.

Michele looked at him askance. "Pizza?" she repeated. He was thinking of food?

"Pizza," Connor repeated firmly. "We could pick one up at a take-out place."

Michele felt as if she had somehow missed a major thread of this conversation. "If you want pizza, we could just have it delivered here," she offered practically.

Connor sighed mightily as he gazed down at the biggest temptation of his life. She had absolutely no idea how seductive she was and how close he was to abandoning his normal caution. "But if we go get the pizza," he murmured in her ear, "I could make a stop at a drugstore."

Michele gazed at him in mystification for several moments before realization came. "You only had one?" she blurted out without thinking. Heat immediately flooded her cheeks at her own naiveté.

Connor didn't know which was more fascinating, her obvious mortification at her ingenuousness, or her perception of him. "How many do you think I should carry?" he asked in amused interest.

Her face was still scorched from embarrassment. "I don't know," she muttered. "I just thought a man like you would be prepared with three or four."

"Three or four," Connor repeated, striving for a straight face. He didn't quite succeed, earning him an indignant glance from Michele. He knew better than to mention what an enchanting shade of crimson her cheeks had become. "Someday we're going to have to discuss this fascinating image you seem to have of me. If truth be known," he continued, lowering his head to nibble at her lips, now pursed in a mutinous pout, "you are the only lady of my acquaintance who could make carrying an entire box a necessary precaution."

Michele couldn't prevent a small smile at his compliment. She looked up into his light green eyes and felt a shiver race clear down to her toes at the desire she so easily read there. He was very blunt and very masculine and very, very sexy. He made her feel sexy, too, she suddenly realized, with his disregard of polite disclaimers, with his honesty. She felt more feminine around him than ever before in her life, and much more certain of her own womanly power.

But for now she knew he was right. She certainly was not in the habit of keeping contraceptives on hand, or of needing them. And the promise in his gaze made her wonder if he was reconsidering the need for caution.

"The pizza?" she reminded him breathlessly, as his lips began a slow descent.

Connor stifled a groan and laid his forehead against hers. "The pizza," he agreed, mentally cursing.

* * *

"This is hedonistic," Michele protested, giggling breathlessly as Connor held yet another slice of pizza to her lips. She bit down obediently and savored the hot tangy flavor. The pizza box lay on the bed between them, and they were leaning against the headboard, freely, wickedly nude. Michele had insisted on sliding beneath the sheet, but Connor was unabashedly stretched out on top of the covers.

"Not at all," Connor countered smoothly, reaching over to pour more wine in her glass. Their goblets clinked a toast before he continued. "Now, if we were lying naked in bed, eating caviar and drinking imported champagne, that would be hedonistic. But pizza and wine? No way," he declared.

Michele sipped from her glass consideringly. "Maybe you're right." They munched and sipped in silence for a while, before Connor reached down and swept the empty box out of the way. He took the half empty glass from Michele's hand and sipped consideringly. "Oh, 1993. A good year," he declared, and Michele laughed again. But her laughter caught in her throat as Connor pulled the sheet away. "But I'll bet I know how it would taste even better," he whispered before tipping the glass and allowing a trickle to run down between her breasts.

"Connor." Michele's protest was lost as he followed the path the ruby liquid had taken, scooping at it with his tongue. Michele gasped as his hot fiery mouth made a sharp contrast to the cool wine on her suddenly fevered skin. And the meal was forgotten as they proved that it was a fine year indeed.

Connor lay awake long after Michele was wrapped in exhausted slumber. He couldn't remember ever being so content just holding a woman. He had never been interested in much cuddling after lovemaking. Yet each time he found himself unwilling to release Michele. Holding her as she slept seemed so right that he decided not to question it. He finally fell asleep himself, with his arms still around her.

It was several hours before the sounds of her terrified screams woke him.

Chapter 11

Connor came awake with a start. Michele was whimpering now, her head tossing back and forth on the pillow in mute denial of the nightmare that was rolling before her closed eyelids.

Connor froze for a moment, sick inside. He knew from the last experience what these episodes did to her. He sat up and reached over, cradling Michele on his lap. Could it be harmful to wake her too abruptly from these damned dreams? he wondered frantically. All he knew was that seeing her in such obvious torment made his guts knot painfully. He began to rock her gently, his hard arms providing a gentle shelter for her trembling form.

"Shhh, shhh, baby, it's all right. Wake up, Michele. You're dreaming, honey. Wake up now." His low voice crooned soothingly to her in a constant steady murmur.

But when, after long minutes, her eyelids finally fluttered open, Connor felt a finger of ice trace each of his vertebrae. Her eyes were opaque, flat, with a silvery sheen and the intensity in her voice, devoid of inflection, sent that chill skating through his body. "They took another one, Connor. And she's so scared, so terrified." Her voice broke then, and the trembling intensified, making words impossible.

He felt as though he had taken a blow to his midsection. If these episodes of hers were so chilling to witness secondhand, how much worse must they be for her? He gathered her more tightly in his arms and with one hand pulled the covers more closely over them. "It's all right. It's over now," he whispered as he continued holding her, rocking her, keeping up a constant stream of reassurance. He didn't even know what he said; his senses were geared only to the woman in his arms, to the gradual lessening of the severe shaking of her body.

The trembling of her limbs had not completely dissipated when she spoke again, her voice urgent. "Has there been another kidnapping that hasn't been released to the media, Connor?"

He felt a fist clench in his midsection at the question he'd known was coming. Yet he couldn't lie to her, even knowing how painful the truth was going to be. His gaze was steady as he met hers. "There haven't been any more, Michele. We could never keep something like that from being made public."

She stared at him, trying to make sense of the dream, the aftermath of which still shook her entire body, making speech difficult. "But how can that be?" she whispered wonderingly. She had often cursed these dreams, wept over them, but she had never doubted them. There had never been any reason to. Since she was a child they had been proven accurate time and again. What could possibly have thrown her so off-balance that she was now dreaming about things that had never happened?

It can't be, she thought. This dream was the same as the rest, yet even more urgent, more vivid. She had felt as if she had been there, a helpless spectator to the girl's terror.

She shook her head disbelievingly, looking at him earnestly. "It must be. It *has* to be," she stressed, her voice quavering. "Connor, as much as I hate this...this curse I'm afflicted with, it's never wrong. Maybe the girl's parents don't realize she's missing. I don't know. Maybe they think she's with a friend, but she's not, Connor. She's not!" Her voice broke, and the trembling strengthened. His mouth flattened at her obvious distress and her body's reaction to it.

He hated this, hated what it did to her, what it put her through. He pressed her head into the niche of his shoulder. He tried to keep his voice as gentle as possible; he didn't want to add to her suffering. "Michele, you have to accept it. This time it just went haywire."

Michele shook her head mutely against him. Didn't he know how much she would give to be able to believe that? But she had lived with this all her life. She could still see the girl in her dream. Her frantic struggles and screams of terror still reverberated inside her head. "I wish I could believe that," she whispered. She drew a breath, then released a long shuddering sigh. A thought suddenly occurred to her, and she looked up at him. "When did you last check in at the station?"

Connor caught her drift immediately and frowned impatiently. "Michele..." he started to protest.

"When, Connor?" she pressed.

"Not since yesterday," he admitted. "But I left your number at the desk. Someone would have called if there had been anything to report."

The significance of his leaving her phone number occurred to Michele, but she didn't address it. Urgently she pressed him, "Call now, Connor. Please. Please!" she stressed as she easily read his unwillingness.

Connor looked at her for a long moment before heaving a sigh. He reached for the phone on the bedside table, punched in the number of the station house and waited a few moments. "Yeah, Lieutenant McLain here. Let me talk to Michael Riley, will you?"

Michele waited with bated breath until Connor spoke again. "Yeah, Mike, how's it going? Never mind why I'm not sleeping late. Listen, has anything new come up in the investigation?"

Michele felt her breath hiss out in frustration as he listened and then replied, "Nothing at all? There hasn't been anything else reported, has there? Okay, you have the number where to reach me if something comes up. Thanks. You too."

With two fingers Connor dropped the receiver back onto its cradle. His gaze, when he looked back to her, was curiously gentle. He said nothing, but Michele thought she could read his thoughts in his eyes, and she couldn't prevent the stab of betrayal she felt. He was, she reminded herself bleakly, an eminently practical man, concerned always with evidence and proof. Had she really even entertained the notion that he would believe her when no proof was available? She knew that didn't negate his concern for her. But it would have been wonderful to be able to read trust as well as concern in his eyes.

Michele thrust the hopeless yearning away. Despite what he thought, despite what had or hadn't been reported, she was wearily certain that another little girl was desperately in need of help. Now all she had to do was convince him of that fact.

"She's only about nine or ten, Connor." Her voice when she spoke was quiet but sure. He looked away at her words, but she continued, determined to be heard. "She's wearing navy sweatpants, a white Penn State T-shirt and tennis shoes."

"Michele, stop it," Connor demanded, his voice tortured.

"She has straight light brown hair, blue eyes," Michele continued, "and a slight build. She was on a playground, throwing rocks through a basketball hoop."

Hard hands grasped her delicate shoulders, and he gave her a shake. "Don't keep doing this to yourself."

"She'd just finished delivering papers. The empty carrier bag is lying by the fence."

For an instant, looking into those fathomless gray pools so close to his own, the scene she'd described flashed before Connor's eyes. Just as Michele had drawn it in her verbal picture, Connor could see the deserted playground, empty now except for the canvas bag, lying in a crumpled heap by the chain-link fence.

He was stunned by the accompanying sweep of desolation at the flick of visual imagery. It was the closest he could ever come to understanding the unconscious torture she endured. He pulled her into his arms and held her tightly to him, as if by the sheer power of his presence he could banish all future demons from invading her unconscious.

"Let it go," he ordered, pleaded with her. "Don't let it torment you."

Michele rested her head wearily against the muscled plane of his chest. "I don't have a choice, Connor," she murmured. "I never do."

Despite Connor's best attempts to calm her down, to distract her from her earlier nightmare, Michele remained jittery and on edge for the next few hours. And when the phone rang as they read the morning paper, she stared at it sickly, unaware of the impatient glance Connor threw her way when she made no attempt to answer it herself.

Barely restraining a curse, he yanked the receiver off the hook. She couldn't blame him if his answering her phone proved to be an indiscretion she had to explain later to a curious friend or relative.

His impatience faded quickly as he listened to the caller and after a few moments dropped the receiver back on its cradle. His movements when he turned back to her were slow, labored, like those of an old man. And when he looked at her, she knew what she would read in his face.

Connor's visage was grim, his eyes bleak when he faced her. "Well, aren't you even going to ask?" he demanded.

Michele said nothing as she stared steadily back at him. There was nothing to ask. She knew what the message was, even if she couldn't tell the identity of the caller. She knew what had put that look in his eyes, the one she hadn't seen since her childhood, the look of fascinated horror that people turned on her when she was proven correct.

Her silence goaded Connor even more, the sheer helplessness of the situation washing over him. "That was Riley. There are some parents at his desk, demanding that we do something. Seems they think their little girl is the latest victim of the kidnapper. Seems she never came home from delivering her papers this morning."

Michele closed her eyes then, forcing away the memories of the early-morning nightmare that threatened to come flooding back, seeping into every facet of her consciousness, enveloping her once again in the icy terror.

Two hard hands grasped her shoulders, and Michele's eyes flew wide as Connor shook her, hard. "Say something, damn you!" he bit out. "Tell me again where we'll find her empty canvas bag, what she was wearing."

Michele tiredly moved herself out of his grasp. "You already know," she told him quietly. "You don't realize how much I would like to be wrong."

He surveyed her for a moment longer, his frustration fading away as he became aware of how tautly she was holding herself, as if she had become suddenly brittle. He became belatedly aware of the way he was lashing out at her and how she was likely to read his reaction as something else. "Michele..." he started, reaching for her again.

But she moved out of his range. "You'd better go," she reminded him distantly. "I'm sure you'll want to talk to the parents."

Connor stood there for a moment longer, feeling like a bastard. He had reacted out of the sheer helplessness he felt, both with the situation and with his inability to understand her uncanny knowledge. "This could be a false alarm, you know. She may have wandered off. She could be with a friend..." His voice trailed away as they both remembered her words earlier as she'd striven to convince him.

Michele didn't respond to his attempt to reassure her. "You'd better go," she repeated quietly.

After a tense moment Connor cursed and strode over to get his jacket. Shrugging into it impatiently, he turned back to her and gathered her close, despite her stiffness. His lips touched her hair as he murmured, "Stay here, will you? I'll check in when I can. We need to talk."

Michele nodded mutely but didn't respond. She watched his departing figure numbly. After all, what was there to talk about? They seemed to have come full circle. And she was more than certain of what he would have to say to her when he returned.

Connor watched the girl's parents depart and felt tired. Down to the bone, soul-deep weariness. Their panic, their desperate need for reassurance, had drained him of every bit of emotion he had. He dropped down in his desk chair and wiped both hands over his face.

"So, Houdini," drawled a voice from the door. "Mind telling me how you knew about this?"

Connor looked up to see Cruz standing in the doorway, holding up a plastic evidence bag. Even from a distance Connor knew there would be a canvas newspaper bag inside.

Cruz closed the door to the office and sauntered into the room.

"That should have been sent to the lab," Connor remarked tensely, ignoring the question.

"On my way, on my way," Cruz retorted mildly as he dropped into a chair opposite Connor's desk, the bag still hanging from one long index finger. "But not until you answer my question. How the hell did you know to tell us to check the playgrounds in the vicinity of her route home?"

Connor feigned a bored tone. "That's pretty standard. You know that, Cruz. She could have been there, may still be for all we know."

"Tell me another one," scoffed his partner, before turning deadly serious. "You forget, I know you, *amigo.* Quite well. You knew we'd find something, and I think you even knew what it would be. Now give. You know something more than you're telling."

Connor surveyed his best friend silently, mentally debating. He knew he could trust Cruz. Hell, he'd trusted him with his life on occasions too numerous to mention. And God knew he needed someone to run this by, and who better than Cruz?

He regarded his friend soberly for long moments while weighing his answer. When he spoke, his voice was devoid of inflection. "You're right. I knew where to look, and I knew what we'd find there. I already knew what Susie Kimberly looked like, what she was wearing and what she was doing when she disappeared. And, yeah, despite procedures and checking out her absence, I'm already sure that she's the latest victim of the kidnapper."

Cruz rubbed his chin reflectively as he watched his friend. "Well, old buddy, I knew you were on to something. What I still don't understand is how you knew all that. You must be becoming psych—Michele!" he said with certainty and leaned forward eagerly. "That's how you knew, isn't it? Michele dreamed it, or whatever, and told you. When? How long have you known this?"

"Since early this morning," Connor told him wearily. "Hours before it was reported. Probably around the time it happened, the way it sounds."

Cruz cursed admiringly. "I'll be damned. Now how do you figure that?"

"How I figure it is that I've been a jerk," Connor told him shortly. "I wouldn't believe her, I made her feel like a freak when the call from the station came, and I found out she was right."

"But you have to believe her now, Connor, and this is great," enthused Cruz. "What are you waiting for? Let's get her in here. Maybe she can remember more, something that we can use. She may know more than she's even aware of."

"Absolutely not!"

Cruz blinked at the growled command. "Why the hell not?"

"Because I said so, that's why not," Connor retorted, rising from his desk threateningly. "I'm in charge of this investigation, buddy, and you report to me, not vice versa. We run this my way, and I say we're leaving Michele out of it. Now, get that evidence bag to the lab and get on with your job."

Cruz's eyes narrowed at Connor's tone. They had been partners and then friends for more years than he cared to count. Connor's rise as an officer had never mattered in their relationship, because Connor never pulled rank, not with him. This display was way out of character for him, and it was that fact that kept Cruz from snapping back. There was more here than met the eye, but he was confident that eventually he would ferret out the whole story. He always did. He rose slowly and silently left the room.

Connor opened the door hours later, and his men filed out one by one. He closed the door after them and leaned against it wearily. How was it possible, he thought bleakly, for each scenario to be so similar? The officers who had worked out on the street gathering information all had similar reports. Everyone on Susie's route had received their papers on time. Most hadn't been awake yet; those who had, hadn't noticed anything different. No one so far claimed to have even seen her that morning, except for a couple of kids who saw a girl on the playground as they rode by on their bikes. They had seen no one with her.

He crossed to his desk, across which was spread a map of the city. Blue dots were filled in near the places where the kidnappings had taken place. A sixth had been marked today, designating Susie's disappearance. Connor picked up a red pen and made one more circle in the area Davey Lockhart had disappeared from.

The boy might or might not be related to the incidents, but Michele seemed to think he was a victim, and she had sure been batting a thousand today, he thought grimly. He studied the map closely for the hundredth time, but no obvious pattern jumped out at him. The sites of four of the kidnappings were within a twelve-block radius of each other, but Davey and Susie had been snatched miles away from the others.

Connor bit out a curse and pushed the map away from him. If sitting and staring at the damn thing would bring him closer to catching the perpetrators, he would have had this case solved weeks ago. All the information on the victims, their families, their day care, their schools—everything—had been fed into a computer. He had hoped that the computer would spit out any parallels between the kids, but so far that had been fruitless. Some of the kids lived in the same neighborhood, a couple had even gone to the same school. But none of the leads had panned out yet.

"Lieutenant?"

Connor looked up at the detective with his head poked through the door and motioned him in.

"This just came in on Davey Lockhart's father, sir. We just located him in a town outside of Tallahassee, Florida. He's been in the county jail there for the last month on bad-check charges."

Connor sighed and held out his hand. The officer placed the report in his outstretched palm. "The sheriff down there gave me his last address, and I called down there. Seems he's been living with some dancer, and she swears he hasn't even talked to the kid in over a year. He didn't even know he was snatched."

Somehow this latest news didn't surprise Connor. Michele had undoubtedly been right about this, too. "Call the boy's mother and tell her, will you? See if she has any other ideas. And in the meantime, feed his information into the computer with the rest of the kidnap victims."

The detective's eyes opened wide in surprise, and he started to speak, but one look at Connor's closed expression obviously made him change his mind. "Yes, sir, Lieutenant," he mumbled and backed out the door.

Connor sank into his desk chair, folded his arms behind his head, leaned back and contemplated the ceiling. As days went, this one couldn't get much worse. Dealing with the parents of the missing children was always tough. Dealing with the media was an added headache. Thank God the police commissioner was taking care of the press release about this latest snatching.

And the worst part about it was that his usual single-minded concentration was shot. No matter what he was involved in, a part of his mind continued to linger on Michele, to wonder how she was, what she was doing. His distraction from the urgent matters at hand was as puzzling as it was frustrating. He'd never before had a problem eliminating a woman from his mind until he had time for her. But thoughts of Michele had been as tenacious as a bloodhound ever since they'd met.

Remorse flooded him as he thought again of his reaction when Riley had called that morning with the news of the latest kidnapping. He couldn't even begin to catalog his feelings when he had witnessed firsthand the accuracy of Michele's dreams. He'd reacted poorly, he had known that even as he acted, but he hadn't seemed able to prevent himself. He hadn't been himself since he met her, he acknowledged. Rarely did he lose the famed control he was noted for, but it seemed to happen on a regular basis where she was concerned.

A quiet rap on the door interrupted his musings, and he cursed silently as he wondered what else could possibly go wrong today.

"Come in," he ordered none too welcomingly.

When the door opened and Michele walked through, Connor's chair came forward with bone-jarring force. "Princess," he murmured in amazement. "What are you doing here?" He drank her in hungrily. It seemed like days since he'd left her that morning.

Michele came inside and shut the door almost hesitantly. "Hi," she murmured, and leaned against the door, surveying him. He looked as though he'd aged five years since leaving her that morning, and she fervently wished that she could wipe those creases from his brow. She didn't dare give in to her inclination, more than a little unsure as to his state of mind after the way he'd left her that morning. His next words allayed her fears.

"Come over here."

At the softly growled command her eyes flew to his, widening slightly. After a moment's hesitation she walked slowly around his desk. He lifted a hand and pulled her unresisting form onto his lap, then wrapped his arms around her, burying his face in her hair.

Connor felt as though a huge weight had been lifted from his shoulders just at the feel of her in his arms. He rubbed his hard cheek against the silky skeins of her hair and inhaled deeply. He couldn't put into words the rightness that entered his world at her touch, the way his worries seemed to shrink when he held her.

Michele's personal composure, her constant equanimity, seemed to ripple out and affect those close to her. Maybe that was why she made such a good psychologist. He didn't know. All he knew was that holding her like this was getting to be a habit, one he didn't know how to break.

Finally he heaved a sigh and started to speak, his voice muffled by her hair. "You called it right all the way, Michele. Her name's Susie Kimberly. She never came home from delivering her morning papers. Your description was perfect to a T. And no one saw a damn thing."

Michele's voice was soft. "The parents...?"

"The family's been visiting relatives in New York. The first time they even heard of the kidnappings was this morning, when they started calling around, trying to locate their daughter."

Michele's heart ached with the frustration she heard in his voice. "You don't know how much I wish I was wrong," she whispered, but Connor heard her and raised his head, tipping her face up to his with a long finger.

"I told you not to feel guilty about this, damn it! You were right this morning, and I was a jerk. If I had just listened to you, maybe she would be—"

"Just as gone as she is now," Michele asserted firmly, seeking to wipe the self-recrimination from his countenance. "Connor, the most frustrating thing about my..." She hesitated, searching for a word. "...sight, is that it's always after the fact, and I don't seem able to see enough to be of any help. That's as frustrating for me as your lack of clues is to you."

Connor objected to the comparison. "You're tortured by those dreams—do you think I'm not aware of that?"

"But at least they wouldn't be in vain if anything I had to tell you was something solid, something you could follow up. If only..." Her voice drifted away while she mentally debated with herself. She was unsure how to approach Connor with her idea. A knock sounding on the door told her that her time for talking with him alone was over.

Michele disentangled herself from his arms less than gracefully and was just slipping into a chair when the door opened and Cruz's dark head popped in.

"Not interrupting anything, am I, kids?" His devilish grin and sparkling eyes told them both that they had separated too late. "I can always give you more time. Never let it be said that I can't be subtle."

Connor eyed his friend with exasperation. "Never let it be said that you have a brain cell above your zipper," he corrected mildly. "Did you hope to interrupt an orgy or something?"

Cruz, sure of his welcome, stepped into the room and propped his tall form against a wall. "I had hopes, to be sure, but I should have known better with you, Connor." He addressed Michele. "Our lieutenant here is a methodical man, Michele. No short cuts for him. I knew you were safe in here for five minutes or so."

Connor said nothing, just stared hard at Cruz, who pretended not to notice and continued to address Michele. "Did he tell you that you were right on the mark about the Kimberly girl?"

"Yes," Michele murmured, her gaze sliding back to Connor.

Connor's gaze was ricocheting from one to the other. "You never did tell me why you came down here," he said slowly to Michele.

She drew a deep breath. He was always painstaking in his work; his mind was a steel trap. "Cruz called and asked me to," she admitted.

"Is that so?" murmured Connor sotto voce, his hard gaze settling on Cruz. "And why is that?"

Cruz returned his gaze and answered steadily. "Because I think we can use her, Connor. She's been proven right time and again. You trust her. So do I. We've been ignoring a source of possible leads for long enough. I think we should explore how much Michele really does know."

"Oh, you think so, do you?" Michele winced at Connor's biting tone, even though he still appeared to be addressing Cruz. "And did you also think that you would take over the investigation, start making all the calls yourself?"

"You know better than that."

"And you know how I feel about Michele being dragged into this! I specifically told you that we wouldn't be involving her in this case."

"I chose to become involved." Both men continued glaring at each other, and Michele gritted her teeth. She hated to be ignored, and she especially hated people talking about her as if she wasn't there. She continued on. "When Cruz called, I agreed to come in. I'd like to help if I can."

Connor shot her a fuming glance. What the hell was she doing? he thought fulminatingly. He wanted to spare her all this—she had said she wanted to be spared it—and now she agreed to *this?* "Michele," he started, placatingly, "I don't see what you hope to accomplish here. You've already told me everything you know—" He broke off as he intercepted the look passing between Cruz and Michele. "What? Is there something you haven't told me yet?"

Cruz spoke quickly, before Michele could. His voice was reasonable. "Well, yes and no. As I was pointing out, we really don't know if she's told us everything, do we? She may know more than she's aware of."

Connor had a feeling of foreboding that he knew where this was headed and hoped fervently that he was wrong. His worst fears were realized at Cruz's next words.

"Michele's unconscious brings her these images, right? In sleep, her most relaxed state, she sees these things happening. So what would happen if we simulate that unconscious state and see what she remembers under skilled questioning?''

Connor blew up. ''We are not, *not,*'' he stressed, looking hard at Cruz, ''going to have Michele hypnotized. Where the hell did you come up with this hare-brained scheme, anyway?''

''Connor, it's worth a try, isn't it, buddy? We're not out anything by trying, and we stand to gain quite a bit. What's the harm?''

''Not a chance.'' Connor's voice brooked no argument. ''I won't allow it.''

''I don't think you understand, Connor.'' Michele's voice was soft, but firm. ''I've already agreed to do it.''

Chapter 12

Both heads swiveled at her words, but it was Connor's gaze she held.

"You can't be serious." His voice was flat.

"Yes, I am, Connor," she answered firmly. "When Cruz suggested this, I—"

"Cruz," Connor's tone was scathing, as was the look he sent his friend, "has more imagination than sense. He had no right to even mention this to you, much less drag you down here."

Michele's stomach plummeted at his unyielding attitude. In seconds the man she was growing to know and love seemed to fade away, and in his place was the icy, intimidating police lieutenant she had first met. She had been certain that Connor would not welcome this idea, but his scathing dismissal of it was worse than even she had expected. He obviously had no faith in the possibility that she had anything valuable to offer to the case. Just as he had once dismissed the possibility that her dreams were credible at all.

Pain flooded her at the realization, and she stiffened defensively at the sudden knowledge of how he must perceive her. As a freak. A spook who could sometimes call them right and wasn't that the most amazing coincidence? But not as someone who could really help. Not as someone he would allow to be of help.

From long practice she forced the pain down for the moment, tucked it away, so she could focus on the need at hand. "I don't care how you feel about this, Connor. I'm going to do it.'' She read his incredulity in his widened green eyes. ''And don't blame Cruz. I'm the one who made the decision to do this.''

Cruz spoke up then. ''Where's the harm, Connor? Michele may give us some more leads. Maybe one that will take us right to the perp.''

''I can speak for myself,'' Michele put in, annoyed at the way the two men's silent communication excluded her. ''And I say yes.'' She cut off Connor's protest with a sharp gesture that was reminiscent of Connor's own. Cruz recognized it as such and grinned. ''You may be in charge of the investigation, of making the decisions about it, but you don't make them for me.''

''I decide how the investigation will proceed, Miss Easton,'' Connor said between clenched teeth. ''No civilian comes into my office and tells me how to do my job. *I* decide what's good for the case, and I don't see how this will aid it.''

Michele's chin came up bracingly at his gibing tone. ''Can you tell me how I could hurt it?'' she countered. Her question hung in the air between them, the answer unspoken. Michele took a deep breath and asked in a calm voice, ''Can you honestly tell yourself that your reluctance to pursue this avenue has everything to do with professionalism and nothing to do with me, personally?''

''What's that supposed to mean?'' Connor snapped.

''I think you know,'' was her quiet answer.

And he did. They all knew. Because she was right, damn her. He didn't know how he would feel if this were really necessary and he was faced with the decision of asking her to do this for the good of the investigation. He wasn't certain that he could say he would react any differently. For sure he would feel just as sick inside as he did right now as he thought about her voluntarily undergoing an experience that would bring those nightmares back to haunt her.

But that wasn't the case. He didn't see the need to put her through this. She and Cruz were pursuing a slim chance. And to his mind the risk to Michele was far greater than what they might gain, even if she did manage to remember something else. He knew what she would have to undergo if Bruce successfully put her under. He'd witnessed firsthand the ordeal those dreams represented for her. He'd held her, comforted her, in their aftermath.

Was it unprofessional for him to want to spare her that? Especially when the outcome was as dubious as it seemed to be? He didn't think so. Damn Cruz for going ahead on his own and calling her. And damn her for not understanding that he was trying to spare her, that he couldn't bear to see her in such torment.

Even so, her question hit Connor right where he was most vulnerable. It seemed as if he had been fighting a losing battle between his job and his growing feelings for her ever since he had met her. That didn't mean he welcomed it.

"I know how you stand on this," Michele said, interrupting his thoughts. "But how would the chief of detectives feel about it? Or the police commissioner?"

Connor's eyes widened in amazement at her meaning. "You can't be serious, Michele."

Her gaze was steady. "I'm completely serious."

"Even knowing that going over my head may deny you the privacy you long for?" he baited her.

Michele closed her eyes briefly before nodding. "I don't want that, Connor. You know that. Don't make me go to them."

"Bruce is in his office right now," Cruz said tentatively, as the silence in the room lengthened. Connor shot him a look, which Cruz returned unflinchingly. Connor knew without asking that Cruz had also taken the liberty of calling Bruce and arranging his presence. "You've been quite a busy boy," observed Connor narrowly.

Cruz's next words verified Connor's suspicion. "I called him after talking to Michele. He's willing to try it."

Connor addressed Michele, who was gazing at him silently. "Even if I don't want you to?" he asked quietly, unable to admit to the slight tone of pleading that had entered his voice.

"Are you going to stop me?" she returned. At the brief flash of pain in his eyes, she attempted to try to make him understand one last time. "I need to do this, Connor. I may be of no help at all, but I have to try."

"You have to try to relive that torment again?" asked Connor, feeling goaded.

Michele's answer was resigned. "I relive it every time I dream. I'll continue to relive it until this case is solved. If I could be of any help at all, it would make the whole thing worthwhile. It would be the only way that any of this would make sense."

Silence reigned for the next few moments. Neither Connor nor Michele noticed when Cruz left the room. Connor rubbed one hand over the back of his neck and heaved a sigh. "I want to spare you this, Michele," he said quietly. And she read his meaning more clearly in his tone than in his words.

"You can't," she answered just as softly.

"At least I'll be there with you," he asserted, and his eyes narrowed as she shook her head.

"I don't think that would be a good idea. I'm not sure I'd be able to concentrate with you there."

"You mean you don't trust me not to interfere," interpreted Connor, annoyed.

Michele's hand went to his arm. "Wouldn't you? The minute you thought I was getting too upset, the moment you saw me start to relive what I've seen, you'd want to call it off. Admit it."

And he couldn't deny it. Hell, he knew he couldn't handle seeing her like that again, watching her voluntarily undergoing that torment, observing the effect it would have on her physically and not go to her aid. He was uncomfortably aware that his emotions at having to witness her trauma would be impossible for him to hide, impossible not to act on.

Frustration slammed into him. He disliked this whole situation. He wished that Michele was at home, under guard, and that he was on his way to her place to check on her. His impatience got the better of him, and he reached for her, pulling her tightly against him.

His kiss was deep and hard, almost fierce. Michele tasted his frustration, his impatience, and met it with her own unique serenity. She tempered the fire fueled by his impatience and welcomed the passion that burned beneath it.

For the first few moments Connor was blind to all but his churning inner fury. His tongue swept her mouth arrogantly, not waiting for a reaction but demanding it. But at the first sweet taste of her, his initial intentions faded away and he reveled in the simple pleasure of kissing her.

He tore his mouth away finally, an awareness of their surroundings returning to him. For the first time he was thankful that his office had no windows and the thick glass in the door was impossible to see through. He leaned his forehead against hers. "I don't want you to do this," he whispered rawly.

"I know," Michele answered, her gray eyes sad. And she did. Whatever else he might feel for her, she had to be aware that he cared about her feelings. That knowledge made it a little easier to face what she was about to do. "Cruz can come in with me," she told him, and he nodded shortly. Obviously his friend's part in this was still bothering him, but Michele was frankly glad for it. She felt better about trying this with someone she knew in the room, and Cruz felt like a friend, even if she didn't know him well.

A quick rap sounded at the door, and Cruz's head popped in. "Bruce is all set, Michele. Are you ready?"

A quick glance at Connor's tautly pressed mouth made her barely suppress a sigh. "I'm ready."

As she turned to join the man at the door, Connor called involuntarily, "Michele?"

She turned to look inquiringly at him, and Connor found his throat suddenly full. There was really nothing for him to say. He couldn't stop her; she wouldn't let him. He couldn't spare her the pain she was about to undergo, no matter how much he wanted to. His eyes cut to Cruz, and he said shortly, "Bring her back here as soon as it's over."

Cruz's dark eyes were full of understanding. He nodded and said, "I'll take care of her, *amigo.* We'll be back in a flash."

Connor sank back into his chair at their exit. Waiting wasn't something he did gladly, although often it was a necessity in his job. But this time it required far more from him than usual.

When his door opened again an hour later, Connor sprang up and was at the entrance to usher Michele and Cruz back in. His sharp eyes raced over her, noting the ashen cheeks, the bloodless lips and the furious trembling of her limbs. Someone had placed an ugly red-and-yellow-plaid blanket across her shoulders. Connor silently cursed himself for listening to Michele and not being in there with her. He could have told them that the blanket wouldn't do any good, that what Michele needed was to be held, tightly, for a long time, to hear another's voice whispering to her, forcing the demons back into the deepest night.

Except that it wasn't the middle of the night, and they weren't in Michele's home. And this hadn't been a dream-induced session but one Michele had voluntarily undergone. He barely managed to restrain himself from slamming the door behind the two of them. He took Michele by the arm and led her to his desk, where, regardless of their onlooker, he dropped into the chair, pulling her with him.

Michele, though, was more aware and pushed at him. "Connor," she whispered warningly, but he ignored her protest, and she gradually relaxed as her body involuntarily was drawn to the furnacelike heat of his. Eventually warmth began to creep into her own icy limbs.

Cruz, looking a little frayed himself, dropped down into another chair.

"I'm fine," Michele insisted as the shaking abated somewhat.

Connor's voice twisted deridingly. "You look fine, sweetheart. You surely do." He would have loved to ask nastily if it had been worth it, but he was unwilling to bring it all back after Michele had finally shown signs of calming. Once Cruz opened his mouth to speak, but Connor threw him such a black look that he subsided without saying a word.

It wasn't until much later, when Michele had left the office to go to the rest room, that the two men spoke. It was Cruz who broke the silence. "I'll be honest with you, buddy. It was no picnic in the park."

"Did you think it would be?" asked Connor bitingly.

Cruz shrugged. "I didn't know what to think. Bruce didn't have any trouble putting her under, and I had a list of questions prepared to ask her, although I had a devil of a time getting them out, I can tell you."

"What do you mean?"

"I know you tried to warn me, but I never imagined what it would be like for Michele, you know? I've seen a lot on the beat, but listening to her describe what she sees, hearing the sound of her voice, seeing the look in her eyes..." He wiped a hand over his face. "It was definitely chilling to observe."

"Much less to experience firsthand," Connor said softly.

Cruz threw him a quick look. "Right. I can't imagine now why she even agreed to do this. If someone had suggested that I put myself through that, I'd punch him out."

"Yeah," Connor admitted, suddenly drained. And that had been exactly how he had felt when Cruz had suggested it to Michele. And when she had agreed to it. "So was it worth it?"

"Might be," Cruz affirmed, reaching for his tablet. "She gave a positive ID on one of the cars used, and it matches exactly the one we found abandoned."

Connor nodded, not even surprised. The car had yielded some minuscule strands of hair, and the lab results were back on them. What still puzzled Connor was that they didn't match the test results on the letters that had been delivered to Michele. So that meant that either the letters were unrelated to the case, or that there were at least two people involved in the kidnappings. Connor suspected the latter. Which meant, of course, that Michele was in a great deal of danger.

"Then we focused on where the children were being held. It's a good thing we didn't spend a lot of time looking downtown," he added.

"Why?"

"Because Bruce had Michele mentally walk to the window in the place, the one that was boarded up. He had her look out the crack between the boards and tell him what she saw. It's obviously in some sort of rural area. And it has a bell out front."

Connor's interest sharpened. "A bell?"

"The way she described it, it sounded like an old church or a school," Cruz said. "That's what it brought to *my* mind, anyway."

"Okay, we'll check that out," Connor said. "Start with the area closest to the kidnappings and fan out."

"Too bad we don't have more men," Cruz said.

"I'll see what I can do," Connor promised, not knowing if he would succeed. "Anything else?"

"Just one thing. She described a bumper sticker on the fender of the car used to abduct Susie Kimberly. It was yellow with red print."

"What did it say?"

Cruz's voice was wry. "It said For The Sake Of The Children. Pretty ironic, considering."

"Yeah," drawled Connor musing. "Real ironic." He pondered it for a few minutes, something about the description bothering him. "That slogan sounds familiar to me," he said slowly. He cocked a brow at Cruz. "Ever heard it before?"

Cruz thought for a moment and then shook his head. "Nope, I don't think so. It sounds like one of those commercials from TV, where they ask for money to feed a child overseas. You mean you think you've seen a bumper sticker like that yourself?"

Connor shook his head. "I don't think so." The memory he was trying to summon teased at his brain, advancing and retreating coyly. "It's the words, I think. Like I've heard them before." He thought hard, trying to use the sheer force of his will to bring the memory to his consciousness, but finally he gave up. It would spring out when he least expected it, most likely. Still, it was odd, the vague familiarity of those words.

"So what's next?" questioned Cruz.

"Nothing more for tonight." Connor rubbed the back of his neck. "It's been a hell of a day already." The door opened, and Michele reentered the office. "We'll pack it in for today and start fresh tomorrow with the search for the building Michele described."

Michele's eyes flew to Connor's, startled. She had expected that Cruz would give him a full report of the session with Bruce and, like a coward, had decided to leave them alone for it. As much as she detested admitting it, even to herself, the session had shaken her more than she had imagined possible. But now it seemed as if Connor was actually going to act on the information she had given; she saw the confirmation of that in his eyes.

A slow ball of warmth started in her stomach and promised to chase away the rest of the memory of the recent events. He believed her, he wanted her to know that he valued her involvement, and Michele felt some of the chill in her limbs fade away.

Connor noticed that she was beginning to sway and frowned. "I'm taking Michele home," he said abruptly to Cruz. "She's dead on her feet."

There he went again, making decisions for her, Michele mused. She was too tired to even summon up the irritation she knew she should feel. "I drove my car here," she protested mildly.

"I'll bring you over in the morning to get it," Connor said firmly, his voice daring her to object. Michele didn't. She was shaky, and she really didn't want to drive, anyway. All she wanted was to crawl into bed, pull the covers over her head and sleep for twelve straight hours. Tomorrow she would deal with the events of the day. Right now she didn't think she could handle anything more even if she had to.

"All right," she conceded.

Her easy acceptance of his plans for her eased Connor's mind a little, but not much. Normally Michele would have responded with a spirited protest about him running her life. The fact that she hadn't probably had more to do with her exhaustion than any change in her attitude toward him. But that was all right. He would deal with that later. Right now he was going to take care of this woman, and he didn't care if he had to throw her over his shoulder to do it.

He found that such drastic means weren't called for after all. Once in his car Michele leaned her head back and closed her eyes. Connor turned on the heater, despite the balmy temperature outside, knowing that her body was still shaking with occasional chills.

They rode in silence, and it wasn't until she felt the car ease to a stop and heard Connor cut the engine that she opened her eyes. But instead of seeing her slightly dilapidated duplex, they were in front of a small restaurant. The flickering neon sign proclaimed it as Guido's.

"You need to eat." Connor staved off any objection she might have voiced. "Then it's home to bed."

Michele sighed and opened the car door. He was really into this bullying today, and exhaustion was no longer a good enough excuse to allow it to continue. "I'm not sure I can eat anything," she warned him as they walked to the front door.

He studied her as he held the door open for her. "Just try. I won't push—honest," he added when he saw the disbelieving look on her face.

Michele walked by him. "I guess it will be worth it just to see you try to keep that promise," she threw over her shoulder.

Connor guided her through the dimly lit room to a small booth in the corner. Michele looked up in surprise as he slid in next to her, instead of seating himself across from her, but after taking one look at his face she said nothing. He was trying to take care of her with a vengeance, she thought with an inward sigh.

After placing their order with the waiter, they lapsed into silence again. Connor racked his brain when the silence stretched into minutes. He wanted to take Michele's mind off what she had to be thinking, off reliving what had happened to her in Bruce's office. But what was there to say? He didn't want to discuss the case with her; that would be a surefire way of bringing it all to the surface again. What did he and his frequent dates even talk about? he wondered in amazement. He certainly didn't talk about his work, and he rarely talked about anything of a personal nature. He thought hard for a few minutes, but all he could come up with was listening to his dates chatter on about their work or their lives, or conversation that was rife with innuendo. That was what he was good at, what came easily to him. Never divulging anything of himself but making the woman feel as if he had.

He slanted a glance at Michele. Neither seemed appropriate for her. Usually she made this easy on him, drawing him out about himself without his even being aware that he was disclosing anything personal. She had a gift for making people comfortable, for getting them to talk about themselves, and for listening, really listening, to everything they had to say. He'd seen its effect time and again. But tonight she seemed disinclined to start a conversation. He felt frustratingly tongue-tied. It was damn hard to break the habit of a lifetime of being closemouthed, even as he was reaching for a way to calm her.

Michele sipped slowly from her water glass, becoming belatedly aware that the silence between them had stretched into minutes. She peeked at Connor and was surprised at the almost fierce expression on his closed features. He must be thinking about the investigation, she thought sympathetically, and it was second nature to her to want to soothe him, take his mind off his troubles.

She touched him lightly on the arm. "Do you know this place well?" she asked.

Connor's eyebrows went up, and he looked almost shocked that she had removed the burden of conversation from him. Not that he had been doing such a bang-up job of it. "Yeah, Cruz and I discovered it a few years ago." He stopped out of habit, not revealing any more, until he realized with a start that an avenue of conversation had opened to him. He pursued it with a vengeance. "We had picked up Guido's son for some punk crime, vandalizing a school building with a bunch of kids."

Connor found himself telling Michele the whole story, of how Tony was the only one of the kids who hadn't had a rap sheet a mile long.

How he and Cruz had decided that it was a matter of him falling in with the wrong crowd and had gone to bat for him to get him community service instead of probation.

"We got him lined up as a junior counselor for a city recreation program. Guido was embarrassingly grateful. In fact, we're darn lucky he's not around tonight, or we'd be treated to the house special and a shameful amount of personal attention." He stopped, amazed at himself. She'd done it again, just by looking at him with her head cocked that way, her gray eyes alight with interest and amusement, encouraging him to share more.

And there was no more awkwardness after that. They talked all through the breadsticks, the salad and the main course. They spoke of mutual interests in working with kids and disagreed as to whether all kids were redeemable. But they agreed on more than they didn't. They agreed that all kids deserved a chance and shared a frustration with the lack of programs to provide them with outlets for their activities.

Connor was almost sorry to see the waiter return to clear their dishes away. It had been an enjoyable hour, yet he was too aware of how little Michele had eaten. She had done more rearranging of the food than actually eating it. But he kept his word and didn't remonstrate with her about it. He was pretty sure her mind was off the events of the day, and he was certain by the droop of her eyelids that the next immediate need was for her to get some sleep.

Michele smiled to herself on the way home. When Connor had first begun to speak, his words had almost seemed labored, an effort he was determined to make. But he had forgotten his reticence after a few minutes. She had noticed that before about him, each time he had spoken to soothe her after one of her dreams. His voice had seemed rusty at first, as if he were unused to using it other than to issue commands. But he made a point of talking to her, and she knew intuitively that he was more open with her than he was with most people, letting out more about himself than perhaps even he was aware. Without his telling her, she thought she could identify each of the people in the photos in his house, because she had heard him talk of his parents, his sister, his nephew and his close relationship with Cruz.

She smiled secretively to herself. To some it might not seem like much, such sharing of mundane information about oneself. But from Connor she had the feeling it was precious and rare, and she hugged it to herself as an uncommon gift.

She walked up to the front door of her house in a mellow mood. She stood docilely by, not even growing annoyed at the way Connor insisted on walking her to the door and unlocking it for her. He stepped in and turned on the living room light, and she started to follow him, thinking in amusement that she was really going to have to object to his machismo. Tomorrow, she decided, swallowing a yawn. Tomorrow she would be back to herself again.

Connor stood stock-still in the doorway, his piercing look sweeping her living room in a second. "Go back to the car," he ordered softly.

Michele was astounded, He really was carrying this too far. He was blocking her entrance into the house, his broad shoulders making it impossible for her to pass by him. "Connor..." she started.

He never turned to look at her, and her eyes grew round as she saw him reach for the gun at the base of his back and draw it out. "Damn it, Michele, don't argue with me. Get back out in the car. Now." His order was given in a whisper, but it was no less commanding for that.

His tone conveyed an urgency that dissipated her annoyance, and she craned her neck to see beyond Connor to her living area. She swayed on her feet at the sight. The normally neat area was now anything but. Sofa cushions had been tossed to the floor, her bookcase turned over, pictures knocked off the wall. It was as if a giant infant had thrown a temper tantrum and left the upheaval for all to see.

"Get back, damn it!" came Connor's terse whisper, and Michele swung her shocked eyes to him and unconsciously moved back out to the porch. Her compliance was all he needed. He didn't spare a glance to see that she obeyed the rest of his command, and Michele didn't. She stayed on the porch, as if rooted to the floor.

Connor went in low, in police stance, both hands on his revolver. There was no sign of an intruder in the living area or the kitchenette beyond. He advanced to the open doors of the bedrooms, each time approaching carefully, then swinging his body around with both hands aiming the gun. He repeated this with each room of the house until he was assured that no one was there. Only then did he holster his gun and go back to the car for Michele

Except that Michele wasn't in the car. She was still standing on the porch, and his mouth flattened in disapproval at the way she had disobeyed him in a situation that could have been very dangerous. "Damn it, Michele, what's wrong with you, huh? Do you have a death wish?"

At her silence he looked more closely at her and noted how stiffly she was holding herself, the way she was biting her lip to still its quivering. He consciously reined in his temper. "There's no sign of anyone now. Let's go back to the car so I can radio this in."

He held out an encompassing arm, meant to turn her and guide her in the direction of the car. Michele ducked under his arm and slowly walked into her home.

She moved from room to room as if in a trance, noting in dismay the willful destruction that had been wrought. Connor sighed but didn't try to stop her, as if aware of the fight he would have if he tried. "Don't touch anything," he warned her, but he needn't have bothered. Both hands were clutched tightly in front of her, as if she couldn't control their trembling any other way. Her gasp as she reached the bathroom was audible, and Connor pulled her back against his chest.

Someone had scrawled across her mirror with a lipstick: "I warned you." With a dispassionate part of her mind she registered the fact that the lipstick had been carelessly dropped afterward, its smooth point flattened from the abuse. She remembered inanely when she had bought it. Frivolous Fruit it was called, and she had wondered at the time who came up with such ridiculous names for products.

Connor's hands tightened on her shoulders, and only then did she become aware of his presence behind her. "Come away, Michele." Her eyes met his green gaze in the mirror. "C'mon," he repeated softly, and she allowed him to lead her from the house and back out to the car.

She sat quietly in the seat, unaware of the worried glances Connor was shooting her way while he spoke on the radio. He asked her once, "Did you notice anything missing?"

Michele shook her head and was proud that her voice was steady when she answered him. "The TV, the stereo and the microwave were there. I'll have to look closer than that to tell if anything else was taken."

She felt as if any second she was going to fly apart into a million pieces, and she held on frantically to the remnants of her sanity. She remained collected while the patrolmen came and checked her home for fingerprints and clues. She followed them from room to room, opening drawers, checking to see if jewelry or anything else was missing. Nothing was. She watched with outward calm as the officers taped cardboard to a living room window that had been smashed to gain entry.

His princess had something more solid than ice in her, Connor mused. She was pure steel. Any other woman would have dissolved by now after everything she had been through that day. She was still outwardly composed, too damn pale for his liking, but calm nonetheless. He wasn't fooled, though. He could see that she was near her breaking point—hell, any person he knew would be. That was why he cut short the questioning and bundled both her and Sammy into his car. He drove her quickly and expertly to his house and escorted her inside and to his room.

Her silent acceptance of his actions worried him more than anything else could. He efficiently and impersonally stripped her and tucked her into his bed. Then he doffed his own clothes and climbed in after her. He pulled her close, as close as he could get her and wrapped both arms around her, hoping to convey comfort, to provide his warmth.

And when the stiffness failed to leave her body, when her breathing failed to reach the even rhythm that spoke of sleep, he turned and moved over her. Then he proceeded to make love to her with the most earnest expression of absorbed concentration on his face. And it was that look that finally reached Michele and sent the tension fading from her limbs. It was in that moment that she knew that she loved him beyond all bearing.

Chapter 13

When Connor took her home the next morning, Michele mentally braced herself to face the disarray of her apartment. But despite her trepidation, she was shocked anew when she entered the front door. For far from the chaos of last night, her home had been returned to order. Cushions had been replaced, the bookcase rearranged. A surreptitious peek showed that even the bathroom had been restored to neatness, with no sign of the intruder's message remaining.

Connor spoke over her shoulder as she surveyed the renewed neatness in amazement. "I gave Cruz a call after you fell asleep last night. He stopped by early, got your key and cleaned up for you. Dropped the key off again before you'd even awakened."

Michele felt tears fill her eyes. She had dreaded returning home again to the mess, to be struck anew with the feeling of fear and anger that someone had violated her home. She was touched at the thoughtful gesture, on behalf of both Connor for making it and Cruz for carrying it out.

"It was a sweet thing to do," she told him as she turned and twined her arms around his neck.

Connor looked at her quickly, uncomfortably aware of the tears choking her voice and welling in her eyes. He searched for something, anything, to forestall their inevitable shedding. "I didn't want to leave you last night, and Cruz didn't mind doing it. Hell, it's the least he could do after putting you through that session with Casel."

"I'll thank him the next time I see him," Michele affirmed, searching his face. "But you're the one who thought of it. Thank you, Connor." She took his hard cheeks in her hands, tilted his head down and pressed a soft kiss to his mouth.

Connor couldn't ever remember having been the recipient of gratitude from a woman he was involved with. Quite the opposite, in fact. But that didn't keep him from being moved by her kiss, nor from responding to its sweetness.

After long moments Michele broke away with a sigh. "I really have to get ready for work if we're going to leave enough time for you to take me to my car."

Connor cleared his throat uneasily. "Uh, Michele, there's really something we have to discuss."

"Can it wait until we get in the car, Connor?" Michele called over her shoulder as she strode toward her bedroom. "I'm going to have to rush as it is."

"No problem," he muttered to her disappearing back. He shoved his fingers through his hair, turning to walk back to the living room. It was his own fault for pussyfooting around the forthcoming subject, but he knew Michele would hit the roof when she heard what he had to say. And after last night he was loath to bring up any controversial subject, no matter how sorely it needed to be discussed. But her safety was his utmost concern, and she was going to listen to him, regardless of her views.

Last night had brought home to him in the most chilling way possible that Michele was in a great deal of danger. She was obviously being stalked by a nutcase who was becoming progressively more violent. And Connor knew in his gut that all of this was somehow tied to the kidnappings.

He shuddered to think of what Michele's intruder might be capable of. Or of what would occur if Michele happened to be home the next time he came calling.

His mouth flattened. No way was he going to allow that to occur. Without her knowledge, he'd assigned a man to watch her house after the second message had been delivered. And in spite of that, the officer didn't have a damn thing to report. He hadn't seen a thing.

It was all so maddening, but Connor was unused to allowing mere circumstances to dictate his choices to him. Michele needed protection; he would protect her. That was all there was to it. She would buck him on this, she was maddeningly strong-willed, but he was going to insist.

No way was he going to allow her to return to this house and be at the mercy of that creep the next time he sprang a surprise visit. She was moving in with him, no argument.

A warm glow set in at the thought. Moving in with him. He had only lived with one woman in his life, and his ex-wife hadn't made it a pleasant experience. But he was looking forward to having Michele entwined even more closely in his life. Looking forward to it too much, he reminded himself sternly. This was merely temporary. He had to keep that in mind. How many times had he told himself that he was no good for her, that she deserved better? But as long as he kept that thought in mind, he was free to relish the experience. Because something inside him wanted very much to wake up every morning next to Michele Easton.

Living together would also make it much easier to keep personal watch over her twenty-four hours a day, another item of his plan that he expected her to fight him on. But he wasn't going to be moved. He would not allow her to be hurt, and he couldn't be sure of her safety if he didn't have her within reach at all times.

"I'm ready," Michele breathlessly informed him, rushing by to scoop up her purse. At his silence, she turned back to him inquiringly. "So overcome at my speed that you're speechless?" she teased.

She was half correct; he *was* speechless. Connor swallowed around the lump in his throat at her appearance. She was wearing a belted dress in a pale peach color that clung softly to her curves and accented her coloring. She looked heartbreakingly beautiful, and he knew in that moment that he would do whatever it took to keep this woman safe from harm.

Michele was puzzled at the almost fierce expression on his face. "Connor? Shouldn't we be going?"

She was even more puzzled when he wrapped her close for a moment, holding her tightly. Then, without a word, he led her to the door.

Her sense of wonder quickly mounted as they rode back to the district headquarters to pick up her car. She listened quietly to his terse explanation. "You want me to move in with you?" Her voice was thin.

Connor glanced quickly at her. "It'd be safest for you," he reiterated. "I've had someone watching your house, and he didn't even see that creep last night. And I sure as hell don't want to take a chance on you being there if he returns."

Michele digested this information in shock. The thought that her home had been penetrated despite police protection was horrifying indeed. She shuddered involuntarily. Connor's voice was flat, devoid of expression, and she wondered wistfully if her safety was the only thing motivating his suggestion. The thought of living with him sent shivers of anticipation down her spine, but she found no corresponding emotion on his face. His suggestion had been delivered in the same calm way he might have suggested that she take her coat along in case it rained.

She sighed silently. She was already painfully aware that all the feelings in their relationship were embarrassingly one-sided. She hadn't intended to fall in love with Connor McLain, and she didn't expect anything but heartache to follow. She was certain that living with him would give her a tantalizing taste of permanence, a permanence that would never materialize. But she was going to savor that taste and hope that it helped the heartache when his job was done and he walked away from her.

"All right."

Connor froze at her words, too shocked to take his eyes off the clogged highway, too afraid of what she would read in his eyes. "You agree?" he croaked, silently damning the incredulity in his voice. Way to convince her, McLain, he derided himself mentally. Sounding like you can't believe she's going along with something you just told her makes complete sense.

Michele felt a tiny smile creep across her face at the abject disbelief in his voice. So, the great detective wasn't as emotionless about this decision as he would have her believe.

"Yes, I agree," she affirmed. And then she admitted, "I've always prided myself on being a strong person, Connor, but I'm finding that I'm not a particularly brave one."

"What you've been through lately would throw anybody." He swiftly defended her. "Don't feel like a coward just because you have a normal sense of caution."

"I just don't want to inconvenience you," she murmured as she gazed unseeingly at the traffic whizzing by her window. "Maybe I should find another place to stay."

"No!"

At his emphatic reply she turned to look at him, but he was still staring straight ahead. Only his grasp on the steering wheel, knuckles white with the strength of his grip gave away his consternation.

"What I mean is, it makes sense for you to stay with me. You would have to explain to someone else why you need to get out of your house for a while, and besides, it will make it easier for me to keep an eye on you."

Michele was amused. "Keep an eye on me? That sounds ominous, Detective."

Connor didn't share her levity. "I'm serious, Michele. Someone needs to be with you at all times. I don't want you going anywhere by yourself. So I'll be with you."

It took Michele a few moments to interpret his meaning through her sense of amazement. "You'll be with me? I don't need a bodyguard, Connor. And I certainly am not going to let you curtail what I do in my free time."

"That's exactly what you're going to let me do," answered Connor imperturbably. This was the reaction he had expected from her, and it was somehow easier to deal with since she had agreed so readily to moving in with him. "The only way I can ensure your safety is to watch over you, and that's what I'm going to do."

She was speechless at his effrontery. "There is no need for that," she gritted, when she recovered her voice. "You're busy with the investigation, and I have commitments. I cannot wait around until you're free to take me everywhere I need to go."

This time he did take his eyes off the road to shoot her a warning look. "Use your head, Michele. Your house has been hit when you were out of it, which means that the perp is probably watching it. If that's so, it won't be long before he figures out that you're no longer staying there. Which means the next step will be for him to contact you some other way."

His words gave her a sick feeling. "You think so?"

Connor didn't spare any regret for the fear he knew his words had rekindled in her. She needed to face the facts, and the sooner the better. This was going to be difficult enough without her fighting him every step of the way, and he meant to instill enough fear in her to make her cautious. "I know so." His voice was flat. He frowned consideringly. "It's probably safe enough for you to drive to work today, but afterward I want you to pack what you'll need and go over to my place." He reached into his pocket with one hand and pulled out a spare key, which he offered to her. "And after today I don't even want you driving anywhere."

She was openmouthed at his arrogance and made no move to take the key from him. After a moment he reached for her purse and dropped the key inside. She strove to stay calm, to use reason. "You cannot honestly expect me to wait for you to take me to work, pick me up and follow me around on whatever professional commitment or errand I happen to have. For one thing, our schedules will never allow it. What happens when I'm ready to leave for the day and you aren't?"

"No problem," he answered with more assurance than he felt. He had been wondering the same thing. He maneuvered the car onto a ramp that would take them downtown. "When I can't make it, Cruz will take over for me."

"Oh, great," Michele said sarcastically. "I not only have one but two watchdogs. Get serious, McLain."

The look he shot her convinced her that humor was the farthest thing from his mind. "I'm utterly serious, Michele, and I won't take any flak about this. Anywhere you have to go I'll accompany you, or *you* won't be going, either. So the best thing for you to do is to clear your calendar as much as possible and give me a list of the things you absolutely can't get out of, so I can arrange my schedule to include them."

Shock had receded, to be replaced by simmering anger. Of all the high-handed assumptions, this one took the cake. She knew arguing with him wouldn't faze him; he was like a bulldozer when he wanted something. Quiet satisfaction filled her. When he heard her next words, she fully expected him to retreat with humorous haste from his intractable demands.

"All right, Connor," she said with such studied sweetness that he glanced at her cautiously. "Then your duties can start tonight." She felt elation fill her at his obvious shock.

"What's going on tonight?"

"The city fund-raiser for the homeless is having its annual gala," she informed him mischievously. She knew instinctively that he would detest the glittering affair, with its masses of people and social dragons. She herself never looked forward to it, but, ironically, this ostentatious extravaganza brought in more money for their cause in one night than all their fund-raising for the rest of the year. As chairperson for the committee, she had to be present.

Connor's tone brooked no argument. "Get out of it."

"I'm afraid that's impossible," she told him with mock regret. "Since I helped arrange it, my presence is mandatory. Of course, there's no real need for you to come along. I couldn't be safer than in a crowd of five hundred people."

If she had hoped to convince him of the ludicrousness of his plan, her effort was in vain. Connor was exploring another aspect of her news, and it didn't please him at all. "How long have you known about this?" he asked, his tone tight.

"It's been planned for months, and I simply can't get out of it. But it doesn't matter. I was just trying to point out that I don't need you to—"

He speared her with a glance so angry that she stopped, midsentence. "And just who," he growled in a voice so low she had to strain to hear, "had you expected to accompany you tonight?"

Michele was at a loss to interpret his inexplicable fury. "No one," she said at last. "That's what I'm trying to tell you. It isn't necessary for me to be escorted everywhere I go."

"Who did you go with last year, Michele, as if I couldn't guess?" he said with a sneer, and she found herself flaring up in response.

"James accompanied me, since he is active in the organization, too. I don't see what possible relevance that has."

Connor concentrated on driving and kept his jaw clamped so tightly it ached. He didn't trust himself not to berate her any more than he had, but his guts were twisting with an unfamiliar emotion, and he knew exactly what that emotion was.

Okay, he was jealous, damn it, he admitted savagely to himself. Forget that she was talking about the kind of social event he hated. Forget that he had done everything possible while married to avoid those events. The fact remained that she had not mentioned it to him before, probably realizing that he wouldn't fit in. James was the kind of man who would shine in such a setting, who would feel at ease there. And the fact that she had deliberately withheld the choice from him meant that she hadn't considered him an appropriate escort.

He couldn't help the cold knot that formed in the pit of his stomach. But right now there were more important matters at hand. Because, despite what he was feeling, there was no way in hell that he was going to allow Michele to attend that ball alone, or, even worse, let James take her. "What time do I have to be ready to go tonight?" he asked abruptly.

Michele felt at sea. His civil tone was at odds with the muscle jumping in his jaw, and she wondered if it was possible for him to be this angry over her little maneuver. "That isn't necessary, Connor, I was just going to make a brief appearance and then make a quick getaway."

"What time?" he grated.

"Eight o'clock, but really, there's no need. I keep trying to tell you..."

"I assume it's formal," he continued, his voice hard.

"Yes." She sighed. It was hard to carry on a conversation with someone intent on not letting you complete a sentence. From his terse replies she was certain he was furious at having to attend the type of function he hated, and she was impatient with him for feeling the need. She certainly wasn't in the mood to deal with his anger, however, and the rest of the ride was completed in silence.

Upon arrival at her car she turned to him, not even knowing what to say. But before she had the chance to formulate a sentence, he was speaking.

"Not to worry, Miss Easton." He bared his teeth at her. "Believe it or not, I can actually be half-civilized when the occasion demands it. I won't embarrass you tonight."

"Connor," she protested, but he slid out of the car and slammed the door. She got out, too, more slowly, staring at his back as he swiftly strode away toward the headquarters.

So that was it, she thought, after getting into her own car and driving to her office. Impatience and pity warred within her. He wasn't angry because his own fears for her safety were forcing him to attend an event he detested. He was furious at her. He must think she had deliberately kept this commitment from him because she was ashamed to be seen in public with him.

Impatience won out for the moment as she felt the sudden urge to throttle him for his leap to such an erroneous conclusion. How was it possible for one man to be so obtuse? What woman in her right mind wouldn't die for the chance to walk into any function on the arm of such a devastating man? At the thought, she half feared for his safety when some of those female piranhas got a look at him. She knew women who would take one glance at him and immediately move in for the kill.

His stupid conclusion was based on one thing, and it all came back to the kind of woman he was adamant that she was. And that hurt most of all, that his idea about her hadn't changed, even as close as they had become.

Her mouth softened as another thought struck her. How ego-bruising it must be for a man like Connor McLain to think that a woman felt he was her social inferior. She would just have to make it her goal tonight to prove to him that he was, instead, her first choice.

She was preoccupied at work for the rest of that day, causing even Julie to cast impatient looks her way when she had to repeat some questions two and three times. And when James entered her office late that afternoon, Michele had the sinking feeling that things were about to get worse.

Her fears proved well-founded when, after a few minutes of polite small talk, James asked, "I assume you're going to the gala tonight, Michele. I hope we can forget our personal differences long enough to go together and represent our business."

Michele hoped her smile didn't appear as forced as it felt. "I'm afraid I can't tonight, James, I'm sorry."

His polite smile never wavered. "You can't? Why ever not? You are planning on going, aren't you?"

"I am, yes, but I already have an escort."

"A date?"

Michele felt like gritting her teeth at his continued prodding. She knew that he would use his gentle interrogation tactics until he extracted the information he wanted. "A date, yes."

"You don't mind telling me with whom, do you?" he asked genially, sinking into a chair facing her desk. "Or is it a surprise you wish to save for tonight?"

As much as Michele wanted to avoid the upcoming scene, she wearily decided it was better to tell James now than to risk a possible scene this evening. "Connor McLain," she responded evenly.

His well-bred face expressed mild surprise. "Ah, yes." He waited a heartbeat before adding, "The police detective."

Michele stared at him in shock. He gazed back at her imperturbably. "I did a little checking after you so politely turned me down a few weeks ago." He made a self-deprecating face. "Call it a snit, if you wish. At any rate, you didn't convince me that there was nothing between the two of you. I sensed it the day you introduced him to me."

"We weren't even dating at the time," Michele answered slowly, in a masterful understatement.

"Well, he must have had some reason for being here," James replied. "He was pursuing you?"

Michele's mouth went dry. Better that James think she had purposefully misled him about her personal life than find out the truth.

"In a manner of speaking," she responded evenly, returning his gaze steadily.

"At the risk of sounding like sour grapes, he doesn't seem your type," James told her gently.

Another understatement, she told herself. She kept her voice light as she responded, "Well, perhaps it's true that opposites attract, James. At any rate," she continued, as she rose to signal that their discussion was over, "we'll see you this evening."

She escorted him to the door, but he turned before exiting. "Forgive my nosiness, Michele. I truly have your best interests at heart. I doubt your involvement with this man will bring you anything but pain. Heed my warning. I would hate to see you get hurt." Without waiting for her reply, he turned and left the room.

Michele shut the door with only a modicum of the force she would have liked. She turned around and leaned back against it, arching her head back wearily. Was it really possible that she had engaged in an argument with Connor about James and with James about Connor in the very same day? She shook her head in chagrin. She, Michele Easton, had never before had to explain herself to any man, and now there were two men in her life demanding explanations.

Not that she owed any to James. A tiny frown marred her forehead, and she unconsciously worried her bottom lip with her teeth. There had never been anything personal between them, despite her long-standing suspicion that he would like it to be otherwise. She hadn't dated anyone seriously since she had begun working at Psychological Associates, preferring instead to concentrate on her job and her volunteer work. And she had never given James any reason to believe that she would welcome a closer relationship with him. She had known intuitively that it would be a bad idea, leading to all kinds of complications.

She sighed aloud, determined to be honest with herself. Because the bottom line was that she had never been tempted to date James, never been drawn to him, never felt a spark of electricity with him. And, to continue telling the truth, she had never felt those things with any man.

Except for Connor McLain.

Her mouth went down in a self-deprecating moue. There wasn't just a spark between herself and Connor, there was an entire electrical storm. Just thinking of him sent a warm river of sensation flooding her system. Whether they were fighting or loving, talking or silent, when she was with him she felt more vibrant, more alive, than ever before.

She loved him, she admitted achingly to herself. And she thought he felt something for her. At least, she wanted to believe that. She knew he had surprised himself on occasion by his openness with her, even when he hadn't yet trusted her. She thought she could read genuine caring in his attitude toward her.

But maybe she was just fooling herself. How many other women had told themselves the same things? How many had fallen in love with him, only to have their hearts shattered by his eventual indifference?

Michele shivered. There were plenty of warning signs that the same thing would eventually happen to her. Connor hadn't had a close relationship with a woman since his ex-wife, and she wasn't sure he was even capable of one.

How, then, had calm, steady and cautious Michele Easton lost her heart to him? She, who had made it a goal in her adult life to avoid taking risks, to ignore temptation, was totally, achingly in love with a man who could do more damage to her emotionally than her stepfather ever had physically.

What a convoluted mess their relationship was, Michele admitted. Yet she couldn't help smiling as visions of a different Connor, a more tender Connor, danced across her brain. An image of the Connor who had saved Guido's son from a road heading to a delinquent home. A picture of the Connor who had sheltered and rocked her, calming her after her dreams. An echo of his voice, almost rusty from disuse, telling her of events from his childhood, pushing the demons back into the night. An image of his tortured face as he tried to talk her out of putting herself through the nightmares with Bruce. How could she deny that side of him, those images of him?

She couldn't, Michele thought simply. Every ounce of sweetness with him was worth the chance of future heartbreak. And she was willing to take that chance, no matter what James or anyone else said about it.

Michele's reverie was interrupted by someone tapping on the door and turning the knob. She moved away from the door, and it was opened by Julie, who eyed her quizzically as her wheelchair moved through the entrance. The secretary's eyes went knowingly from Michele to the door and back again.

"So, were you trying to keep me out or make sure James didn't get back in?" she asked wryly as she moved past Michele to put a sheaf of paperwork on the desk.

"How'd you guess about James?" Michele sighed as she headed over to her desk to glance sightlessly at the pile of papers Julie had set there.

"Didn't you know? I'm psychic." Julie laughed.

Michele's expression froze at her secretary's choice of words, but Julie went on blithely.

"Plus there was the thundercloud brewing on James's face as he stormed—ever so civilly, of course—out of your office and past my desk."

Michele relaxed and answered, "Well, we did have a little disagreement."

"Before the fund-raiser tonight?" Julie *tsk*ed. "That wasn't a smart move, Michele, to argue with your escort. You don't want to wind up going alone, do you?"

Michele was used to Julie's personal chatter and, in fact, at most times encouraged it. They were friends as well as co-workers, but at this moment she wished fervently that Julie was up to her eyebrows in typing.

"That's what the disagreement was about," Michele answered shortly.

Julie looked up at her, the confusion on her face quickly chased away by enlightenment. "You have another date!" she crowed triumphantly, then read her answer on Michele's pained face. "Wonderful! I'm always telling you to get out more. I hope it's with someone great."

Michele dropped wearily into her chair. "I'm going," she announced, feeling as if it were for the hundredth time, "with Connor McLain." She waited for her friend's reaction. It wasn't long in coming.

"Oooo-whee," Julie sighed. Her eyes closed in delight, and she smacked her lips in delectation. "That hunk who stopped in here a few weeks ago?"

"I'm surprised you remember," Michele murmured dryly.

"Who could forget a face like that?" asked Julie with interest. "Or the body. That man sure does look good walking away."

"Julie!" scolded Michele, heat scalding her cheeks. But privately she had to admit that she was partial herself to Connor's well-formed behind.

But her secretary's lightninglike mind was already off to other matters. "But as great-looking as he is, I'm not too sure it was smart of you to antagonize James like that. I've always had the feeling that he had the hots for you himself."

"I had no intention of antagonizing James," Michele responded stiffly. "But there's no way I could go with him tonight."

"Connor's the jealous type, huh?" Julie asked understandingly. "Well, you have to do what you have to do. And I can't blame you for wanting to keep that hunk of manhood happy." She winked up at Michele's frozen expression, chattering on. "I'll clear up as much as I can for you, so you can get out of here at a decent hour. You'll want to leave plenty of time to get ready."

She wheeled her chair around and motored toward the door.

Michele's mind barely registered the click of the door behind her. It was too busy toying with the idea planted by Julie.

Jealousy. She turned the possibility over and over in her mind. Was it possible? Though hardly a noble emotion, it was certainly a human one, and she found herself examining the possibility minutely. To believe that Connor was jealous of James would make one wonder if he harbored deeper emotions for Michele than she had at first believed.

As the door opened again, Michele closed her eyes in dismay. What else could possibly go wrong today? She felt a little guilty for her impatience when Scott stuck his head in the room.

"Miss Easton? Okay if I empty the t-t-trash?"

She managed a wan smile. "Sure, Scott, come on in."

The janitor shuffled in carrying a large plastic bag. As he busied himself emptying her waste can, Michele asked kindly, "How's your mother, Scott? Is that new medication helping her?"

Scott had told her once that his mother was crippled with rheumatoid arthritis, and Michele made it a point to ask about her frequently.

He straightened from his task and shrugged a little as he answered, "Helps s-s-some, I think."

"That's good news." Michele smiled. The janitor fidgeted in front of her, shifting from one foot to the other. Michele waited in silence, aware he had something to say, and that prompting only made his stutter more pronounced.

Finally he asked, "Are you going t-t-to that b-b-ball tonight?"

"Why, yes, I am, Scott. It's for a very good cause, don't you think?"

He ignored her question and pursued doggedly, "With Dr. Ryan?"

Michele closed her eyes, unable to believe this comedy of errors. It was a good thing, she reminded herself whimsically, that she had no more clients scheduled today. At the rate this was going, they, too, would feel free to quiz her about her social life.

"I'll see Dr. Ryan there, yes," Michele answered evasively.

But Scott didn't stop there. A frown worried his forehead, and he asked, "You m-m-mean you'll m-m-meet him there?"

Silently asking herself why she was doing it, she explained, "I have a date taking me, but I'm sure we'll see Dr. Ryan there tonight."

"D-D-Dr. Ryan is a f-f-fine m-m-man," he said doggedly. Michele cocked her head at his doggedness in pursuing the topic and the strength of his feelings about it.

"Yes, he is, isn't he, Scott?"

The janitor shrugged and looked at a point beyond her left ear. After long moments he muttered, "Okay," and turned and left the room.

Michele leaned back in her desk chair and shook her head in amusement. She had never had so many people take such an interest in her private life before. James would be absolutely appalled if he knew that Scott had taken it upon himself to plead his case with Michele.

Eventually her thoughts drifted away from her co-workers and back to Connor. She thought again about what Julie had said about Connor being jealous of James. Hugging the idea to herself, she busied herself with the mound of papers she needed to work through. This evening, Connor McLain was going to become aware of how much she valued him in her life. She would make sure of it.

Chapter 14

Connor barely looked up when the door to his office opened.

Cruz sauntered in and dropped into a chair opposite the desk. "What's the good news, pal of mine?"

"There isn't any," Connor said shortly. "The creep who broke into Michele's last night must have worn gloves. No prints or anything else that would lead us to him."

Cruz cocked a dark eyebrow. "Nothing? How's Michele this morning?"

Connor sighed. "Fine. She appreciated your cleaning up her place for her."

Cruz waved the thanks away. "*De nada.* But if she's okay, why do you look like you'd like to go a few rounds with this year's heavyweight champ?"

"I'd rather," Connor explained darkly, "take him on than Michele."

Cruz chuckled. "Packs quite a punch, does she?"

Connor's thoughts went back yet again to the bombshell she had hit him with earlier, and he felt an immediate tightening in his gut. "In her own way," he responded cryptically.

Cruz waited for further explanation. When it appeared none would be forthcoming, he prodded his friend. "How'd she take the suggestion of moving in with you?"

Connor squirmed uncomfortably. He hadn't exactly presented it to her as a suggestion, more as a demand, really. "Amazingly well, considering," he responded finally.

Cruz cocked an eyebrow. "Yeah? And she didn't buck you on the idea of you or me as temporary companions?"

Connor closed his eyes in memory. "That's where I kind of lost her," he admitted.

"But you explained it was for her safety, right?" prompted Cruz. "You told her it was the only way we could make sure that nut doesn't go any further than he has with her?" As he received no reaction from Connor, he stopped and invited, "Feel free to jump in here with an answer anytime."

Connor looked up, after being absorbed in his own thoughts again. "She doesn't see the need for it," he said shortly, rising to pace the small area. "Says she won't wait around for one of us to accompany her everywhere. Probably afraid we'd cramp her style," he added bitterly.

Cruz frowned at his friend's obvious consternation. "But you insisted, right? Because it really is the only way."

"Yeah, I insisted. And she *will* have one of us with her at all times, whether she likes it or not."

Cruz, sensing there was more to his friend's foul mood than the argument with Michele, sat back. "So what's the plan for tonight?" he asked lazily. "If you have to work, I'll be glad to watch her for you. I could take her out to this cozy little French restaurant I know of...."

"Not a chance," Connor shot back. He stopped, recognizing the glint of humor in his friend's eyes, and said, "Besides, she has bigger plans than that for the evening. She's attending the city's annual fund-raising ball for the homeless."

Cruz whistled tunelessly through his teeth. "Well, la-di-da," he mocked. He grinned at Connor, his teeth a white slash in his bronzed face. "Just the kind of affair you love, buddy. Bet you get to dress up in a monkey suit and everything, don't you? Couldn't you talk her out of it?"

"She's chairperson for the committee or some damn thing," Connor grumbled. "And as for your next question, have you ever tried to talk Michele out of anything?"

Cruz's grin flashed again. "Well, no, I didn't think you'd approve. But there was that little waitress we both met. I was able to—"

Connor looked pained. "You know what I mean. There's no way to change Michele's mind once it's set. She's going, and I get the idea that I'm the last person in the world she wants as an escort, you know?"

Cruz regarded his friend more soberly. Here, at last, they were getting to the crux of what was bothering Connor. He knew how much Connor hated high-society events, but he also knew his friend well enough to know that having to attend one in order to see to Michele's well-being wouldn't have put him in the mood he was presently in. He very much resembled a man who would like to put his fist through the wall, and Cruz couldn't remember the last time he had seen him like this. "What makes you think that?"

Connor's expression grew savage at the question. "Well, it's pretty apparent, isn't it? These things are arranged months in advance, but today was the first I heard about it."

Cruz regarded him lazily. "Maybe Michele knows how you feel about these functions."

Connor whirled around and bit out, "Or maybe she doesn't want to be seen with me with all her friends and colleagues around. She probably had Ryan all lined up to escort her and schmooze all the social lions for contributions. Maybe I'm good enough to call when some nut is threatening her, but not to escort a real live ice princess."

He crossed his arms across his chest, his face twisted with self-disgust. "Hell, I knew the score all along. I'm not the kind of guy Michele needs. She should have someone like her, a professional who enjoys the opera and the ballet, not some cop who's seen too much to match her ideals, whose idea of a good time is floor seats at a pro basketball game. I'm mighty good enough to be her stud, but—"

"First time I heard you complain about that," Cruz put in, tongue-in-cheek.

Connor glared at him. "You know damn well what I mean. We're too different. Anyone can see that."

"Too different for what?" Cruz asked quietly.

Connor stared hard at his friend, realizing the trap he had just been led into. Because he knew exactly what Cruz was getting at, even if he refused to give an answer. He had never before cared much what, if anything, he and his frequent dates had in common, other than mutual attraction. He had never looked for more, had never wanted more.

His mind shied away from what that meant. When he finally spoke, his voice was bleak. "It doesn't matter. She needs me right now, but when this thing is over, so are we. That's the way it has to be."

"You know," Cruz said soberly, "I haven't seen you this twisted up over a woman since Tricia, and you married her."

Connor's mouth went down. "I distinctly remember you trying your best to talk me out of that decision."

Cruz shrugged. "Michele isn't Tricia. And there's a major problem with being alone, *amigo*." He waited a heartbeat. "It's damn lonely."

"How profound," Connor grumbled.

"Decide what you want and go after it. That," said Cruz, as he rose to leave the room, "is what you're noted for, isn't it?"

The closing door made barely a ripple in Connor's concentration. Yeah, that sure as hell was what he was noted for. But how did he go after what he wanted when he wasn't even sure what that was?

He shook his head in finality. Cruz didn't know what he was talking about. Connor knew in his gut what was right for Michele, and he wasn't it. He was going to have to pull away, maintain some distance between them. That would be difficult given their current physical proximity, but he would have to try. Then maybe it would be less painful when this whole thing was over.

Maybe, but he doubted it.

Michele checked the clock once more, then turned away, satisfied that they had plenty of time before she was due at the fund-raiser. Connor had arrived home less than an hour before. They had exchanged hardly a word before he'd brushed by her to go get ready.

She frowned as she looked in the mirror for the last time. He had seemed withdrawn, and she wasn't sure whether that was due to work or to his aversion for the affair they were about to attend.

She made a face. She could certainly guess. She knew how he felt about functions like this one, but she had promised herself that she would leave no doubt in his mind about who she wanted to be with tonight, and she was going to do that.

Her reflection mimicked her, biting her lip reflectively. Michele caught a look at herself and stopped, muttering a curse. She quickly reapplied her lipstick, then put the lid on it and dropped it into her bag. She had arrived at Connor's long before he had, thanks to Julie's help in clearing her desk. She had made a quick stop at home first, but she hadn't lingered there, packing only a few clothes and toiletries. Later she and Connor could go back for more of her things, but the house had seemed too eerie to her after Connor's warnings for her to be comfortable enough to take her time.

She smoothed her long white formal gown with one hand, turning this way and that in the mirror to check for wrinkles. The dress left one shoulder bare and most of her back, as well. It fell to the floor, sheathing her body sleekly. It was gathered between her breasts, emphasizing her high bosom. Her hair was pulled up in a smooth knot, and diamond studs glittered at her ears. Taking a deep breath, she left the room to wait for Connor.

He didn't keep her waiting long. She heard his footsteps coming toward her and whirled around to face him, her breath stopping in her chest. He was incredibly handsome, and her heart kicked into a faster rhythm at the sight of him. In shorts and a tank top, chinos or jeans, he was a virile, unmistakably sexy male. In a tuxedo, Connor McLain was heart-stopping.

The austere contrast of the snowy white shirt against the black tux should have tamed him, should have made him look a bit more civilized, a little more conventional. Instead it contrasted with his dangerous good looks, highlighting them. His gold hair brushed the satin sheen of his collar in back and provided a vivid contrast to its inky shine.

He looked like a magnificent lion, petted and preened and forced into a civilized setting, but the formal clothes merely highlighted his wildness. Michele swallowed hard. She wasn't used to having to combat an urge to undress a man before they went out the door for the evening!

Connor stopped when he saw her, his chest growing tight as he surveyed the vision before him. Here was the epitome of his fears, Michele looking as ethereally lovely as he had always imagined her. She looked as comfortable in her designer dress as he'd always known she would, and though she looked gorgeous, he couldn't tell her so. His throat was too full. If this didn't prove he'd been right about her all along, he didn't know what would. Soon he would escort her to a place where she would fit right in, further setting her apart from him. And though that was exactly what he had told himself he wanted, he was reluctant to see it actually happen.

They stared silently at each other, each lost in their own thoughts, for long minutes, before Michele noticed the missing studs on Connor's shirt.

"Did you forget something?" she asked teasingly, and he blinked at her before belatedly remembering the trouble he had encountered earlier.

"I never can get these blasted things," he muttered, thrusting the handful of studs at her, and she smiled as she took them. She moved closer and worked each through its buttonhole slowly. She recognized the ruffled shirt as the one she'd worn the first night they'd made love, and the sight of it evoked heated memories. She peeked up at him through her lashes and saw that he was staring straight ahead, holding himself rigid.

Connor stood still under her touch, scarcely daring to breathe. She seemed to be taking the devil's own time with those studs, and he wondered if it was because she, too, remembered the time when she had worn this shirt. Even as he'd shrugged into it, he'd been ensnared by the image she'd presented wearing it, the memory of how it had draped her lovely form, and how that evening had ended.

There was a muscle jumping in his cheek, and Michele smiled to herself. He might be trying to hold himself back from her, but he was not unaware of her. Judging by his heightened color and rapid breathing, her nearness had more effect on him than he was willing to admit, and it was a heady feeling indeed.

"There," she finally said, smoothing her hands down the front of his shirt. "All done." Then all teasing left her face as he looked at her, really looked at her. The air around them seemed charged, and she forgot her plan, forgot everything but Connor and the effect he had on her.

"You're beautiful," she whispered, sliding one hand along his freshly shaven jaw.

"God, I hope not," he muttered, giving her an aggrieved look. "That's not exactly the look I was trying for."

"No? What look were you trying for?" she asked.

"Early Spencer Tracy, maybe a dashing Clark Gable."

"Well—" her voice was shaky "—I think you've surpassed dashing."

"You think so?" he asked huskily, moving one hand up to cup hers and bring it to his lips.

"Definitely."

Connor pressed a kiss to her palm. He couldn't maintain a distance from her, not a physical or an emotional one. It was impossible for him to be unmoved by her, and he was stupid to think otherwise. Why the hell should he even want to? Better to enjoy to the fullest each moment he had with her. To hell with tomorrow. "And you are breathtaking," he whispered, his face drawing closer to hers. "Like an angel, so perfect that I'm afraid to touch."

"Don't be," Michele breathed as he hesitated a fraction away from her lips. "Because I want to be touched by you. Very much."

His mouth pressed lightly against hers, stealing the words from her lips. Michele moved closer, seeking more from him. When he would have moved away, she slid one hand around his neck and kept his mouth on hers, twisting her own sweetly beneath him.

Something more than desire curled through Connor, and he gathered her closely, trying to stay mindful of her dress and carefully arranged hair. But it was hard to keep his hands off her completely, and he stopped trying. Their mouths moved together, their tongues meshing wildly, before he finally broke away.

He rested his forehead against hers, their breathing labored. "We'd better stop or we'll never leave here,'' he murmured, touching her mouth regretfully. ''Your lipstick is smeared.''

''All over you,'' she returned softly, one finger tracing the fullness of his bottom lip, which was smeared with traces of vivid color.

Connor pulled his handkerchief out and wiped the telltale marks away slowly, watching as she went to the mirror in the hallway and repaired her mouth quickly. He felt almost regretful when she finished. He would rather have arrived there as they were, branded by each other's passion, a visual reminder to all of their involvement. He shook his head at his own fantasy.

Without any more words they collected their coats and left the house, the bond between them stronger than ever.

Their seats were at one of the head tables, and Michele could feel Connor tighten when he saw that James would be seated on her other side.

''Who's he bringing tonight?'' he asked suspiciously.

Michele slid her glance to him. No way would she let on about the conversation she had had with James earlier that day. ''I have no idea,'' she responded calmly, turning to look fully into his eyes. His head was bent, a slight frown marring his face, and she sensed that he would have liked to pursue the matter further. Her next words sidetracked him. ''The only escort I have any interest in is my own.''

Her words, delivered in an intimate voice, and the warmth in her direct look caught him off guard, as did her actions for the rest of the evening. Far from ignoring him, as he had been wearily certain would happen, she made sure he was at her side the entire night. She left him only once, to converse with some of her committee members about their part in the program. But even that was for only a few minutes.

Connor felt himself visibly relaxing at being the center of her attention. Michele treated him no differently here than when they were out alone, introducing him to each person who came up to speak to her. It was far more than he had expected, far more than he had hoped for. He even unbent enough to slip his arm around her waist, and she didn't resist. In fact, she seemed to welcome his touch, moving closer to him.

''McLain, I certainly didn't expect to see you here tonight,'' a jovial voice hailed them, and Connor turned slowly, his face tightening once more. ''Mayor,'' he said, greeting Larry McIntire laconically.

The politician eyed him shrewdly. ''Not your usual choice of gatherings,'' he noted.

''No, it's more yours,'' Connor returned easily enough, but Michele noted that neither men wore a smile that reached his eyes. She looked between the two of them confusedly, aware of the tension radiating between them but at a loss to explain it.

Connor gestured to Michele. "Have you met Michele Easton, Mayor? She was on the committee that arranged this fund-raiser tonight."

Michele found both her hands grasped in Larry McIntire's. "It's a pleasure, Ms. Easton," he told her, not relinquishing her from his grip. "And from what I've seen so far, you and your committee have done a wonderful job here tonight, a wonderful job. Through your diligence I'm sure funds will become available for even more shelters for the poor homeless souls who roam our streets. I can't tell you how much the work you people do is appreciated."

"Thank you, sir," she replied simply, extricating her hands gracefully. Fortunately his attention was called away by someone else, and within seconds he was striding away.

"I have never trusted that man," Michele muttered as an aside to Connor, and his eyes widened. "He's entirely too smooth to be believable."

"You're an excellent judge of character," he allowed. At her raised eyebrows he elucidated. "I've known Larry McIntire for years, and he's the smoothest son of a bitch I've ever met. I wouldn't trust him any further than I could throw him."

"There seems to be bad blood between the two of you," Michele observed.

He snorted. "I wouldn't let him stand in back of me holding a sharp instrument, if that's what you mean."

Michele frowned, disturbed by that image of the man in charge of running their city. "You must be grateful the Reverend Carlson is giving him a run for his money in the mayoral race, then. At least the people will be given a clear choice this time around." At the look on his face, she demanded, "You are going to support Carlson, aren't you, feeling the way you do about McIntire?"

Connor, noticing that people were drifting to their seats at the tables, started to gently guide Michele to hers. "Nope," he replied, artfully dodging other couples in pursuit of their chairs. He wasn't a political creature, and party politics didn't interest him. But Michele pursued it. "Why not?"

He looked down at her. "Because I don't trust God-squad types, either. Better the devil you know, sweetheart," he responded. His cryptic remark silenced her, and she allowed him to seat her, troubled by his cynicism. She had always known that Connor possessed a wealth of knowledge outside her scope of experience, known that it had hardened him. She couldn't imagine the frustration of going to work each day, doing your job to the best of your ability and being thwarted by your own superiors. She mulled that over as they waited for the crowd to be seated.

Dinner passed pleasantly enough despite the fact that James, seated on her other side, seemed determined to monopolize her attention. She tried to focus on Connor as much as she could, but she could tell that he was withdrawing from her. He became steadily more uncommunicative, and she despaired for the outcome of the evening. It wasn't until the first course had been served that she was struck with an idea. As they both ate, she dropped her left hand below the table and moved it to the region of Connor's rock-hard thigh.

He reacted as if he'd been scalded, turning his head to look sharply at her, his eyes narrowing. But Michele just smiled sweetly and bent toward him, speaking banally of the meal.

Connor was unable to take in her words, so aware was he of that small hand lying inches away from where heat was rapidly pooling. He stared hard at her before gradually relaxing. She had done everything she could this evening to show him her pleasure in his company. He might not understand it, but he was sure he liked it. Damn sure.

The rest of the meal passed unremarkably, Michele once more feeling the tension ebb from Connor. He even managed to mask his boredom with the speeches, wearing a polite, blank mask while listening to speaker after speaker jovially invite the audience to be generous in their donations, in addition to the five hundred dollars a plate they had already paid for their dinner. His attention sharpened, however, when the guest speakers introduced were none other than Larry McIntire and his opponent.

Connor inwardly groaned and settled back in his chair. It promised to be many more long minutes before they were released from their boredom, and he picked up Michele's hand, absently playing with her fingers as his mind drifted away from the speeches. Being here tonight hadn't been as bad as he'd feared, certainly not as awful as his memory of similar functions. He even enjoyed, primitively, the looks of admiration and envy Michele had elicited from men, knowing that she was his and reveling in her attempts to show him that she was glad to be with him.

It seemed that he'd been wrong about her this morning, and maybe wrong about other things, as well. The cool mask that always infuriated him had been present more than once this evening, but not with him, never with him. It dawned on him suddenly that it was her way of withdrawing, a defense mechanism when she felt uncomfortable or threatened in some way. He understood because he tended to do the same thing himself.

Connor's attention wandered back to the stage, where Carlson was winding down his speech. "...the future of our society depends on the present we can provide, especially to the youngest members of our city." He joined in the polite applause and restrained a groan as Larry McIntire rose. The mayor used the forum to make a thinly veiled campaign speech. "As my worthy opponent has noted, children are our future. This city has made children its main concern, as evidenced by our new parks, schools..." Connor drifted off again.

After the speeches were over the band tuned up its instruments. Connor would have liked to ask Michele to take a walk for some badly needed air, but once again she was being monopolized by James. He heaved a sigh. The woman on the other side of him tried to engage him in conversation, but his replies were terse to the point of rudeness. There was only one woman he was interested in talking to, holding, leaving with. And that woman was sitting on the other side of him.

He leaned over again, interrupting the conversation she was having with James. "Excuse me," he said, getting up and pulling Michele's chair out. "Shall we dance?" She smiled her acquiescence, and they left a fuming James glaring after them.

Being in Connor's arms felt like heaven, and Michele was content to float there indefinitely, held against his strong chest. The music surged around them, but the rest of the people faded away. It was as if she and Connor existed in their own charmed world, one where doubt and confusion had never existed.

After dancing for a long while, Connor whispered huskily, "Ready to go home?"

Home. Michele's heart gave a little leap at the word. She wasn't going to analyze his meaning; she was going to savor it instead. She smiled mistily up at him, her smile a sultry promise to match the desire she read easily in his eyes. "Yes."

Connor felt the passion that had existed between them all evening develop a sharper edge. He only hoped he could get her through the crowd and home before he embarrassed them both.

With one arm around her waist, he guided her through the mob of people, impatient with each person who stopped them to talk or to thank Michele for her work on the project. He managed to rein in his impatience, barely, but his civility was wearing thin.

It snapped when they were very close to the door and Michele was stopped yet again. He stood tensely behind her, wondering savagely how angry she would be if he just threw her over his shoulder and headed out the door with her. The fantasy definitely had some advantages, he decided, when a voice spoke behind him.

"Rushing Michele away so early, Detective McLain?"

Mentally cursing, Connor turned slowly and returned James's look with a glacial stare. "We're going to call it a night," he replied steadily.

"That's a shame. Michele does so love these events. It's unfortunate that you've allowed your own discomfort to interfere with her pleasure. I'd be glad to see her home myself, in order that she may stay and enjoy herself longer."

Connor mentally counted to ten before answering. Nothing would have given him greater satisfaction than to smash his fist in this man's well-bred face. "That won't be necessary. I'll see to Michele's enjoyment myself." The sharp intake of breath at his side told him that she had heard the double entendre.

"Connor, let's go," she hissed, dragging at his immovable arm. She might as well have tried to move a slab of granite. He didn't budge.

James dropped all pretense at civility. "I don't know what hold you have over her, Detective, but in the long run you will mean nothing at all to her. You are of no real importance in her life."

Connor crossed his arms, returning the man's gaze. "You sure of that, Doc?"

"Both of you, stop now!" Michele demanded in a furious whisper, aware that their threesome was drawing curious stares. When neither of the men moved, only continued relentlessly staring at each other, she whirled around and walked quickly away. After fighting her way through the people, she finally made it to the women's rest room.

Muttering a curse, Connor turned on his heel and strode after her, his progress hampered by the crowd. He stood outside the door to the ladies' room for several minutes, but Michele did not emerge. When several other women did, he earned himself some odd glances. A few of them looked at him as if he were some kind of pervert.

Ah, the hell with it, he thought. She was mad already; he couldn't make it much worse. With that thought he reached into his jacket's inside pocket and withdrew his shield. With it in visible view he opened the door of the rest room and walked in.

The women in the sitting room looked at him openmouthed, but he delayed their words. "Lieutenant McLain, ladies, Philadelphia P.D. Please clear this area. I repeat, please clear this area."

Michele couldn't believe her eyes. Or his audacity. She groaned aloud. "Connor, how dare you?"

One woman in a strapless dress sauntered by him and asked in a sultry voice, "May I be of any help, Lieutenant?"

Connor grinned, actually grinned, damn him, and answered, "No, ma'am, the woman I have to detain is right there."

The lady in black glanced back at Michele and heaved a mighty sigh. "Too bad. Well, come on, ladies, you heard the man."

Michele felt slow heat travel up her breasts, her neck and then climb to her face as the women hurried by her, some of them throwing her skeptical looks. "I will kill you for this, Connor," she promised through gritted teeth. "I will really, really, murder you this time."

Connor slipped his shield back into his pocket and leaned against the door to prevent anyone else from coming in. "Threatening a police officer is a criminal offense, Miss Easton," he commented finally. "Don't make me run you in."

"Don't make me run you over," she flung back, still busily plotting his demise. "And get away from that door. I'm leaving."

"With me."

"I'd rather walk on hot coals." Her voice dripped ice.

"Then I'm not moving," he returned implacably.

They glared at each other for long moments before a knock on the door jarred them both. "Connor," she snarled in exasperation as the knock was repeated, a little more desperately this time. "This is not the place."

"I agree," he said promptly. "Let's go home."

Michele closed her eyes and prayed for strength, but it was hard to concentrate on divine intervention when the door sounded as if a battering ram was being used on the other side of it. "All right," she gritted.

She sailed by him, and Connor thought that if he hadn't stepped aside she would have walked right through him. As they opened the door and hurried through, the very pregnant lady on the other side glared at Michele accusingly. When Connor moved into her view, her mouth dropped into a wide O, and she stared after them.

As they retrieved their coats, Connor made the mistake of attempting to help Michele with hers. The look she shot him would have frozen flame. "If you so much as touch me," she purred lethally, "I will shatter both your kneecaps."

As Connor followed her slowly out the door and waited for the car to be brought around, he wondered dismally how the hell he was going to get out of this one.

Chapter 15

An Arctic wind would have provided welcome warmth in the glacial silence that enveloped them throughout the ride home. Connor made no attempt to break it, aware that he had already pushed Michele further than was wise. He also didn't trust himself not to make it worse. Actually, he felt he had exercised remarkable restraint earlier. He hadn't annihilated James, which would have given him the greatest satisfaction. And he hadn't made a scene.

Well, he fidgeted uncomfortably, not much of one. He shot a surreptitious look at Michele's frozen features. Prudently, he kept his silence, hoping she got over her pique quickly.

When they entered his home, she dropped her purse, hung up her coat and, leaving him staring after her, strode past him to the door of the second bedroom and shut the door with a decided slam.

Well, hell, Connor thought aggrievedly. If she wanted to pout, she could go right ahead. He knew for certain that he wouldn't be able to sleep, so he headed to his bedroom, changed into shorts and tennis shoes, and stomped down the stairs to his gym. Two could play at this game.

Michele lay on her back on top of the bedspread, still in her finery, and contemplated the ceiling, wondering furiously when she had ever been this angry at another human being. He deserved to be boiled in oil, she thought waspishly. No. She wished she could hire a huge thug to beat him up. That would teach him a lesson.

She rolled over and propped her chin on her hands. That idea lacked satisfaction, as well. She couldn't stand to see Connor hurt, although the thought of thrashing him herself would go a long way toward alleviating some of the frustration he made her feel.

She pounded the pillow impotently. He made her so mad! No other man, no other person, had ever had the power to make her react so quickly, so violently. Only Connor McLain could take her on an emotional roller coaster, from euphoric heights to the depths of fury. Her fist stilled. Taking her from cool, calm composure to instant heated passion.

She groaned inaudibly. The very chemistry between them defined the emotional power he had over her. And although that thought was frightening, even more frightening was her doubt that the power was mutual. Though she had admitted to herself that she was in love with him, she had never uttered those words to him. She hadn't dared to. Even as she derided herself for being an emotional coward, something inside her would not allow the words out. She couldn't risk being more vulnerable than she already felt with him.

She stared unseeingly at the carved headboard. Admitting her love for him would carry an additional risk, as well, she thought gloomily. Most likely it would send him backing away from her so fast that he would stop traffic. She knew how he felt about commitment. He'd certainly sent out enough warning signals.

So what did his behavior today mean? she asked herself confusedly. He'd certainly seemed jealous of James. He wasn't an obsessive man, he wasn't mean-spirited, so surely that pointed toward him harboring something other than territorial feelings for her.

She shook her head in mingled frustration and puzzlement. The man was more complex than a maze. And as much as she tried in the next few hours, she didn't feel any closer than before to figuring him out.

A couple of hours of intense physical exercise hadn't dimmed Connor's frustration at all. If anything, they had heightened it. Afterward he'd been just as frustrated, but also exhausted and sweaty. Finally he'd called it quits and taken a quick shower. But even that had failed to calm him. He lay wide-eyed in bed for too long before muttering a curse and sitting up. Reaching for the tux pants he'd worn earlier, he pulled them on carelessly before padding barefoot to the living room.

He crossed to his stereo and squatted down on his heels, flipping quickly through the selection of CDs on the shelf below. He selected one that suited his mood and put it in, turning on the power and lowering the volume simultaneously. He opened up the living-room drapes, allowing the light from the full moon to spill unencumbered into the small room. Pulling up a chair, he sank back into it as the low mournful wails of a saxophone came from the stereo. He listened to the music with one ear as he stared out into the night.

He'd screwed up royally tonight, he admitted sourly. He was uncomfortable with the acknowledgment, and even more uncomfortable with the panic that welled up inside him at the thought. He'd never been this primordial with a woman before, willing to go to such lengths to protect her. Only Michele could rouse this kind of incomprehensible emotion in him.

Michele. He gazed unseeingly into the night as he grappled with her specter in his thoughts. He was completely unsure of himself with her, and that scared him to death. He had always been the cool one, the one who held on to his emotions with a tight rein and walked away easily when a relationship threatened to get sticky. Yet walking away from Michele was the one thing he didn't want to contemplate, the one thing that terrified him. Even more terrifying was the possibility of her walking away from him. Something besides logic told him that if that happened, he wouldn't be cool and emotionless.

He shook his head wryly. It was all well and good for him to tell himself that he was going to keep his distance, not let her get to him. He'd been kidding himself all along, allowing himself to believe that he'd ever really had any control over his reaction to her.

The truth was, he admitted, his thoughts as morose as the shadows outside, he had never had any power at all over his behavior toward her. Michele Easton had hit him like a ton of bricks, and his every word, his every action, had been dictated by his reaction to her. It was time to cut the thoughts of emotional damage control. There was no such thing with her. She'd gotten to him the first time he'd laid eyes on her. He'd fallen faster, harder, than ever before in his life, and he had probably been the last one to realize it.

That didn't change anything, though, he thought gloomily. And the sooner he talked to Michele about this, the better off both of them would be. It was still the best thing for her to get as far away from him as soon as possible. The case was winding down; he could feel that with every instinct he had. It wouldn't be long now before the danger to her was over and she was back in her own home, in her own life.

Once things were back to normal she would be able to step back and look at things more clearly. And when she did, he was sure she would be appalled at how involved she had gotten with him. Connor would make damn sure he was long gone by the time she reached that conclusion.

Deep in thought, he was startled by a sound behind him and rose instinctively, turning. Michele stood there observing him silently, wrapped in a starkly white terry bathrobe. At the sight of the object of his musings, he stared, suddenly tongue-tied.

Michele spoke first. "I couldn't sleep."

Connor cleared his throat. "Me either."

She gestured toward the hallway with one hand. "I thought I would take a shower."

Though no answer was required, something forced Connor to speak. "Go right ahead."

Michele made no move, unable to tear her eyes away from the sight he made. The bright light of the moon silhouetted him against the window, gilding his bright hair while leaving much of his body draped in shadows. With one of night's tricks of light and shadow, the moonlight reflected off his bright head, creating a surreal halo effect.

Yet there was nothing in the least angelic about him. He much more resembled a modern day Lucifer, the devil of temptation. Lean, hard and sexily dangerous, he wore only his unbuttoned tuxedo trousers. They rode tantalizingly low on his lean hips, and her heart tripped alarmingly at the sight. She was mesmerized by the ribbon of silky hair that meandered teasingly down past his navel and disappeared in the unfastened pants. She remembered too well the softness of that hair, what it felt like under her wandering fingertips.

She pulled her eyes away with difficulty and turned jerkily to flee to the bathroom. If she stayed much longer she was very much afraid that she would forget how furious she was with him tonight.

Seeing her turn away, Connor felt panic well up. This was his chance to talk to her. But what came out of his mouth wasn't in the least diplomatic.

"So, have you gotten over your sulking?"

As she froze at his words, he mentally groaned. Obviously that hadn't been the most sensible way to detain her. He wouldn't be able to talk sense to her if he got her mad all over again.

When she finally answered, her tone was precise. "I was *not,*" she stressed, "sulking."

Connor gave a mental shrug. At least they were communicating. He let amusement creep into his tone. "No?"

Darned if she didn't feel like smacking him again! Michele strove to respond calmly. "You're mistaking emotional restraint for sulking. I was merely endeavoring to allow us both the time we needed before discussing your boorish behavior."

"No time like the present," he invited.

Michele's eyes widened, then narrowed at his flippancy. "All right," she agreed, moving toward him until she met him almost nose to nose. Gray eyes spat sparks into green. "Why don't we start with you? Would you like to explain what motivated you to behave like such an utter lout tonight?"

She glared at him, their faces close together. One electrically charged moment passed, then another. Finally Connor cleared his throat and asked, "Ahhh...could you be more specific?"

Michele ground her teeth. "Fine, Connor, how about if we start with the fact that you intruded into the ladies' room and put on your Lieutenant Bunko act? Those ladies probably think I'm a felon!"

His lips twitched at the memory. "I think most of those ladies had a very clear idea of what your 'crime' was."

"And then there was what you said to James," she went on, mastering the barely audible tremble in her voice. "How could you?"

At the hurt so apparent in her eyes, in her voice, Connor knew the time for flippancy was over. He responded simply, "Jealousy."

Michele gaped at him, but his eyes continued to meet hers steadily. "You...I...what?" she sputtered in disbelief.

Connor reached toward her and picked up the tie of her robe. He flicked it back and forth. "You heard me, Princess. I was jealous. You must have had a clue, after all." He slanted a glance at her. "Isn't that why you paid such close attention to me all evening?"

Despite her earlier anger, Michele was disarmed by his honesty. "No," she replied softly, with equal candor.

"No?" He cocked a brow at her.

She shook her head and continued bravely. "I wanted you to know how much I wanted to be with you. To show you how much you mean to me."

Connor squeezed his eyes tightly closed at the sweep of emotion that followed her words. She was so open, so giving, and he didn't deserve her. And she damn sure didn't deserve a bastard like him.

"You shouldn't feel anything for me, Michele. It would be better that way."

Michele's lips trembled at his words. She had known, of course, that any indication of her feelings would send him running. But somehow that didn't make it any easier for her to listen to this.

"I'm not the kind of man you need. Tonight should have shown you that. I don't fit into that pretty, glittery world we were in for a few hours. That was pretty obvious."

"Yes," she whispered, almost to herself. But not the way he thought. He seemed to think that a lack of wealth and a prep-school education were what set him apart from the other men who'd been there tonight. He couldn't be further from the truth. He was a world unto himself. He immediately drew eyes, and not only the women's. Men, too, seemed to recognize the air of authority, the hard edge of experience. And the invisible sexuality that radiated from him was impossible for anyone to ignore.

Connor swallowed hard at her slight sound of agreement. "You belong in that kind of life." He forestalled her protest, even as she opened her mouth. "Even if you weren't born to the privileged upbringing I had assumed, everyone can see what kind of woman you are."

"And what kind is that?" A chill skittered down Michele's spine in anticipation of his answer.

One hand slid up into the ebony fall of hair she had released earlier. "Classy," his husky voice whispered. "Refined." His finger slid in a slow caress down her jawbone. "Elegant. The kind of woman who should have caviar and expensive foreign champagne. Opera, ballet, symphony." He shrugged. "All that high-brow stuff." He used the tie on her robe to draw her closer and wrapped his arms around her, burying his face in her hair. "Me, I'm a simple guy. Give me a pizza, beer and a fast-paced 76er's game, and I'm happy. You deserve better."

Michele's arms crept around his bare waist even as she asked, mystified, "Better than what?"

His lips buried themselves in her hair of their own volition. "Than me," he muttered.

But he was so wrong, her mind cried out. He had been all the support she needed, all she wanted, for the past few weeks. He had made her greedy, wanting more even as she knew how impossible that would be. She would never have enough of him, and she was fiercely, suddenly angry that he could dismiss her so easily. She knew he cared, damn it. Why wouldn't he admit it? And why, oh, why, would he not let her be the one to decide if that could be enough for her?

When he said nothing else, Michele murmured, "McLain?"

A muffled "Hmm?" was her answer.

"You're a good cop, aren't you?"

His head rose slowly, warily, to train those glinting hawk eyes in her direction, but he didn't answer.

It was surprisingly easy to continue, even with that unwavering stare fixed on her. She had nothing to lose, not when he was ready to let her down anyway. "You must be. You're awfully young to be a lieutenant."

"So?"

Michele plowed on. He wasn't making this easy for her, but she knew the time was coming when he would try to walk out of her life, so she wasn't going to make it easy on him, either. "So a lot of people had to have faith in you for you to make it as far as you have. They must have believed in you." A heartbeat pause there. Then she went on, her voice as soft as a butterfly's kiss. "Trusted you."

His brows lowered at her words. "What's your point, Michele?"

"My point—" she kissed his chiseled chin consideringly before dropping a chain of kisses along his jaw "—is that you're a worthy man, Connor McLain. Worthy of those medals lining your shelf, worthy of the commendations that I'll bet fill your folder at work." His quick grimace told her she'd been right about that. "You have so much to give, Connor. Why do you believe that the only thing you have that's worth giving is in your professional life?"

"Because that's all there is," he asserted bleakly. Why couldn't she just take his word on that? Why did she have to push for more? Want more? And why did she have to make him want the same?

"I won't make it simple for you to walk away from me," she whispered fiercely, wanting to shake him. "I love you, Connor. I haven't asked you for anything. Let me be the judge of what I need in my life."

He closed his eyes at the tidal wave of emotion that swept over him at her words. Never had he experienced such unqualified acceptance from a woman, and it was heady. But love wasn't something he could accept from this woman, even if he wanted to. He bent his head then and fixed his lips to hers, meaning the kiss to be gentle, a prelude to their inevitable parting. But although it started out that way, he quickly lost control. Their mouths twisted together passionately, lips fierce, tongues wildly mating. When Connor finally pulled away, their breathing was choppy. He scooped a startled Michele up in his arms and strode toward the hallway.

Michele was disoriented by his abrupt breaking off of their kiss. Even more dizzying was finding herself in his arms, clasped against his bare chest. "Connor," she murmured, one long-fingered hand threading through the long hair at his nape. "Where are you taking me?"

"You wanted a shower, didn't you?" he questioned huskily, even as they entered the small bathroom. He put her on her feet, but one arm kept her close to him. Michele found that she didn't mind. She leaned on him, watching bemusedly as he turned on the water and adjusted the temperature.

Satisfied, he turned his full attention back to her. He reached toward her and untied her robe, pushing it off her shoulders and letting it fall to the floor. His eyes swept her form hungrily; he was suddenly anxious to touch her again, to possess her. Maybe then he would be able to convince himself that she was real.

Michele shuddered as he brought her close again and her achingly taut nipples were caught in his chest hair. Her hands closed on his biceps, and she leaned forward and bit one earlobe teasingly. "That's right," she purred with the intimate certainty that came from knowing she was loved, "I'm going to take a shower. The question is, what are *you* going to do?" She ran one finger down his chest lingeringly before twisting nimbly away and stepped into the shower, closing the door behind her.

She stepped under the spray, a small smile tilting her lips as she raised her face to the warm spray, letting it cascade over her face, soaking her. Connor had seemed frozen at her action, and she wondered in anticipation at his next move. She didn't have long to wait. The door opened, and her next teasing comment remained unspoken on her lips.

Connor stepped into the small enclosure and pulled the door shut after him. Immediately his presence filled the small space and made Michele totally aware of him. "You forgot the soap," he said in a gravelly voice, one hand holding a fresh bar out to her. He was still in his tux pants, and Michele laughed, then gasped as he stepped forward and pressed her against the cool tiles.

"I think you forgot something," she managed to utter as his warm lips branded her neck. "Most people undress to take a shower."

By this time he was as soaked as she was, and he reached up to wipe his wet hair back from his forehead. "That's true," he agreed, a wicked note in his voice, "but I felt it imperative to point out an appalling lack in your bathroom etiquette."

It was decidedly difficult to try for a casually interested tone when his mouth was diligently attempting to scoop up the rivulets of water cascading down her neck, but Michele did her best. "And you decided to eradicate that void in my education while half-dressed," she managed in a halfway serious tone.

"But that's the problem, sweetheart," he answered, pushing his hips against her. Michele gasped at the feel of the hard ridge of masculinity reined in by the dress pants. "When someone undresses you, it's common courtesy to return the favor. So I'm here to let you do...just...that...." His breath hissed out as Michele allowed one curious hand to explore his hardness.

Michele could no more keep from touching him than she could stop breathing. Her eyelids were inexplicably heavy, and she surveyed the picture he made with the water sluicing over him. The trousers, although completely modest when dry, were as erotic as a g-string when soaked as they were now. The wet black pants were molded to him, delineating every muscle in his legs and highlighting with intimate detail each centimeter of his manhood. Michele swallowed. Her hand continued its adventurous exploration and her other hand joined it, then released the zipper slowly.

Connor's groan sounded ragged in her ear, but she didn't let that deter her from reaching for him, freeing him from the trousers and cradling him in both hands. She caressed him wonderingly, amazed at the strength and sensuality encased in that velvety hardness. But her musings were cut short as Connor rasped, "Take them off, Michele."

Her gaze tore away from her hands to mesh with his glittering one. "Undress me," he begged huskily.

And she complied. The pants were soaked to his skin and had to be peeled down, and Michele did so, an inch at a time. She knelt on the shower floor to aid in her duty, and the stance put her lips on a level with his throbbing staff.

Connor swallowed hard, but his narrowed gaze never left her. Inch by methodical inch the trousers descended, Michele's hands helping their journey, and her mouth, dear Lord, her mouth was just a fraction away from where he would give a year's salary to feel it. He was barely aware of stepping out of the pants, because in the next moment his dream came true and those pink lips began tracing his masculinity.

Michele explored his strong length with her lips and tongue, licking away the streams of water, an endless task, as the shower continued to provide more. Long minutes passed until Connor couldn't stand it any longer and with two hard hands pulled her up and fastened his mouth to hers savagely.

All finesse was gone, the thought of control laughable. He pressed her against the tiled wall, wanting to brand her with his body. And Michele reveled in it. She couldn't get close enough; she couldn't feel enough. His mouth was everywhere and had a direct relation to her ability to stand. His warm avid tongue swirled the droplets from her nipples, then paused to suck deeply, causing Michele to cry out at the sharp sensation. One hand smoothed her flat stomach and tangled in the silky wet hair at the juncture of her thighs. His intemperate desire ignited her own, and she cried out at the exploring finger he sent inside her.

"Connor," she moaned, almost incoherent with need. But she didn't have to be more direct, because Connor knew exactly what she wanted. What they both wanted. He placed both hands beneath her bottom and lifted her against the tile. Her legs encircled his waist, and he entered her with a surge that drew a moan from both of them.

"You're so hot, Michele, so damn tight," he gasped, his hands at her hips directing their movement. His eyes were slitted open, and he watched in savage enjoyment as Michele reacted in pleasure. Her dark hair lay against her back in a satin ribbon, and her perfect features were twisted in pleasure. She looked like a pagan princess.

Michele's back arched away from the wall, and he drew one nipple into his mouth. And then it was too much for both of them. He pressed her to the wall again, her legs tight around him, and thrust up inside her again and again until they both cried out in unison.

Long moments later Michele became aware that the water running over them was cold. Connor released her, and she slid slowly to the floor, grateful that he didn't completely let go of her, because her knees threatened to buckle at any moment. She leaned against him weakly as he soaped his hands and moved them surely, lingeringly over her. Unbelievably, she felt the first stirrings of desire again.

Connor reached around her and shut off the shower, pushing open the door and drawing her out. One large towel was placed around her, and he handed her another for her hair. She blotted the dampness from her head bemusedly as she watched him tousle his own hair dry with a towel and carelessly run a hand through it. Then, without a word, he scooped her up again and walked back to his bedroom. When he deposited her on his bed they made love again silently, each afraid of where words would take them.

When Michele woke up it was almost dawn, and her teeth were clamped so tightly on her bottom lip she could taste the blood they had drawn there. So cold—she was so cold. Shaking, she reached up with one hand to brush away the tears that had flowed down her cheeks while she slept. And dreamed.

Connor lay on his back, still asleep, and Michele endeavored to still the shaking of her limbs. The blanket was trapped under Connor's hip, and after a couple of ineffectual tries she stopped trying to free it. The last thing she wanted to do was wake him now, but she had to get warm, had to stop the memories of the dream that even now sent fresh blades of ice down her spine.

She forced herself to move limbs that seemed wooden, taking no orders from her. A scalding shower would be the best thing for her, but she didn't even leave the bed before Connor's arm snaked around her waist. Michele sat on the edge of the bed, her breath trapped in her lungs. She didn't turn to face him; she couldn't let him see the terror she knew was stamped on her face.

"Michele?" His voice was raspy with sleep, but she didn't fool herself into thinking that his mind wasn't alert. She didn't answer, was unsure if she could. Her throat felt raw, as if the screams she had dreamed had in fact emanated from it.

No explanation was needed, though. Connor pulled her back against his chest and with one long arm swept the blanket around her, cradling her in a warm cocoon. Then, with both arms firmly around her middle, he asked quietly, "What was it?"

"Blood." She spoke rawly, and both of them reacted to the hoarse, hollow ring of the word. She continued, her voice choked with tears. "Scarlet streamers across a shirt, puddling on a dirty plank floor." Her voice caught, and when it continued, it had the shaky, plaintive tone of a child. "It runs across the filthy floor and drips through the cracks between the planks."

Connor frowned fiercely, his arms tightening protectively around her. "It's all right," he said savagely. "We're getting closer. Michele, we're going to find those children, I promise. We'll find them before another one gets hurt," he vowed.

Michele's head turned then, slowly, wearily, and when she looked over her shoulder into his determined gaze, his jaw clenched at the mirrored emptiness in her eyes. But her next words had him forgetting even that.

"It's not their blood, Connor. It's yours."

Chapter 16

Michele didn't slam down the phone receiver, but it was dropped with a decided ring of frustration. A heavy sigh broke from her, and her pencil tapped the top of her desk consideringly.

Cruz hadn't been much more help than Connor, though she shouldn't have expected anything else. He'd mouthed the same platitudes she'd already heard. About Connor's years of experience on the force. His training, his caution.

Damn! Her pencil broke with the sudden ferocity with which she slammed it against the desk. Why were both of those men so bull-headed? Why did neither of them believe that danger was closing in on Connor with the deliberate certainty of a noose?

Connor had been unmoved by her fear for his safety, Michele remembered morosely. His concern had all been for her, for her peace of mind, her feelings. Why, oh, why, couldn't he spare some of that concern for himself?

"Because it's my job, Michele," he had told her that morning. His voice had been unyielding, despite the warm shelter his arms had still provided for her. "I'm not going to take any foolish risks. I never do. This case is winding down. I can feel it. We know there are at least two people involved in this. It's only a matter of time until we find them."

Michele had known it was useless to try to push Connor any further. He would do what he saw as his job and in the process be killed.

Michele swallowed hard and folded her arms around herself at the thought. If only she could have seen more in that dream last night. As usual, she damned it for the lack of real information it had brought her. Each dream focused on one piece of the puzzle, the rest of the background fading to rippling underwater images. She might not have convinced Connor of his imminent danger, but *she* was certain of it. Just as certain as she was despairing that there was nothing she could do about it.

Or was there?

Her arms tightened. She was suddenly struck with the memory of the episode with Bruce Casel. Under hypnotism Michele had been able to recall information about one of the vehicles that she hadn't remembered from the dream. Was it possible? Was there a chance...?

Goose bumps broke out on her arms, and she rubbed them vigorously. Just the thought of voluntarily reliving those nightmares filled her with dread, but she examined the possibility nevertheless. She had spent her entire life shutting those images out of her conscious thoughts, relegating them to the shadows of her subconscious. Did she have it within her power now to reverse the practices of a lifetime, to invite the images out to be examined minutely?

She raised a shaky hand to push back a tendril of hair. She wasn't sure it was possible. She didn't know whether she had the capability or the strength, but she had to try. Anything was worth the price if it meant protecting Connor. She had been unable to shake off the feeling of impending doom hovering over them since last night.

"Michele, what is it? What's wrong?" Julie's concerned voice tore through Michele's thoughts, and she raised startled eyes to her secretary. She had been so deep in thought that she hadn't even noticed Julie's entrance.

Julie's wheelchair made a gentle whirring noise as it approached Michele's desk. Michele summoned up a shaky smile to reassure her friend, but the sight of Julie's frown told her that she'd failed. "Michele? Are you sick?"

Michele pushed her hair away from her face and spoke reassuringly. "No, of course not. Why do you ask?"

Julie eyed her skeptically. "Well, your face is completely colorless and you're trembling. Do you have the chills? There's been a lot of flu going around lately, you know."

Michele shook her head. "I didn't know," she murmured, suddenly aware that her secretary had just handed her a perfect excuse. "But you may be right. I have been feeling a little shaky this morning." That was certainly no falsehood, she told herself grimly. She pushed aside the guilt she felt at deceiving her friend.

Her foremost concern was Connor, and she suddenly realized that she wouldn't have a chance of even trying her plan in the evening, when he was home. And if she did remember a real clue, when was she ever going to have time to check it out? Between Connor and Cruz she was never alone, outside of work, so the only possible time she would have for this was during the day. When she wasn't working.

While Connor thought she was sick.

She raised her eyes slowly to her secretary's concerned face.

"All right, I'm not going to hear any arguments." Julie spoke authoritatively. "You, Michele Easton, are going straight home and to bed." Michele made a show of reluctance but allowed Julie to bully her into collecting her coat and purse. "Don't worry about a thing, I'll reschedule your appointments for the day, and you can give me a call tomorrow and let me know how you feel, okay?"

"You're wonderful, Julie," Michele said sincerely, even as she was being ushered out of the office. "But I...I didn't drive today. Could you call me a cab?" Julie picked up the phone and began dialing even as Michele spoke. "And I will call tomorrow morning, okay?" Shooed off by her secretary's wave, she let herself out of the office and almost bumped into James in the hallway.

He grasped her elbows and peered concernedly into her face. "Michele, what is it?"

Mentally groaning, she mustered up a wan smile. "Julie's called me a cab. I'm feeling a little under the weather."

James studied her face soberly without letting go of her.

She gently but firmly pulled her elbows from his grasp. "I'm sure it's nothing serious. Maybe just that flu going around. At any rate, a day or two of aspirin and rest should take care of it."

Her babbling didn't appease the worried look on James's face. A frown furrowed his brow, and then he cleared his throat. "Michele I know this is a touchy subject, but are you sure the problem is physical?"

Michele sent him a puzzled glance. "What are you talking about, James?"

He gentled his tone. "Just that physical maladies are often a product of emotional or psychological distress. Perhaps something in your life is causing this. Perhaps..." He paused for a moment. "Perhaps it's Connor McLain."

For a moment Michele's mind froze. How could he know about her fear for Connor's safety? But as his cultured voice continued on, she quickly regained her equilibrium. Of course he wasn't addressing the image of Connor's death that was haunting her. He was talking about the same thing he always harped about...Connor's lack of suitability for her. Her temper seethed as he used his years of experience as an examiner of other people's relationships to dissect, uninvited, what he thought of theirs.

"James?" Her voice had a ring of authority, bringing him to a halt as he cocked his head inquiringly.

"Just stuff it, would you?" And she turned to march toward the front door, where her cab had just glided to a stop, leaving James to gape after her.

Once she was back at Connor's house she stood indecisively in the living room. Although she wasn't at all sure how to go about this, she imagined that the best idea would be to duplicate to the best of her ability the relaxed state she had been brought to before Bruce had hypnotized her. She wished for just one of the countless antistress tapes she had at home before she headed toward Connor's entertainment center.

She put on a soothing classical piece before settling on the sofa. Starting at her toes and working up, she consciously willed each separate muscle group to relax. She remained motionless, eyes closed for several minutes.

Nothing. Her eyes snapped open. What was she doing wrong? Glancing down, she saw one hand knotted on her lap. With a grimace she unclenched her fist. Obviously she wasn't as relaxed as she had thought.

She started again, resolutely releasing each separate part of her body, emptying her mind, allowing herself to be open to...anything.

The music stopped long before Michele finally opened her eyes. She heaved a sigh of defeat. It was clear that this wasn't going to work, at least, not right now. Apparently years of suppressing her dreams had become a habit, a defense mechanism that would be difficult, if not impossible, to change in a single afternoon. If ever.

Admitting defeat for the day, she stood and headed for the bathroom. And refused to put a name to the tiny flicker of relief she felt.

The hot spray felt heavenly on her body, completing her earlier attempt at relaxation. When she finally turned off the water and stepped out, her body felt almost boneless. She actually craved a nap, but she worked at tidying up the bathroom first.

The blinds on the room's single window sent splinters of sunlight across the steamed mirror. Michele used her towel to wipe it off. Although at home she was just as likely to leave a mess and then whirlwind through the house later, tidying it up, she didn't feel comfortable doing that here. After all, this was Connor's...

...blood, dripping off the mirror, into her hands. She pulled her hands back reflexively, staring at them in horror, before raising unseeing eyes back to the sun-mottled mirror. But it wasn't the mirror she saw before her; it was dust motes dancing in the rays that made it through a boarded up window. Connor lay on the dirty floor, his torso haloed in one brilliant ray. Michele was on her knees beside him, and her hands were covered with the blood soaking his shirt and pooling on the floor. Terror warred with nausea, and for one instant she thought she would be sick.

She forced herself to continue with the image, to make it finally work for her. She watched herself get up and walk to the window, then peer out one of the cracks. She forced her focus away from the most horrible aspect and concentrated on making the other, more surreal, images real. She made herself see the gravel road in front of the building, the cracked bell, the farms in the distance and the woods to the left. She made herself look, listen to the sound of water in the background, observe....

Michele felt her knees give out beneath her, and one shaking hand sought the countertop to steady herself. She sank to the floor, arms wrapped around herself, rocking a little to calm the shaking and the icebergs bumping through her veins. After a long while she stood on legs that were still wobbly and forced herself to move to the bedroom and get dressed. And as she dressed she planned her strategy. For she now had a location of sorts to look for. This place, whatever it was, was obviously located in the countryside.

Finished dressing, she grabbed her purse and coat and headed toward the door. Operation Save Connor McLain was now in progress.

Three days later Michele pulled off what seemed like the one thousandth gravel road she'd traveled. She was in a small park. She knew without looking further that this spot, too, was a dead end. Though it was lightly wooded and near a river, there were no buildings in sight. She turned off the engine and reached for the stack of maps at her side.

She chafed at the feeling of desperate hurry that seemed a permanent part of her these days. It seemed as if she barely got started each day before she needed to turn around. Each day she needed to drive back to the city, wash the day's dust from the car and carefully park it in exactly the same spot in front of Connor's house before he was due back from the station.

She felt guilty each morning when she called in to work, letting Julie continue to worry about her. But that was nothing compared to the guilt she felt each night when Connor came home. His concern for her was apparent. He solicitously cared for her, tending to her fake illness, and the slight frown on his brow as he did so made Michele feel like the worst kind of phony. But it also solidified her resolve to keep this man safe from harm.

She rested her forehead against the steering wheel. There was nothing else to do. She was going to have to walk through those nightmares again, trying once again to get one more clue, the one that would turn her in the right direction.

She had gotten better at that with practice. She now had a clear picture of the place where the children were being held. She could easily picture it in her mind now, but she still had to find it! She forced herself into the mode she had perfected in the past three days. Gradually she opened her mind to all possibilities, pushing aside the curtains of caution, of fear. She could feel the specters lurking in her subconscious, prowling the edges like slavering jackals, evil lurking animals of prey waiting for her to lower her guard so they could pounce on her very sanity. She tore at the cloak of her defenses and concentrated on emptying her mind, studying the way the sun dappled through the leaves of a nearby tree, painting the ground beneath with flirtatious shadows...

...the sun's rays made fervent attempts to spread their brilliance, spilling through the cracks of the boarded up windows. Michele made her specter walk to that window again and look out. Ignore the horror, ignore the pain and evil choking the air. Look out through the cracks between the boards and see...

Michele's head snapped to the side, and she screamed faintly as the door on the driver's side opened. Her hands over her mouth, she looked up at Connor in shock, still so caught up in what she'd just seen that she couldn't be sure if he was real or a player in the vision she'd just witnessed. She wasn't left in doubt long. The stream of curses flowing from his mouth assured her that he was indeed very real. And utterly furious.

He ducked and slid into the car, and Michele moved over, to avoid being landed on. He glared at her ashen face for a tense, silent second before snarling, "Surprised to see me?"

Leaning against the far window, endeavoring to calm her image-induced shaking, Michele finally regained her breath. "What are you doing here, Connor?"

He stared hard at her before raising his hands and rolling his eyes. "What am *I* doing here? No, Princess, I think you have that all wrong. The million-dollar question is, what the hell are *you* doing here?" He ended on a roar, eyes blazing at her. "And don't try to tell me that you went for a drive," he sneered. "Somehow, I don't think I'll quite buy it."

"I wasn't going to say that," Michele inserted quietly.

His mouth clamped shut for a moment, the muscle clenching in his jaw attesting to his restraint. After a moment he spoke, his voice controlled. "I was really concerned about you, Michele, you know that? When I thought you were ill, I was afraid that all this had been too traumatic for you, that maybe your body had finally had enough, you know?"

Michele dropped her eyes guiltily.

"So you can imagine how hard it was for me to allow myself to see, really see, what was going on. To make myself wonder at the fact that your car was never in exactly the same spot when I got home at night."

Michele's eyes flew to his in shock. He was watching for her reaction. "It was close, mind you," he continued. "Just close enough to look like someone was trying to put it in the same place. And it was always so damn clean." He paused for a moment, but Michele stubbornly stayed silent. After a minute he went on. "Add to that the fact that I could never reach you during the day. What was that you told me?" he asked rhetorically. "Ah, yes, you wanted to sleep," he stressed the word, "and unplugged the phone so it wouldn't wake you. How could you go on lying to me like that, Michele?"

When she finally spoke, Michele's words were stark. "I was trying to keep you alive. I hated deceiving you. I did," she insisted at his snort of disbelief. "But it was necessary. You would have tried to stop me if I had told you the truth."

His green eyes shot sparks at her. "Damn right I would have, because I've been trying to protect you from the wacko who was behind those incidents at your house, and you make that real damn hard to do when you...are not...where...you are supposed to be!"

"And *I* am trying to protect *you!*" Michele cried passionately. "Why is it that my motives are any less lofty? I want you safe!" she exclaimed vehemently.

His face softened at her words but quickly grew grim again as she went on. "And I'll do anything I can to keep you alive. If it means lying to you, I'll do it. And if it means finding the kidnapper's lair before the police do, I'll do that, too."

"And exactly how did you intend to go about that?" drawled Connor dangerously, but Michele refused to answer. His gaze fell to the floor of the car, and he reached down and grabbed the stack of maps that had been pushed there in Michele's hasty slide across the seat. "Parks and Rec, Agricultural Services, Office of Tourism." He flipped through them before eyeing her balefully. "You were quite the busy little girl, weren't you?" He dodged her attempt to grab them away and shook out first one and then another, intently studying the markings she'd made on them.

After several minutes he raised his eyes. "Seems like you've been withholding some information, Michele," he said quietly. "You knew I've had men looking for days for the building you described. Or are you going to tell me you have no particular reason to be looking for a wooded place in the country, near water?"

Michele sighed in resignation. As much as she damned his intense powers of observation, they were a part of him, probably an important part of why he was such a good detective. And they were all she could count on now to keep him alive. "I've seen it clearly." She spoke with a sigh. "I think I can find it. I know I'll recognize it when I see it."

Connor sat silent for several moments, his mind racing furiously. The first thing he wanted to do was to get her the hell away from here and tuck her away someplace where she would be safe. But even as he acknowledged that wish, he knew it would be impossible. Michele had proven in the past few days that she couldn't be trusted to stay put and let him do the police work. And the last thing he needed right now was to be constantly distracted by wondering where she was and what she was doing.

If Michele was on to something here, and he was forced to admit that there was a strong possibility she was, he needed her, at least until she was able to find the place. Once that was done, he would find his own way to keep her out of harm's way.

"All right," he decided, and Michele gaped at him.

"All right?" she questioned faintly, but his head was buried once again in the maps. "All right what?"

"You can help find the place where they're holding the kids." Her brief surge of elation that she wasn't going to have to fight him on this anymore was squelched by his stern look and next words. "But we do this my way. Once we do find it, you will stay well out of the way. Understood?"

"*If*," she stressed the word, "I decide to do as you say, will you promise to wait for backup before you go in to search the place?" At his silence, her alarm grew. "Connor! I want you to promise."

He sighed and eyed her soberly. "You know I can't promise you that, Michele."

If anything more lethal than a pile of maps had been handy, she would have thrown it at his stubborn head. "Then I refuse," she said haughtily.

It was Connor's turn to gape. "You what?"

Michele sniffed. "You heard me. I refuse. I won't help you. And I'll slip away every chance I get and continue searching on my own."

Connor's hands crumpled the maps as his fists clenched. It had been a while since he'd seen that haughty mask descend over those perfect features and heard that snooty tone, but it still had the power to rouse his instant ire. "You won't refuse, Princess," he crooned softly. "Because if I can't be sure you'll stay put, I'll throw you in a cell for obstruction of justice, and you can just explain that to your dear colleague."

Michele's frosty gray eyes changed to simmering coals. "You wouldn't," her voice dared.

"Try me," he invited flatly. Green eyes glared into gray. It was Michele who looked away first. After a long silence she spoke, her voice soft. "I'm so afraid for you, Connor."

His voice was just as quiet. "So you know how I feel about you. Work with me on this, Michele. I have the manpower to find the place eventually, but with you, I can find it a lot faster. You don't want to subject those kids to any extra moments of hell, I know. All right?"

"All right," she murmured in resignation. Vibrant between them was the understanding that she had never received the promise she had asked for.

Connor's perusal turned back to the maps. "These X'ed areas have already been checked?" At her nod, he asked, "Did you have any special reason to start where you did?"

Michele hesitated. Finally she replied simply, "I had to start somewhere."

Connor nodded. "We'll leave your car here for now and take mine." He got out of the car with the maps in his hand, and Michele followed more slowly. "We'll probably start northwest of the district," he continued, spreading a map over the hood of his car as he planned, "because that's the general area in which most of the kidnappings occurred. If the kidnapper continued in that direction, that would put the place right about in here." He indicated a section on the map. "Doesn't look like you've started looking there yet."

Michele continued past him, around the car. She opened the door and slid in without a word. As she stared sightlessly out the window, she couldn't prevent the feeling that Connor's plan would take him to his own death.

After several hours driving around the scenic countryside, Michele couldn't remember a single trait she had ever found attractive in Connor

McLain. She was tired, she was thirsty and she had found answering nature's call in the tall grassy ditch next to the road humiliating.

Connor was undoubtedly feeling the same frustration, and obviously adversity didn't bring out the best in him. He was sarcastic and downright surly. As the afternoon waned and they still found nothing, his mood worsened.

Michele complained querulously, "For goodness' sakes, Connor, let's pack it in for the day. I'm tired, and I want something to eat and a long hot bath. And I don't know about you, Attila, but the next time I have to go, I'd like to use a rest room."

"Well, look into your crystal ball," he baited back, "and see if you can at least find one of those anywhere around here."

Michele told him in short graphic terms where she would put her crystal ball if she had one, and they continued to drive in silence for a while.

At last Connor spoke. "Well, if nothing else, we've gotten to see a lot of the countryside. Hell, tourists pay good money to come to Pennsylvania and drive through country like this. Maybe you should have brought your camera." At her silence he glanced over at her, and the sight of the frozen expression on her face instantly alarmed him. "Michele, what is it? Michele?" He reached over and touched her still arm. "You're like ice," he muttered as he steered the car to the side of the road and stopped. He turned to her again. "Michele, honey, are you okay?"

Michele looked at the landscape ahead of her as though memorizing it, but that wasn't really necessary. She knew without using her eyes what she would see in front of her. The little farm lay nestled snugly in the distance, flanked by rolling hills. And to their right... She knew already what lay ahead of that stand of trees. She could feel the evil, even if she couldn't see the building itself yet. She felt the hopelessness, the despair, of the children, and something else, something with an almost familiar air about it.

Connor stared hard in the direction where her eyes were focused and suddenly knew without any words from her what was wrong. Despite the warmth outside, he threw the heater on full blast, his only concession to what Michele was feeling, and drove on.

A quarter mile up the road he stopped again. He didn't need to ask for Michele's confirmation; she had described this place too well on too many occasions for him to be unsure about what they had found. He radioed the state police for backup. Then he turned to Michele.

Her gray eyes were wide with terror, and he hated to leave her, but he had to. "It looks deserted," she whispered, staring out at the dilapidated building. And it did. It had obviously been decades since it had served in its original function as a one-room schoolhouse for neighboring farm families. The bell in front was cracked and hung crookedly from its crossbar. The windows were boarded up, and Michele's eyes were drawn irresistibly to the one she had looked out in her dreams. The crack between the boards was there, just as she had known it would be.

"Give me your hand," Connor ordered, and Michele tore her eyes away to turn them to him in confusion, even as she obeyed. As he drew out a pair of handcuffs she guessed his intention too late and frantically tried to withdraw, but he held her hand tightly and snapped one of the bracelets over her wrist and locked it.

"What are you doing?" she demanded.

"Making sure you stay put," he told her imperturbably as he latched the other cuff to the steering wheel. He slipped the key in his pocket. "I'm going to take a look around," he told her as he slipped from the car.

"Connor, no!" Michele implored. "Wait for the others, please. Connor!" She was speaking to his retreating back. She drew a deep breath as she watched him draw his gun and approach the building in a crouched position. He disappeared around one corner, and Michele slammed her free hand against the steering wheel. She waited anxiously for long minutes, but Connor didn't reappear. Peering down the road, she couldn't see any oncoming vehicles, and she knew that it would still be a while before help would reach them.

She yanked ineffectually at the cuff, which held firm. Then she eyed it skeptically. She was small-boned, and it just might be possible....

After several more minutes she gave up. Try as she might, she was unable to worm her hand through the opening. She slumped back in the seat for a minute, then sat up in renewed determination. She reached over with her free hand and opened the glove compartment. She rummaged through the full compartment as best she could, but she didn't find another set of cuffs or another key. That didn't stop her, however. She got down on the floor on one knee and contorted her body so that her free hand was able to search under the front seat.

She grunted in discomfort. She obviously wasn't as flexible as she had thought. Her hand moved under the passenger seat in vain. It was a bit more difficult to search under the driver's seat. She finally had to turn her back and crouch completely under the steering wheel, wincing in pain as the handcuff pinched her flesh at her changed position. Once more her free hand searched, this time with more luck. She pulled out a packet of tools, Connor's shield and badge—and an extra set of handcuffs.

She held the handcuffs up triumphantly and, in her jubilation, sat upright. "Yeow," she moaned as her head met the bottom of the steering shaft. Next she maneuvered her body back to her original position on the seat and, using the key from the extra set of cuffs she'd found, attempted to unlock the ones she was wearing.

By this time she was sweating at the combined effects of her efforts and the heater. She switched the heat off before turning her attentions to the handcuff once again. In moments she was free.

"Finally," she muttered as she rubbed her tender wrist. It was red from the twisting and tugging she had been doing in her efforts at freedom.

She opened the car door and got out, casting a worried look down the road again. Still no cars in sight. Michele made herself look at the building once again, praying to see Connor McLain emerge from around one corner. No sign of him, either.

She stood still and chewed her bottom lip uncertainly. How many minutes had it been since Connor had disappeared? She closed her eyes briefly. Too many.

She walked toward the old school. Toward the scene that had played too many times in her mind to be disbelieved. Toward Connor.

Chapter 17

Michele followed the path Connor had taken around the old schoolhouse, but he was nowhere in sight. There was a back door leading to the inside, mute testimony to where he had disappeared.

She eyed it, shocked by the ice crystallizing anew within her body. This was it; she knew it with a certainty that had nothing to do with the woods to the side or the brook gurgling behind it with an incongruously pleasant sound. The surety rose from something else, the suffering and despair that radiated from the building in waves, enveloping her.

She wrapped her arms around herself and tried to still the shaking that suddenly attacked her body with bone-jarring force. She longed violently to go running back to the car, back to the heater, away from the unfamiliar dementia that surrounded this building.

Michele closed her eyes, struggling with herself. Even as she longed to leave, she knew she would never comply with that wish. All the heat in the world wouldn't warm her now, could never chase away the chill that had permeated her bones. Only finding Connor could do that. Finding him safe. And whole. And alive.

Her hand shook so badly that it slipped from the knob twice before she managed to pull the door open. She somehow wasn't surprised to find that it opened easily, swinging outward without a sound to attest to its age. Peering into the dark interior, she stepped over the threshold.

The door swung closed behind her, leaving her blinking at the sudden blackness. As she stood still for a moment, her eyes adjusted. Because of the bright sunlight outside and the poor condition of the roof and rotting boards over the windows, the place wasn't totally dark. Here and there a wayward ray crept in and provided partial visibility.

Michele moved forward, aware that most of the corners were still shrouded in darkness. She didn't question her knowledge that there was no one in her immediate vicinity, just as she didn't question the ability of her feet to take her directly to a rickety stairway in one corner.

The condition of the stairs as she crept carefully up them made it obvious that whoever had taken such pains to render the door soundless had not paid the same care to the steps. Each step creaked and groaned, and at one point Michele's foot went completely through a tread.

Grimacing, she was silently grateful she couldn't see her feet well enough to examine what was covering her shoe when she finally freed it. The upstairs was almost as dark as the downstairs. As she gazed around tremulously, she was only half aware that she was in some sort of loft. Because her immediate attention centered on the man crumpled upon the floor.

With a muffled cry she rushed to his prone figure, sure that the nightmare was ready to reach up and engulf her, certain that his blood was about to flow over her, just like in her dreams.

But when she reached him, she knew she had been wrong. For once the cursed visions had gone awry. "Connor," she murmured to his still figure, but relief swept through her when she bent low and heard his steady breathing. She closed her eyes briefly in gratitude before moving her hands worriedly over his torso. How had he been injured? What could have happened to him? This place seemed deserted, and she wanted to scream inwardly for the damn backup car to get here already, so Connor could get help. So she could get him to safety.

"Move away from him, Miss Easton."

Michele froze for a moment before looking up slowly. She swung her gaze searchingly around the area, but she saw nothing but shadows.

"Who are you?" Her voice came out as a croak. "What have you done to him?"

"He's not hurt bad. And I told you to get away from him. Now!" the voice commanded her.

Michele stood slowly, her mind racing. She knew that voice. She *knew* it!

"Over there, by the window," she was instructed, and she moved like an automaton, her eyes still flickering about in the darkness. Her eyes widened in shock, then horror, as the owner of the voice stepped out of the shadows, close enough for Michele to recognize him.

"Scott," she murmured, dazed. She shook her head, trying to make sense of the scene before her. "Whatever are you doing here? It doesn't matter now," she continued, worry for Connor taking precedence over her confusion. "You can help me. First we have to see what's wrong with Connor. Then we can get help."

The young custodian approached her, stopping a few feet away. "I already know what's wrong with him," he told her, with no trace of his familiar stammer. "I hit him with this." He held up an old board, then threw it to the side, where it clattered noisily down the steps. "He's out cold."

Michele's numbed mind was having difficulty making a connection between his words and what was happening in front of her. She wondered disjointedly at the certainty that had replaced his usually unsure manner. Not only was his familiar stutter missing, he seemed so decisive, so aggressive. What could have brought about such a change? "You hit him?" she repeated. "But why? Why would you...?" Her voice trailed to a stop as she watched him reach into his belt and pull out a gun.

Her eyes widened in disbelief. She had seen that gun too many times not to recognize it. She'd seen it lying in pieces on the table, being cleaned. She'd watched it being slid into its holster as it was being belted on. It was Connor's.

"What are you doing with that, Scott?" she asked conversationally. She noted the unfamiliarity with which he handled it and didn't know if that was a bad sign or a good one. She devoutly hoped it was the latter.

"Took it off him," the young man boasted, casting a scornful eye in Connor's direction. "The big city detective ain't so great after all. Didn't even have to swing that hard at his head and he was out like a light."

Michele felt nausea rise at his words, so callously describing how Connor had been injured. She forced it down, forced her voice to mildness, as she inquired, "Why would you want to hurt Connor, Scott? He wouldn't harm you."

He snorted at her words. "Think I don't know what he was doing here, what both of you are here for?" he asked scornfully. "But you're too late. The last few kids are gone, and you'll never find 'em now. I was just getting rid of the last traces of 'em. And the great hero detective won't never solve this case."

Michele was aware of a great many things all at once. That she had never really known the person standing in front of her. That he had obviously had something to do with the kidnappings, and that he had no intention of letting them out of here. At those simultaneous certainties, she felt composure slip over her. All she had to do was keep Scott talking. Just keep him busy until the units Connor had called had time to arrive. It shouldn't be too hard. After all, drawing people out about themselves was what she did for a living.

But her life had never depended on it before.

"Why don't you tell me about all this, Scott?" she invited softly. His eyes jerked from Connor's still figure to her. "How are you involved in this?"

She watched as he almost preened with pride. "I knew what was happening all along. Me! Knew more than the cops, that's for sure."

"That's obvious," Michele agreed gently. "How was it you were so clever, Scott?"

"I seen the kidnapper that first time," he explained proudly. "I seen him take that first kid. The cops thought no one seen nothing, but they were wrong. I was there, at the store where he was snatched. It's the same place I pick up my ma's pills."

"So you saw the whole thing," Michele repeated, encouraging him to go on.

"Yeah, I saw, and I knew the guy what did it, too. Seen him at church lots of times. My ma always makes me go," he explained, as if his church-going habits rather than his bizarre behavior warranted clarification. "So I followed him on my moped until I lost him. But after church the next time I went up to Dennis—that's his name," he explained in an aside, "—and I says, 'What'd you do with that kid you took?'"

"And he told you?" Michele asked, genuinely amazed.

"He didn't want to," Scott muttered in remembered anger. "He thought I was stupid. I ain't stupid!" he roared suddenly, his eyes blazing. "My ma says I just think slower, but that don't make me dumb."

"I've never thought you were," Michele reminded him gently.

That stopped him for a moment, and he stared at her, the anger fading from his face. "No, you never did," he agreed. "But Dennis did, at first. Thought he could scare me, make me be quiet and leave him alone. I had to prove how smart I can be before he'd let me help."

Connor stifled a groan as he battled the unconsciousness that had briefly claimed him. He lay quietly, hoping whoever had belted him would believe he was still out. That would give him an advantage, one he would take at the earliest opportunity. As his mind cleared he listened intently to the voices. One he didn't recognize, but it was obvious from the man's words that he was up to his neck in the kidnappings. The other voice was softer, calming. He mentally cursed as recognition flooded him. It was Michele's.

Damn her, why couldn't that woman ever stay put? And how the hell had she gotten free? Her presence complicated matters. He was fairly confident he had a chance to overpower whoever had slugged him. But now he wouldn't be able to concentrate as he should; he would be too worried about Michele.

Michele. She was too damn important to him to allow something to happen to her. He was going to have to come up with a way to get them both out of this without her getting hurt.

He listened to them as he lay still, quickly aware of what Michele was doing. Drawing the bastard out, getting him to talk about himself. Wasting time until the backup unit got to them.

"Tell me why you wanted to help Dennis, Scott," Michele said softly, forcing herself to keep her eyes off Connor and concentrate on the confused young man before her.

Good girl, Connor encouraged her mentally. Just the right tone, nice and easy. There was no judgment in her voice, only a soothing quality that the guy couldn't help but respond to.

"Dennis told me why he wanted to do it. We was helping those kids. We never did nothing to hurt 'em." His voice was emphatic. "Nothing." He looked at her soberly. "We always found the kids on the streets somewhere. Nobody was watching over 'em. Nobody caring about 'em. We took 'em to a better life."

Michele's blood ran cold at his words. Did that mean the children had been murdered? His next words temporarily allayed that fear.

"We listened to what the reverend is always saying, see. 'For the sake of the children.'" He repeated the slogan carefully. "That's why we did it. We only took the kids who didn't have no parents who cared about 'em. Not really. They'd leave 'em in front of stores, in cars," he said scathingly. "Little kids running around with no one to care where they're at. People like that don't deserve kids, Miss Easton. The reverend says we gotta save 'em and that's what we've been doing."

Michele cocked her head, staring hard at Scott. For the sake of the children. That had been printed on the bumper sticker of the car she had identified when Bruce Casel hypnotized her.

Scott continued. "You never shoulda messed in this, Miss Easton. You've always been real nice to me. That's why I tried to protect you, scare you away. You wouldn't listen."

"When, Scott?" she asked quizzically. "When did you try to tell me?" But she was afraid she already knew.

"I give ya that note," he reminded her. "Told ya to stay away from cops, didn't I? You can't say I didn't warn ya. I seen you on TV that day." At her blank expression he reminded her. "The mayor was on TV, and I seen you in the crowd. In front of the police headquarters."

Michele's mind whirled crazily. She remembered the day well, the day she had finally gone and told the police what she knew. How nervous she had been when she had seen the television crew out front. She had convinced herself that no one would recognize her. Even if the cameras had panned the crowd, her face couldn't have been on the screen for more than a millisecond. But Scott had seen her. And recognized her.

"Then I seen that cop—" he gestured at Connor contemptuously "—at the office that day, so I warned ya. I seen his picture on TV all the time about working on those missing kids. I tried to tell ya over and over," he said, his voice rising in anger. "But you never listened to me, didja?"

Michele swallowed hard as she unwillingly remembered those messages, how violated it had made her feel to know someone had been in her home, had touched her things. Thinking about how he had terrified her made anger flare inside her.

Connor waited anxiously for her answer. Don't let him rattle you, stay calm, he told her mentally. He knew that just the memory of those incidents would shake her up.

But when Michele spoke, her voice was even. "But I didn't know it was you, Scott," she told him reasonably. "I was frightened by the messages. I never would have been frightened if I had known it was you."

Way to go, Connor thought admiringly. She could play this guy perfectly.

"I know you would never hurt me, Scott." Michele's voice was soothing, full of confidence.

"I d-d-don't want to," Scott replied, his uncertainty reflected by the returned stutter. "I never wanted t-t-to. Dennis thought I was smart the w-w-way I got in and out of your place. I never left no fingerprints," he boasted. "I wore gloves, and I was smart, too, the way I cut those letters out of m-m-magazines."

"That was clever of you, Scott." Michele's voice held admiration. "That's why I know you won't hurt us. You're too smart for that."

"I c-c-can't let you g-g-go," he answered slowly, obviously trying to follow her line of reasoning.

"But you must, Scott. You haven't done anything wrong, have you? You were trying to help those children. We know that now. But if you were to hurt Connor or me, then that would be wrong, wouldn't it? Then the police would be after you, and you don't want that, do you? To undo all the good you've been doing?"

Connor waited anxiously for the man's reply, his whole body tense. Careful, Princess, he mentally told her. This guy is crazy, and there's no telling what may set him off. You're not in your office now, and he's not a patient. And he has a gun.

Her next words had needles of fear piercing his body.

"Give me the gun, Scott." Her voice was coaxing. For God's sake, don't, he mentally screamed at her. Stay away from him.

Michele took advantage of the confused expression on Scott's face. She had to get the gun from him. Images whirled madly in her mind, flashes from her dreams, flickers of the most horrendous image of all. She had to get the gun away to save Connor.

She stepped closer to him, murmuring soothingly. "It's all right, Scott. We understand, really. Just give me the gun, and it will be all right."

"No!" Scott screamed suddenly, bringing both hands up to hold the gun, shaking, but aiming it at her. "Don't come any closer!"

Connor made his move then. Letting out a loud moan, he moved slowly, bringing a hand to his head as if he were only just regaining consciousness. He let his eyes flicker open slightly. Scott was staring at him now, his attention finally off Michele. Connor continued the farce, slowly rising to sit up, then to stand.

"G-g-get away from h-h-her," Scott ordered him shrilly, and Connor moved a few steps farther from Michele, satisfied when Scott swung the gun to follow him. At least it was no longer pointing at Michele.

Michele's blood ran cold when she saw Scott's shaking hands point the gun at Connor. She was relieved to see that he was all right, but she wished he could have stayed out for just a couple more minutes. She'd almost had the gun. Damn! Where were the backup units?

"Michele's right, Scott. Nobody is going to blame you. Let's just solve this right now. Give me the gun. That's all you have to do, buddy. Put it down, nice and easy."

Connor's voice, slow and soothing, had just the opposite effect on Scott. "No!" he screamed. "I have to b-b-be smart," he muttered frantically. "I have to be s-s-smart." He leveled the gun again at Connor, and one finger slipped to the trigger.

The next few seconds blurred in Michele's mind. A noise came from the stairway, and Scott's eyes swung in that direction. Michele moved, her limbs curiously heavy, as if they were underwater, reaching for the gun. Connor saw her and leapt toward her, yanking her behind him. Scott turned. Movement slowed as if in a slow-motion movie. Eyes wide and terrified, he brought the gun up. His finger squeezed. Connor dived for Scott's feet.

The deafening roar brought an end to the surreal unreality of the moment. Michele rolled from where Connor had thrown her in time to see his body jerk back, then crumple at her feet.

She was unaware of everything else that happened then. The shouted orders from the stairway to throw down the gun. Three state police officers racing up the steps and securing Scott.

She was unaware of it all. She crouched frantically above Connor, whose face was revealed by the ray of sunlight that made it through the boarded-up window. She watched the blood seep from his body, cover her hands and drip slowly to the planked floor. And knew that no dream she'd ever experienced could equal the agony of this reality.

It was nearly a week later when Michele pushed open the hospital door and poked her head in. She didn't want to disturb Connor if he was getting the rest the doctor and staff kept insisting he needed. Her lips firmed when she saw him sitting up in bed.

"Don't you ever sleep?" she scolded good-naturedly, entering the room. Any inclination to berate him was lost when she saw the look on his face as she came in. Pleasure was there, and then those wickedly sexy dimples made an appearance.

Michele sauntered to his side, already affected by that rakish grin and the sensuous look in those light green eyes.

"You know I can't sleep without you beside me whispering sweet nothings in my ear," he bantered, reaching out with his good arm to pull her close.

Michele gave him a soft kiss on the mouth, then ducked adroitly under his arm when he would have held her. She ignored his glower at her move and pulled a chair up to the bed.

Connor cocked a brow at her. "Keeping your distance?" he mocked softly. They were both aware that it would take very little encouragement on his part to coax her back to his side.

Michele's cheeks warmed. "Just trying to keep decorum in mind," she answered tartly. "Which I see has escaped you." She nodded at his bare chest.

The white gauze bandage wrapped around his upper chest and one shoulder was the only covering on his otherwise bare torso. The sheet was spread carelessly across his lap, and Michele had no doubt that he was bare beneath it. On more than one occasion he had told her, and every nurse within shouting distance, that he refused to wear those damn wimpy hospital gowns. Michele turned a resigned look to the corner and saw, as she had expected, the day's fresh gown wadded up.

"You're not still embarrassed about last night, I hope." Connor's voice was low, but full of remembered amusement. His grin widened at the immediate flare of color in Michele's cheeks.

"Last night and every other time I get within two feet of you," she muttered. "Connor!" she cried at his obvious mirth. "It wasn't funny! I'm tired of having people walk in here—"

"At inopportune times?" he finished wickedly. "Is it my fault you find me so irresistible?"

Michele fixed him with a stern look. "Irrepressible, maybe," she corrected. "You've been an absolute dictator since you were admitted, and you know it. I hear the nurses are planning a champagne celebration for the day you're released."

Connor leaned forward, wincing a little as the movement pulled on his wounded shoulder. "And what celebration are *you* planning for me when I get released, hmm, Michele?" he crooned. "I prefer a private one, involving only you and me. Do you want to hear my ideas?"

Although Michele could feel her face burning, she answered primly. "After they finish fixing your body, they need to work on your mind. You have an overactive fantasy life."

"That's not all that's overactive where you're concerned," Connor muttered. If he didn't get released from this white-walled prison soon, he would explode. He had wanted Michele near him constantly after he'd been shot, just to see her, to convince himself that she was safe. And now that he was feeling better, her presence had the power to send all his senses racing. He shifted uncomfortably. All body parts were definitely in working order, and some were working overtime.

The corners of his mouth kicked up as he remembered the times over the past few days when he'd been able to coax Michele close enough for kissing. He had known how concerned she was for him, and he had used that concern shamelessly. Once he had her close, it never took either of them long to forget where they were. But close encounters of the unfinished kind were playing havoc with his libido, which in turn didn't improve his temper. He wouldn't be satisfied until he walked out of this place and he and Michele could finally be alone again.

"Evening, gorgeous," a familiar voice caroled out, interrupting Connor's thoughts. He groaned aloud and glowered at the blond, fortyish nurse who entered the room.

"Get out," he ordered flatly.

Michele and the nurse exchanged knowing looks.

"Sorry, gorgeous, it's time for another antibiotic." She walked to the other side of the bed and prepared a long wicked-looking needle. "Roll over, big guy, before I start to think that you enjoy this."

Connor opened his mouth to tell her exactly where to put her needle before catching Michele's eyes. Her presence there never failed to make him curb the worst of his temper, so he obeyed, rolling over, but still muttering.

"I can't believe you didn't work for a dictator. Haven't you guys ever heard of pills?" He winced at the stick of the needle that he always suspected this nurse injected with just a little too much enjoyment.

"What? And deprive myself of the sight of these gorgeous buns?" The nurse pulled the needle out, smiling as Michele snickered. "Is he always this annoying?" she asked casually.

"No, sometimes he's worse," Michele replied.

Connor eased back to his original position, scowling at both the women in front of him. "Get a different nurse in here from now on," he commanded. "You've got a damned heavy hand with that needle."

"Sorry," the nurse answered good-naturedly. "I'm the only one they can trust not to go ga-ga over your marvelous bod and handsome mug. Add that to your oh-so-charming personality—" she rolled her eyes humorously "—and you're just too much man for most of these gals to resist. I guess you're stuck with me—no pun intended."

Connor's comment made Michele's eyebrows climb to the top of her forehead, but the nurse just laughed as she moved to the door.

"Flattery won't get you anywhere with me, even if you do have the cutest tush on this floor." The door swung closed before the pillow Connor threw could reach it.

He glared at Michele as she calmly retrieved the pillow and tossed it back to him. "You think this is funny, don't you?" he asked sourly.

"Who, me?" Michele's tone was innocent. "You don't see me laughing, do you?" Truth be told, she much preferred this nurse's breezy nonchalance to the attitude of a few of the others she had met. Some of them had been oversolicitous to the point of nausea, and Michele suspected that their concern for Connor had more to do with his virility than with their care for the sick.

Connor eyed her for a moment. "Why don't you come over here and fluff my pillow for me?" he wheedled.

Michele laughed as she recognized his ploy. "Not me, Detective," she drawled. "My mama didn't raise no dopes."

"Hey, *amigo*, is Michele picking on you again?" Cruz strolled into the hospital room and surveyed the two of them, clucking his tongue reproachfully. "Shame on you, Michele. Connor has been shot. He needs care. He needs devotion. Look at that pathetic face," he continued, gesturing at the bed. Connor did his best to look sickly. "He needs your loving care and attention."

"He needs a swift kick," Michele answered, unmoved by the obvious line.

Cruz shrugged and swung a chair over to the bedside and sat down. "Can't say I didn't try, buddy," he whispered loudly to Connor "But the lady just knows you too well."

"Look, Michele," Connor said. "Cruz isn't afraid to sit too close to me."

"That's because he's not in any danger of ending up in a compromising position with you on your bed," Michele answered tartly, before thinking.

The two men laughed uproariously, enjoying the immediate flood of color that rushed to her face. Cruz was the first to regain control. He told her soberly, "That's because he respects me, Michele," and they broke up again.

Michele watched the two men, unwillingly amused by their joke. It was too good to see Connor smile again, to be well enough for this kind of lightheartedness, for her to be impatient with them. She joined Cruz at the other side of Connor's bed.

"So when do you get sprung from here, Connor?" Cruz asked.

"Tomorrow."

"Next week sometime."

Both Connor and Michele had spoken simultaneously. Connor fixed her with a long look. "I'll be out of here soon, no matter what anyone else has to say. I've been poked and prodded enough for a lifetime."

"He's working on a dishonorable discharge," Michele explained to Cruz in exasperation. "Someone needs to tell him that a little charm would go a long way." Privately, she vowed to speak to Connor's doctor herself. She knew he was capable of bullying his way out of here, and she was just as determined that he stay as long as he needed to. They would see who was more stubborn on this issue.

It wasn't long before the conversation turned to the case. "You're the fair-haired boy once again," Cruz told Connor. "Wouldn't be a bit surprised if another commendation came out of this one. McIntire is singing your praises around the station."

"While singing his own on the campaign trail," Connor came back, unimpressed. "This newfound admiration for me will last only until the next time I tick him off."

"I don't know," Cruz countered. "You did him a big favor. The glory of having the case solved this close to election day just might wrap things up for McIntire."

"What's the latest on Dennis Hardy?" Connor wanted to know. The man Scott had implicated had been picked up shortly after Connor had arrived at the hospital. But up to this point he had been steadfastly protesting his innocence.

"You were right," Cruz informed him. "As soon as we hit him with the identical matches between hair samples taken from him and those found in the abandoned car, he crumpled. He's singing like a canary now, despite the public defender's advice."

Connor nodded. He had expected nothing different.

"He's a wacko religious fanatic, but he's shrewd. Once he'd snatched the kids, he scared the bejesus out of them. Told them they'd been bad, that their parents didn't love them anymore and had sent them to him to be punished."

"Oh, how awful," Michele whispered, closing her eyes for a moment. She could easily feel the children's terror and despair. Connor took her hand, and she opened her eyes to meet the understanding in his.

"Yeah, he's pretty sick," Cruz agreed grimly. "After he convinced them their parents didn't want them back, he pretended to be their only friend, offered to get them good homes if they'd follow his instructions."

"Have all the children been located?" Connor asked.

"The state police sent men to each of the addresses to pick them up," Cruz confirmed. "They're in various parts of the state."

Michele shook her head in disbelief. "I still don't understand. Where did he find families for these children?"

"He had quite a system," Cruz answered. "Used the personal columns in newspapers across the state. You know the ones. 'Loving couple wants child to adopt.' He'd call them, pretending to be a lawyer who placed orphaned children for a religious organization. He'd zero in on the ones who were really desperate."

"The ones who had been turned down by every adoption agency in the state," Connor guessed.

"Or the ones who had just about given up hope," Cruz agreed. "He suspected they'd be more willing to take any child they could get and ask the fewest questions. After that, it was just a matter of selecting the ones who would provide the so-called 'moral environment' he was so crazed about."

"Cruz," Michele put in hesitantly, "how's Scott?"

"Seems better since you came to talk to him."

Michele held her breath as Connor swung his gaze to her. She had purposefully neglected to tell him about her trip to the police station a few nights ago. She had spent over an hour talking to Scott, and then to his lawyer. She was now satisfied that he would make a case for diminished capacity on Scott's behalf. She hadn't known how to explain to Connor her feeling of compassion for Scott's plight, in spite of what he had been involved in.

But Connor didn't berate her. Instead he rubbed his thumb over her hand, which he still held. "Are you okay?" he asked, and Michele knew he understood her feelings and was asking if there were any lingering effects from the experience.

"Yes, I'm all right," she murmured back, smoothing his hair away from his forehead with her free hand. She was better than all right. She felt as though the weight of the world had been lifted from her shoulders. For the first time in months she felt complete and utter peace. She looked down at the man holding her hand so tightly. She felt completely in love.

Cruz felt like an outsider as he observed the look passing between them and decided to make his exit.

"Well, better leave you two alone," he said breezily as he rose and headed for the door. "After all, I did get Michele close enough for you to get your hands on her again, and that *is* what you pay me for, isn't it, Connor?" He laughed and ducked out of the room before his friend could respond.

"Sounds like you're going to be a hero," Michele teased, laughing at the grimace that passed briefly over his face.

"You're the one who deserves the praise for solving this case." Connor spoke seriously. "You led me right to the place." He kissed the hand he still held. "Lucky I had you with me."

"That's what I keep trying to tell you," Michele said lightly.

A slight frown crossed his face. "Yeah."

At his look, Michele bit her lip. It had been easy to forget her fears about his leaving her in the last hectic week. But now those fears came rushing back to her, brought on, in part, by his intense expression.

"Connor..."

"Michele..."

They spoke simultaneously, then paused, looking at each other. When he opened his mouth again, Michele quickly laid two fingers against his lips. "No, let me say something."

Connor's face was determined. "I think I'd better go first."

"No, please." Michele smiled tremulously at his surprise. "Hear me out." Taking his silence for agreement, she looked down to where their hands were still clasped. "That night after the homeless benefit, you were quite certain in your assessment of what I need in my life." She slanted a glance toward him. "But you weren't totally accurate."

"I wasn't."

It was a statement, but Michele still shook her head. "No. Actually—" she took a deep breath "—I detest caviar and the opera. I do enjoy the ballet and symphony, but from your collection of CDs, I could tell that you appreciate some classical music yourself. And I happen to love pizza and basketball."

"You do?"

She smiled at his skeptical tone. "I do. So I was wondering...doesn't this habit of jumping to conclusions about people sort of hinder your police work?"

He was amused by her impertinent tone. "I don't usually have that problem with people."

"Then why with me?"

A hard smile tilted his lips. After a long moment he answered wryly. "Self-preservation." At her quizzical expression, he sighed. "Princess, the first time I saw you, I knew I should run as hard and fast as I possibly could."

"You've been doing a pretty good job of that," Michele murmured.

His thumb skated over her knuckles. "I tried. And recounting the differences between us was as much to remind me as it was for you." He looked into her steady gray eyes. "I've spent the last few years perfecting the art of shallow socializing, Michele. Not exactly the gentleman and scholar I'm sure your mother would want for you."

She felt a tiny bud of hope bloom. "Why don't you let me decide what I want for myself?" she asked softly.

His eyes never left hers. "All right, I will. I love you, Michele." He paused for a heartbeat. "My life has been nothing but shadows for too long. And now that I've found you, I'm too damn selfish to do the noble thing and send you away."

Hearing the words she had waited so long for, had despaired of ever hearing, made her feel like weeping for joy. "I wouldn't go even if you sent me," she answered him shakily.

"You'd better be sure of what you want," he warned her, even as he drew her still nearer. "Be very sure, because I don't intend to let you go if you change your mind later."

Michele bent her head. "I'll never change my mind," she informed him firmly. "I love you, Connor. And that will never change."

His eyes were gleaming as he returned her look. "They call me

Maximum McLain,'' he whispered, letting go of her hand to cup the back of her head. ''Are you ready for a life sentence?''

Michele willingly allowed herself to be pulled close enough for their lips to barely meet. Against his lips she answered softly, ''I'd accept nothing less.'' And then words were lost as they sealed their promise with a kiss.

* * * * *

American
HEROES
AGAINST ALL ODDS

1. ALABAMA
After Hours—Gina Wilkins
2. ALASKA
The Bride Came C.O.D.—Barbara Bretton
3. ARIZONA
Stolen Memories—Kelsey Roberts
4. ARKANSAS
Hillbilly Heart—Stella Bagwell
5. CALIFORNIA
Stevie's Chase—Justine Davis
6. COLORADO
Walk Away, Joe—Pamela Toth
7. CONNECTICUT
Honeymoon for Hire—Cathy Gillen Thacker
8. DELAWARE
Death Spiral—Patricia Rosemoor
9. FLORIDA
Cry Uncle—Judith Arnold
10. GEORGIA
Safe Haven—Marilyn Pappano
11. HAWAII
Marriage Incorporated—Debbi Rawlins
12. IDAHO
Plain Jane's Man—Kristine Rolofson
13. ILLINOIS
Safety of His Arms—Vivian Leiber
14. INDIANA
A Fine Spring Rain—Celeste Hamilton
15. IOWA
Exclusively Yours—Leigh Michaels
16. KANSAS
The Doubletree—Victoria Pade
17. KENTUCKY
Run for the Roses—Peggy Moreland
18. LOUISIANA
Rambler's Rest—Bay Matthews
19. MAINE
Whispers in the Wood—Helen R. Myers
20. MARYLAND
Chance at a Lifetime—Anne Marie Winston
21. MASSACHUSETTS
Body Heat—Elise Title
22. MICHIGAN
Devil's Night—Jennifer Greene
23. MINNESOTA
Man from the North Country—Laurie Paige
24. MISSISSIPPI
Miss Charlotte Surrenders—Cathy Gillen Thacker
25. MISSOURI
One of the Good Guys—Carla Cassidy
26. MONTANA
Angel—Ruth Langan
27. NEBRASKA
Return to Raindance—Phyllis Halldorson
28. NEVADA
Baby by Chance—Elda Minger
29. NEW HAMPSHIRE
Sara's Father—Jennifer Mikels
30. NEW JERSEY
Tara's Child—Susan Kearney
31. NEW MEXICO
Black Mesa—Aimée Thurlo
32. NEW YORK
Winter Beach—Terese Ramin
33. NORTH CAROLINA
Pride and Promises—BJ James
34. NORTH DAKOTA
To Each His Own—Kathleen Eagle
35. OHIO
Courting Valerie—Linda Markowiak
36. OKLAHOMA
Nanny Angel—Karen Toller Whittenburg
37. OREGON
Firebrand—Paula Detmer Riggs
38. PENNSYLVANIA
McLain's Law—Kylie Brant
39. RHODE ISLAND
Does Anybody Know Who Allison Is?—Tracy Sinclair
40. SOUTH CAROLINA
Just Deserts—Dixie Browning
41. SOUTH DAKOTA
Brave Heart—Lindsay McKenna
42. TENNESSEE
Out of Danger—Beverly Barton
43. TEXAS
Major Attraction—Roz Denny Fox
44. UTAH
Feathers in the Wind—Pamela Browning
45. VERMONT
Twilight Magic—Saranne Dawson
46. VIRGINIA
No More Secrets—Linda Randall Wisdom
47. WASHINGTON
The Return of Caine O'Halloran—JoAnn Ross
48. WEST VIRGINIA
Cara's Beloved—Laurie Paige
49. WISCONSIN
Hoops—Patricia McLinn
50. WYOMING
Black Creek Ranch—Jackie Merritt

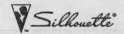

HARLEQUIN® Silhouette®

Please address questions and book requests to: Harlequin Reader Service U.S.: 3010 Walden Ave., P.O. Box 1325, Buffalo, NY 14269 CAN.: P.O. Box 609, Fort Erie, Ont. L2A 5X3 PAHGEN

INTIMATE MOMENTS®
Silhouette®

If you've got the time...
We've got the
INTIMATE MOMENTS

Passion. Suspense. Desire. Drama.
Enter a world that's larger than life,
where men and women overcome life's
greatest odds for the ultimate prize: love.
Nonstop excitement is closer than you
think...in Silhouette Intimate Moments!

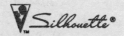

Silhouette®

SIMGEN99

FOUR UNIQUE SERIES
FOR EVERY WOMAN YOU ARE...

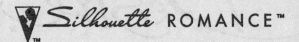

Silhouette ROMANCE™

These entertaining, tender and involving love stories celebrate the spirit of pure romance.

Desire®

Desire features strong heroes and spirited heroines who come together in a highly passionate, emotionally powerful and always provocative read.

Silhouette® SPECIAL EDITION®

For every woman who dreams of life, love and family, these are the romances in which she makes her dreams come true.

INTIMATE MOMENTS® Silhouette®

Dive into the pages of Intimate Moments and experience adventure and excitement in these complex and dramatic romances.

Visit us at www.eHarlequin.com SGEN00

passionate powerful provocative love stories that fulfill your every desire

Desire®

Silhouette Desire delivers strong heroes, spirited heroines and stellar love stories.

Desire features your favorite authors, including

Diana Palmer, Annette Broadrick, Ann Major, Anne MacAllister and Cait London.

Passionate, powerful and provocative romances *guaranteed!*

For superlative authors, sensual stories and sexy heroes, choose Silhouette Desire.

Available at your favorite retail outlet.

Silhouette®
Where love comes alive™

passionate powerful provocative love stories that fulfill your every desire

Visit us at www.eHarlequin.com SDGEN00

Silhouette ROMANCE™

What's a single dad to do when he needs a wife by next Thursday?

Who's a confirmed bachelor to call when he finds a baby on his doorstep?

How does a plain Jane in love with her gorgeous boss get him to notice her?

From classic love stories to romantic comedies to emotional heart tuggers, **Silhouette Romance** offers six irresistible novels every month by some of your favorite authors!

Such as...beloved bestsellers **Diana Palmer, Stella Bagwell, Sandra Steffen, Susan Meiner** and **Marie Ferrarella,** to name just a few—and some sure to become favorites!

Silhouette Romance—always emotional, always enjoyable, always about love!

SRGEN99

Silhouette®

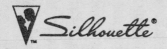

where love comes alive—online...

Visit the *Author's Alcove*

- Find the most complete information anywhere on your favorite Silhouette author.
- Try your hand in the Writing Round Robin—contribute a chapter to an online book in the making.

Enter the *Reading Room*

- Experience an interactive novel—help determine the fate of a story being created now by one of your favorite authors.
- Join one of our reading groups and discuss your favorite book.

Drop into *Shop eHarlequin*

- Find the latest releases—read an excerpt or write a review for this month's Silhouette top sellers.
- Try out our amazing search feature—tell us your favorite theme, setting or time period and we'll find a book that's perfect for you.

All this and more available at

www.eHarlequin.com

on Women.com Networks

SEYRB1